I0536157

I GUESS I LOVE YOU

MISTY MALONE

Published by Blushing Books
An Imprint of
ABCD Graphics and Design, Inc.
A Virginia Corporation
977 Seminole Trail #233
Charlottesville, VA 22901

Misty Malone
I Guess I Love You

eBook ISBN: 978-1-64563-918-3
Print ISBN: 978-1-64563-919-0
v1

CHAPTER 1

NEW YORK, 1862

"Martha, are you about ready to go so we can get our shopping done?"

"Almost, Uncle Franklin. Let me grab my shawl and I'll be right down."

A few minutes later he turned to see his eighteen-year-old niece descend from the stairs and into the kitchen. "It took you that long to get ready and that's what you decided to wear?"

She looked at her uncle with a pout on her face. "What's wrong with it? It's clean, and it's not torn anywhere, is it?"

"No, but young ladies around here don't wear those split skirt things much. They wear a pretty dress and do their hair up some fancy way, hoping to catch the eye of a single young man."

"Well," she said, puffing her chest out and standing tall, "if I ever decide I want to catch the eye of a man I'll keep that thought in mind. In the meantime, are you ready to go, or do you want to argue about what I chose to wear again before we leave?"

Franklin Welch looked at his niece, whom he loved dearly, and sat down in a chair at the table, sighing. "No, honey, I don't want to argue again. Would you please sit down for a few minutes, though? I think it's time we have a talk."

Martha could tell her uncle had something on his mind, and immediately sat down across from him. She loved her uncle and truly didn't want to argue with him any longer, either. "Certainly. You look concerned about something, Uncle Franklin. Is it anything I can help with?"

"Maybe," he said as he reached over and patted her hand. He took a moment to consider his words before meeting her eyes and squaring his shoulders. "Martha, it's been two years now since your father died and you came to New York to live with me. I hated that your father died. I know you loved him and miss him; I miss him, too. He was my brother, and I loved him, as well. I'm glad you were able to come live with me. I've enjoyed having you here, and I think we've helped each other get through it."

"I'm glad you invited me out here, too," she said quietly. "I don't know what I would have done back in Missouri on the farm alone."

"I think it was easier for both of us to face his death since we knew each other so well. We truly were family before you came out here to live."

"I've known you my whole life. Since you and Aunt Helen owned the farm next to ours, we saw each other all the time." She paused and swallowed hard before continuing. "I was so young when my mother died that I don't remember her at all. Aunt Helen was like a mother to me growing up. I missed you both when you moved here."

"I know you did, and trust me, we missed you, as well. After your mother died we spent as much time at your house as at ours, helping my brother through the loss of his wife, and learning to care for a baby not even a year old yet. Helen did most of the care at first, but your father learned quickly. You became closer to us than just a niece. When Helen got word that her parents had been involved in a freak carriage accident and were hurt badly, it was a tough decision for us. They needed someone to take care of them, but her father also asked if I would take over running his business until he was able to get back to it. We hated to leave you and your father, but her parents needed our help."

"We hated to see you leave, but Father and I understood. They needed you."

"Yes, they did. We thought we would be able to come here and help them out for a little while until they were back on their feet and able to take care of themselves and their business again. We intended to go back to our farm."

"We thought you would be back, too. I remember Papa said you were lucky when you found someone who was looking for a place to stay, and agreed to run the farm for you while you were gone."

"We were lucky. We told them our guess was we'd be gone three or four months, and they were happy to do it, thinking that would give them time to find a job and a place to live."

"Did you have any trouble learning the business? It had to have been hard, stepping in and running it."

"We'd been here visiting her parents on several occasions over the years, and every time we were here he took me down to the plant with him. They were both hoping we'd move back here, and he constantly offered me a job helping him run it. I'm pretty sure he thought if he showed me the business and how it runs I'd accept his offer."

"Did you ever consider it?"

"Not really. I loved running the farm, and we were both happy in Missouri. After helping him every time we were visiting them, though, I had a pretty good idea how to run it. He was hurt pretty badly, but he'd have a day here and there where he was doing better. Every time he had one of those days we'd talk about the business, and he answered any questions I had."

"Did he ever get well enough to go back and help with it again?"

"No. He started improving and we thought he was about ready to go back for a couple of hours a day as long as he didn't overdo it. His wife was slowly improving, as well, and was able to get up and go sit at the kitchen table and talk to Helen for an hour or so at a time while she was cooking. But then sadly he and his wife both caught that awful influenza that was going around. The doctor said he thought it was because they were in a weakened state to begin with, and unfortunately, neither of them lasted very long after that."

"And Helen caught it from them while she was taking care of them?"

"That's what the doctor thought, yes. I still don't know how I managed to avoid it, but I never did get it."

"I'm so sorry things happened as they did, Uncle Franklin. I about cried my eyes out when I heard Aunt Helen passed, but here you were, out here with none of your family close by, and all three of them passed away. Papa said they all died within a couple of weeks. That had to be awful."

Franklin took a deep breath and patted Martha's hand again. "It was, but it's behind me now. What I wanted to talk to you about is our future. I think it's time I stopped living in the past and we look ahead."

"What do you mean?"

"It's obvious to me you're not happy here in New York."

"Uncle Franklin, that's not really true. You've been so generous and kind to me."

"Thank you, Martha, but that doesn't mean you're happy here. I appreciate your kind words, but this is nothing like the area you grew up in, and nothing at all like a farm. The thing is, seeing you and watching you try to fit in has made me realize I'm not a whole lot different from you."

"I don't understand."

"I came to New York because I was needed here. I wasn't comfortable, but I didn't have much time to think about it because I had a business to run. If I wouldn't have been so busy trying to run a business and help your aunt care for her parents, I would have realized I was much like you are now, like a fish out of water, not happy here. Then when your aunt passed away and I inherited the business, I carried on, doing what I had to do, without really thinking or feeling. I think in a lot of ways I was living in a daze."

"I'm so sorry."

"When I got the telegram about your father's sudden passing, in a way it was like I somehow came back to life. I had a new reason to live. I got to Missouri as quickly as I could and started focusing on what all needed to be done. I talked to the man who had been running my farm and then bought it when it became apparent we would be staying there longer than we'd planned. He made it clear he and his son would very much like to purchase your farm, as well, so we packed up what you wanted to keep and came back here. Since we've been here, though, I've gradually come to see things differently. I stayed here to run the business, but watching you struggling to fit in has made me see that I still don't really fit in here, either."

"You don't?"

"No. As I thought about you and I saw you floundering, trying to fit in, I realized I'm still doing much the same. I've never felt at home here, like I did at the farm in Missouri. I had a business to run so I never allowed myself to think about it, until I've watched you. Now that I've seen you and know you're not happy, it was easy for me to see that I'm not happy here, either. Furthermore, I've been staying here because of the business, but it isn't my business, something I started and am proud of. We both would have been better off, happier if I would have sold this business and moved back to Missouri and run your farm. Now that I realize that, I can do it now. I can sell this business and we can move. Your farm has been sold so we can't move back here, but we can still move."

Franklin watched Martha as her eyes lit up, something he hadn't seen in way too long. "You would be willing to sell it and move?"

"Absolutely. Life is short, and happiness is very important. Although this business has provided me a nice income, my heart's not in it. I would rather sell it and we can take that money and move someplace where we feel more at home, and find something to do that makes us happy."

"Like what, and where?"

"We'll have to talk about that and decide. If you have friends back in Missouri and would like to return there, I can always write a letter to the sheriff and ask if there are any farms for sale in the area."

She thought for several moments before shaking her head. "No, I don't think I want to go back there. Our farm was a ways outside of town so I didn't see the kids except for at school."

She was quiet, and her uncle rubbed her hand. "I know some of the girls used to make fun of you because you didn't do most things girls did," he said. "Your Aunt Helen felt bad about that, and that's why she tried to teach you how to cook and sew."

"I appreciated her teaching me those things, because they were things I needed to know to take care of myself and Papa. But I didn't really like doing most of those things."

Franklin laughed as he thought back to that time. "I know. You were much happier on a horse than you were in a kitchen."

"I still am," she admitted, "even though now I can take care of a house, too. But I never had any close friends back there, so if we're going to move, unless you want to go back there, I'd rather go somewhere else and make a new start. If we go back there I'm

6

sure it will bring back memories of Papa taking me to the general store, or on a picnic, or to eat at the restaurant when we went to town to get our supplies."

"I understand, and I agree with you," he said. "It'll bring back memories for both of us. Let's give it some thought over the next few days and see if we can come up with somewhere else we might like to move to."

"Okay. Do you want to buy another farm? The money we have from our farm, together with the money you get from selling your business should be enough to buy another farm, shouldn't it?"

"The money from your farm is your money, Martha. I put it in the bank in your name because it's yours and I want to make sure you have it. I should get enough from this business to buy any farm or business I may decide I want, but thank you for your offer."

"But you should have it for allowing me to live with you. You're providing everything for me."

"Because I love you and I want to," Franklin said quickly. "We were never blessed with any children and we both thought of you as the child we never had. We felt fortunate that your father shared you with us. That money is for you, in case you ever need it, or when you get married you and your husband will have some money if you need it to purchase a home or business. But like I said, I'll have enough when I sell the business, so we won't talk about this any further. What I'd rather talk about is where we want to go and what we want to do."

"I'll do some thinking," she promised him, a big smile on her face.

"Good. I will, too, and in the meantime, I'll put the word out that I'd like to sell the business."

"Do you think it will take long to sell?"

"I don't think so. It's a good business and it's making a good profit, so I think it should be pretty easy to sell. We better start thinking, so we have some kind of plan when it sells."

"Okay." She started to get up, but paused. "Are you sure you want to do this? I don't want you to do it if it's just for me."

"Nonsense. I would do anything to see you happier, Martha, but honestly, this is for me, as well. You made me see that I've just been going through the motions of life, and it's been passing me by. I'm excited about making a change in my life, too." He got up, kissed her forehead and asked, "Now, are you ready to do our shopping?"

OVER THE NEXT several days Martha gave a lot of thought to her uncle's words. She hadn't been happy in New York, but she was surprised that he knew that. She'd been truly thankful he took her in, and he'd been so very kind. She tried not to let her unhappiness show. Apparently she hadn't done a very good job of hiding it.

She was ashamed of herself, though, for not seeing that he wasn't happy, either. Thinking back on it, she admitted to herself she'd been so busy trying to hide her true feelings, she hadn't noticed several signs she should have picked up on. He wasn't as jovial as he was when they'd all lived in Missouri. He laughed a lot back then and always seemed to have a twinkle in his eyes. He didn't have the spring in his step she was used to seeing, though she wondered if that was due to his being older and having been through so much over the last five or six years.

Now that she knew this, she was determined to make it up to him. She planned to give this serious thought and come up with an idea that sounded good to both of them. Then she would help him get ready to move, and make the move as easy on him as possible.

They talked about it nightly, but failed to come up with any ideas they both liked. They agreed they would both like to go back out west, quite possibly to another farm or ranch, but neither of them knew much about anywhere out west other than Missouri, and they didn't want to go back to the general area they lived before. They weren't opposed to another area in Missouri, but they didn't know where or how to start looking for a farm for sale in a safe area. They had heard stories of areas out west where Indian uprisings were fairly frequent, and other areas that didn't yet have any law in the area, which made it a dangerous place, especially for ladies. They wanted to avoid areas like those.

Martha sat down and wrote some inquiries to sheriffs in several towns out west, explaining they were looking to return to the west and asking if they knew of any farm or ranch in their area that might be for sale. If so, she asked for a little information about their area. She wasn't actually expecting to receive any replies, but knew at least this way she had a chance of gaining some valuable information. The next time they went to do their shopping, she went to the postal window at the mercantile to post her letters.

While she was doing that, Franklin went to talk to his banker. Local bankers often knew of people in the area looking for a business to purchase, or that might be interested in investing in them if it was the right kind. He told him of his desire to sell his business, knowing if he didn't know of anyone right offhand, he would get the word out that the business was for sale. Franklin knew he would try to find a seller, hoping to keep the business as a bank customer. There would also be a chance the bank could make a loan toward purchasing the business. As Franklin expected, the banker was certainly interested and vowed to help him find a buyer.

While he was talking to him, he also asked if he knew of any areas out west that might be suitable for them to look for a ranch or farm to purchase. The banker didn't have any immediate suggestions, but assured Franklin he would start asking questions and see what he could find. He knew of several men who had businesses that required them to travel out west occasionally, and they might have some ideas for him.

Now that they'd laid the groundwork, Franklin and Martha just had to sit back and wait for a response from someone. That proved to be the difficult part. They busied themselves in an attempt to make the time go quicker. Franklin got the business in order, making sure the books were all up to date, and kept the bills all paid as soon as he received them. He also had a few people paying extra attention to cleaning the shop. He wanted to be sure the business made a good impression in every aspect.

While he was doing this, Martha set about going through the house. She separated things that were special to them and knew they would want to take with them, from things they could do without. She gave serious thought to several items, knowing moving across country would be a difficult and expensive task. Depending on where they bought land, things would need to be packed, and could be sent on trains part of the way, but would then have to go by private wagon. It would probably be easier and more economically feasible to sell much of their furniture and other items here and buy new once they arrived at their new home.

Franklin waited two and a half weeks, then started going to the bank two or three times a week to check with the banker. At this point he was more interested in finding someone who might be helpful in deciding on a general area they might want to concentrate on when trying to find a farm. Finally he was given the name of a man who had traveled quite a bit to a few places in the west, including the Nebraska territory. Ralph Amherst said he would be happy to talk to him and share what information he had.

Franklin sent him an invitation to have supper with them a few days later, and was happy when he accepted. He wanted

Martha to be able to hear what he had to say, as well, and to ask any questions she might have.

Martha worked diligently to prepare a fine meal for Mr. Amherst, and make sure their house was spotless. As they sat down to eat, Mr. Amherst explained his business and the parts of the west he was fairly familiar with, including the Nebraska territory. They had a good conversation, during which their guest readily answered every question either of them had, and spoke frankly. The three of them had a very enjoyable evening, and Franklin and Martha thanked him for his help. By the time he left, they had a lot to think about.

Over the next few days as they talked about what they'd learned, they decided to focus their search on Nebraska. There were parts further west that appealed to them, as well, but much of that territory seemed too untamed yet. It sounded like there was good farmland in the Nebraska territory, however, and overall it sounded like it was more civilized, which equated to more ladies in the area. That was important to both of them. They'd heard stories of towns with only a few ladies, and they couldn't walk around town alone safely.

Several days later Martha was again at the mercantile picking up some supplies, and stopped by the postal window to see if they'd gotten any replies. She was surprised to hear she had two. She put them in her pocket so she could read them and absorb the information later, once they were home. She and her uncle finished their shopping and headed for home.

Once they were out of the busy part of town she shared her news, pulling the two envelopes from her pocket. Both were eager to hear what the sheriffs had to report, so she opened the first one, which was from a small town further west from the Nebraska territory. She scanned it quickly, then read the disappointing letter to her uncle. It basically warned them of what they'd heard; that part of the area was sparsely populated, and most of the residents were men, some of whom were not to be trusted around ladies.

She folded it back up, returned it to its envelope and turned to the next one, which was from a town in central Nebraska. It was much more encouraging. It was from a Sheriff Thomas Hanley from Gulley Ridge. He reported good farmland in that area, and he knew of two farms for sale at the moment. He described their town a bit, which sounded good to Franklin and Martha. He also said there was more land further west that was available to be claimed yet. It would require some hard work to build a house and barn and turn the land and prove it able to be farmed, but it would be theirs once that happened.

As they talked the next few days, the idea of claiming land was tempting. As long as they lived on the land and farmed it, they didn't have to pay for it, which would be nice. Instead of using part of his money to purchase a farm, Franklin thought he could use his money to purchase the equipment, animals and seeds he would need for his first year or two of getting a farm operating. As nice as that sounded, they realized that would mean living on land that had no house and the land would need to be cleared before it could be tilled, which would be a big job.

Both of them felt they would probably be able to do it and were up to the challenge, but there were some unanswered questions. They didn't know what kind of wildlife they might encounter and how much of a problem they might be. They also didn't know if there would be an abundance of trees to use for building houses, or if there was a sufficient number of creeks and rivers to provide water for livestock. They would definitely need to get answers to those questions before undertaking such an adventure.

CHAPTER 2

A few days later they were at the mercantile again to do their weekly shopping. Martha checked at the post office window, but hadn't received any more replies. Franklin, however, received some news on his business. The banker had put the word out, and two men had approached him about possibly buying it. Both men had the means and were very interested. Both wanted to talk to Franklin as soon as possible. Franklin made arrangements to meet with them the next couple of days. He would show them the business, let them see his books, and answer any questions.

With two men interested, he knew he and Martha would have to make some decisions soon. One of the men told the banker he was looking for a house in the area, as well, and asked if Franklin's home would also be for sale since he was moving. The request caught Franklin a bit by surprise. He did want to sell his house in New York eventually, but his intention was to wait until they had solid plans made. Then he would put word out that the house was for sale. If it didn't sell before they left, he would simply have the banker sell it, send him the papers to sign, and put the money in the bank. He could contact him and make arrangements to send Franklin a bank draft once he knew where he would be receiving his mail.

While selling his house to the same person that buys the business was something he hadn't considered, he had to admit it would have its advantages. He could finish his business here before leaving, and could take a bank check with him. That would ensure he had the money available to purchase everything they would need once they had a place. Even if he purchased an existing farm, he would still need additional money to purchase additional animals or equipment, feed to winter the animals, and seeds in the spring. They would need money to live on until the farm started producing an income, as well. Knowing he had that would surely make it easier to concentrate on the work they would need to do.

That option was certainly exhilarating, but it would require them to be ready to move sooner, once the deal was made. If he sold the business and the house now, where would they go? He decided to have another serious talk with Martha this evening, and if they talked it over, perhaps they could come up with a solution. If not, he would just have to hold onto the house a bit longer while they made their plans.

Martha finished her order at the mercantile and turned to leave, when something caught her eye as she passed the list of notices near the door. She paused to read it, and went back to the counter of the store. "I'm sorry, I need to make a note of something. Would you have a pencil and some paper I could purchase, please?"

"If you just need to make a single note, I'll give you a sheet of paper and lend you a pencil," George said with a smile as he handed her what she needed. "I'll get your purchases loaded in your buggy while you do that."

"Thank you," she said, returning the smile. She went back and read the notice again, and jotted down the important information. She wasn't sure it would help them any, but it gave her something else to think about, and she and her uncle could certainly discuss it. She returned the pencil with a smile and another word of thanks, and hurried out the door. Her uncle was just leaving the bank, heading to their buggy.

Once their purchases were loaded, Franklin started the horses toward home. As they left the busy downtown area, he started a conversation. "I have some news about the business."

"A possible buyer?"

"Yes. In fact, two of them," he said with a smile.

"That's wonderful."

"Possibly. One of them is interested in purchasing our house, as well." Franklin watched her reaction, which was mixed. Initially she had a big smile, obviously excited by the news, but as she thought a moment, some of the excitement seemed to diminish. "Your smile is vanishing. Does that mean you're not in favor of that, or simply that it means there's more to think about with that option?"

She met her uncle's eyes with a grin. "You know me well, Uncle Franklin. It's wonderful news, but it also causes me to pause a bit. It would mean –"

He waited several moments, and when she didn't continue, he tried to help finish her thought. "That we have to have some plans as to where we're moving to?"

"Exactly," she confirmed. "Do you have any thoughts about that?"

"Nothing other than further west in Missouri. Or Kansas or Nebraska both sound nice to me. Those aren't plans we can actually act upon, however," he said with a bit of a sigh.

"Maybe, maybe not," she said with a bit of a mischievous grin. "How daring are you?"

He looked over at her, knowing there was something behind that grin. "What do you have in mind?"

"Well, as I was leaving the mercantile I saw a notice hanging there, and I took down the information. I'm not sure if you're interested in it, but I got the information anyway, just in case."

"What kind of a notice?"

"It's a notice of a wagon train leaving out of Missouri, heading west. They plan to travel from Missouri through Kansas, and into the new area known as Wyoming, and beyond."

Franklin looked at his niece, a bit of surprise mixed with worry on his face. "Are you saying you would like to go that far west?"

"No, but according to the notice, they plan to stop close to several towns along the way so they can pick up additional supplies if needed. They say individual wagons can leave the wagon train at any time if they choose. Perhaps we'll find an area we both like, and we could go into the nearest town and see if there are any farms for sale in the area."

Franklin was quiet for several minutes, and Martha could tell he was giving the idea some serious thought. "That sounds like it might be a good solution, except for one problem I see. What if we do that, but find there are no farms for sale. Then what will we do?"

"According to the notice there will be another wagon train heading the same direction three weeks later. If you stop along the way to visit family or look at the area, you can join the next one when it goes past three weeks later."

Franklin considered that idea, and Martha watched as a slight smile appeared, and slowly grew. "Now, that might work," he said with a nod of his head. "What do you think?"

"I haven't really had a lot of time to digest the idea fully, but apparently my thoughts are running real close to yours. According to the notice, there will be a series of three wagon trains, each departing from St. Louis, Missouri, three weeks apart. If we could make it to the first one, that would give us two opportunities to stop off and look into opportunities, and still be able to join back up if it didn't work out. That would be nice. My biggest concern right now is can we be ready to go in three weeks?"

They talked about it the rest of the way home. "Let's get the buggy unloaded first. Then I'll take care of the horses, and if you want to make us a quick dinner, we'll see if we can talk this out," Franklin said. She nodded and picked up a box of supplies and headed to the house. He followed behind with another box. "I'll get the rest of this stuff, Martha, so you can fix us something to eat. I always think better when we can talk things out over a meal."

She giggled, noticing the smile on his face, and agreed. It was good seeing him smile again. "Okay, I'll start on some dinner for us. It's already a little after noon."

Less than an hour later their supplies were put away, the horses were taken care of, and they sat down to enjoy their noon meal. "Before we even delve into what all we would need to do before we could leave, let me ask, does this idea appeal to you?" Franklin asked, giving his niece a serious expression.

"As I've thought about it more, I have to say I do like the idea. In fact, it's exciting to think we could travel to the area I've grown up in, and go beyond that. We can see the country we haven't seen before, and we may find a place that feels special to us, and we can stop and look around more. I think if we find there is a farm or land available in that area, we'll know we're home."

"I think it may be a good opportunity for us, as well," he said, allowing a small smile to grow. "I want to be sure we agree on what type of place we're looking for, though. If we agree on that, then we'll see what all we have to do before we can leave. If it's all feasible, then we need to get busy."

"I agree," Martha said, beaming, "but I'm not sure I know what you mean by what type of place we're looking for. I thought we agreed we liked living on a farm, or we would be willing to try a small ranch."

"We do agree on that, but there's more to it than simply being a farm. It's important to me that it's not too far from the nearest town."

"You used to like being out in the country where you didn't have a lot of people around bothering you. Is this what living in the city has done to you?" she asked with a chuckle.

"No, I'm looking forward to getting back to country living. I'm thinking of you, though, and I want to be close enough to a town that we can attend church on a regular basis and get our supplies. I want you to have other ladies you can meet with, and the possibility of meeting a young man."

"Uncle Franklin, I've told you, I'm not looking for a husband."

"I know you aren't looking, and I'm not trying to match you up with someone. But I also don't want you to miss out on the chance at a life with a special man. I consider myself a lucky man. Your Aunt Helen and I loved each other, and it made life very special. I'm not saying you can't be happy without meeting the special man for you, but I am saying life can be even better with him. I'm not planning on pushing you toward any man, but I do want you to have the opportunity to meet a few men and see if that magic happens for you. You're too special to me to keep you isolated, assuring that magic doesn't happen."

Martha was quiet for several moments, and Franklin noticed her fighting tears. He reached over to pat her hand, but she caught his hand and squeezed it. "Thank you, Uncle Franklin. I wasn't looking to get married, but that was such a nice thing to say, I'll remember it, I promise. And I approve of looking for a place not too far from a town. I do enjoy visiting with other ladies after church."

"Good," he said in an easy tone to lighten the mood. "Then if we agree that we both like the idea of the wagon train, and we agree on what type of place we're looking for, we better make a list of what all we'll need to do before we can go. It may not be feasible."

"Oh, I hope we can work it out. Knowing it's something we both want, I'm getting more excited just thinking about it. How long do you think it will take to sell the business, and possibly the house, as well?"

"I'm meeting with one gentleman tomorrow. I'll set up a meeting with the other man for as soon as he's available. Hopefully he can look at the business and house in the next couple of days, as well, and then we'll just have to wait and see if either or both of them make an offer."

"And while we're waiting for that we can decide what we're going to take and what we aren't, and get things packed."

"We'll also need to get a wagon," Franklin said. "And different horses. Ours are fine for a buggy or small wagon, but we'll need to get a larger wagon and some large horses or a team of oxen."

"Where will we get them? Can you even get oxen around here?"

"We'll probably have more luck finding a larger wagon and better horses or oxen when we get to Missouri. Several wagon trains leave from the St. Louis area, so I'm sure wagons, good horses, and oxen are easier to find there. We'll trade our horses there."

"How about the wagon? We could trade our buggy for one there, but our things won't fit in our buggy."

"No, they won't. We'll trade our buggy for a wagon here. The wagons around here aren't as large as what we'll find there, but we can get one here to carry our things to St. Louis. We can get one large enough to carry everything we decide to take with us, then trade that wagon for a larger one once we're there. We can transfer our things to the larger wagon and still have room to carry all the supplies we'll need, which we can buy there before we leave."

"Okay," Martha agreed. "Then I guess the next obstacle will be to decide what we have to take along and what we can either do without or replace once we reach our destination, wherever that turns out to be. Then once you get a wagon, we can load it full, without needing to leave room to store a lot of supplies."

"I'm thinking we'll be safe doing that. So once we have an idea of things we'd like to take, we'll get a wagon and put on as much as will fit. They warn you not to take too much on a wagon train because it will be too difficult, especially the further west you go. Since we're not planning on going that far, though, I think we should be okay."

"I hope so. I hate to think of how much we're going to have to leave behind. We have some beautiful furniture, and I know we can't take it all with us. Do you suppose we'll be able to replace it with like things, or will we have to replace it with more simple things?"

"I've wondered that myself," Franklin admitted. "I have a feeling furniture wherever we settle will be more basic, like we had in Missouri."

Martha nodded in agreement. "You know, thinking about that made me realize something. I grew up with simpler things and was happy with them. It wasn't until I moved out here and saw some of your beautiful pieces of furniture and pretty dishes that I even gave such things much thought. Now that I've seen them, it will be hard to give them up. As I've thought about that, I can't say I'm very proud of those thoughts."

Franklin patted her hand. "I know what you're saying, Martha, and I've had the same thoughts. The fancy things here were Helen's family's things, not mine. They are very pretty, and once you get used to them, you can't help but appreciate them. However, I'm willing to give them up in order to move back to a farm and have neighbors that genuinely care for each other."

Martha thought about his words several moments before responding to them. "Uncle Franklin, thank you for making me think of it in that light. These things are very nice, but to keep them we stay here, and that means having neighbors that are neighbors only because they live close. Out there our neighbors were our friends, and we all helped each other when they needed it. Now that I'm seeing it that way I'm sure it will be easier to leave these nice things behind in order to have good neighbors and friends again."

"With that thought, maybe this would be a good time to start going through our house and picking out the few things we would like to take with us." Martha nodded, and the two of them got some paper and a pencil and started going through their large house with a pragmatic eye, determined to whittle the list down to what they truly felt they needed to take with them.

THINGS MOVED QUICKLY for them from that point on. Franklin showed the business to the two men that were interested, and both made him an offer within the next day or two. The one that also looked at his house made an offer on both the business and his home. Franklin was more than a little surprised with the two offers. He hadn't expected as much. The banker felt they might want to wait and see if anyone else showed an interest, thinking they might get a higher offer. Franklin was more interested in selling it soon so they could get their plans underway. They had a lot to accomplish in a short amount of time if they wanted to make it to St. Louis to join the first of the three wagon trains. He accepted the offer of the man wanting to purchase the business and his home, liking the idea that the same man would purchase both.

The new buyer was ready to take over and move in immediately, which was fine with Franklin and Martha, so as soon as the papers were signed, they got busy. Franklin traded their buggy for a wagon and traded their horses for two larger horses to carry their belongings to Missouri. While he was doing that, Martha busied herself packing her trunk with her clothes. She knew she wouldn't need the gowns she'd acquired since coming to New York, but she sorted through the rest of her dresses.

She was determined to limit herself to one trunk for her clothes, and she hoped to use one trunk for all their bedding, table coverings, towels and curtains, although she wasn't sure she would take curtains. It might be easier to buy fabric and make curtains to fit their windows once they had a home. After her talk with her uncle, she was finding it much easier to leave many of their nicer things behind, now willing to get used to simpler things again in exchange for leaving the big city. She'd grown up on a farm, and the country was calling to her again. She was eager to get back to it.

After much hard work and making many difficult decisions to leave some of the things they liked behind, they had their new wagon loaded up and ready to leave. Franklin took enough money with them for what they felt they would need until they got settled, and the rest was put in a bank note. He was assured any bank would accept it and it would in effect transfer his money to a bank near his new home.

They said good-bye to the friends they had in New York, knowing they had to keep moving if they wanted to reach St. Louis in time to trade for a bigger wagon, and acquire another team of horses or oxen, get registered with the wagon master and purchase their needed supplies before the wagon train left. If they missed the departure time, they would have to wait three weeks, and they would only have one chance to stop along the way and still catch the next train heading west. They felt it was important they be part of the first train leaving, so they set off, determined and hopeful.

Driving the wagon all day wasn't fun, but they were determined. They helped and encouraged each other, reminding them it would be worth it to find a place where they wanted to live. They pushed ahead, getting as far each day as they could, and were happy when they finally reached their destination a bit earlier than they'd planned. They got there in the evening, and would have two full days to prepare. The wagon train was set to leave at sunup on the third day.

Franklin wasted no time, locating and talking to the wagon master first thing the next morning. The wagon master was very helpful and told him of a place he could trade his wagon and suggested what kind he should get and why. Franklin followed his advice and traded for a large covered wagon and purchased a set of oxen. The wagon master initially advised against getting a second team of animals because it would require them to carry extra oats to feed them and would be extra work every evening caring for them, making sure they had water and were fed. However, when he learned Franklin and Martha didn't plan on going any further than Kansas or possibly into Wyoming, he understood why he wanted them, and left the choice up to him.

Franklin had heard oxen and large work horses were rather scarce the further west you go, and thought an extra team would not only be helpful if they had an animal come up lame during the trip, but would provide the animals they would need for farming once they found a home. He decided the extra work during the trip would be worth it to have two teams of animals when they found a farm, especially if they staked a claim on unclaimed land. Turning land into a farm was hard work and two good teams of animals would be a lot of help.

They made friends with others they would be traveling with, and a couple of the men helped Franklin transfer their things to the larger wagon. Martha talked to others about what all supplies they should get, and made a list. They took her list with them to the mercantile to be sure they got all the items they thought they would need. They found a place to store it all on their wagon, and their second day there they went to bed tired, but full of hope. They were now ready to head out with the wagon train the next morning.

CHAPTER 3

$\mathcal{T}$raveling with the wagon train wasn't as bad as they thought it might be. It certainly wasn't easy, but the other people made traveling all day not quite as difficult. The ladies often walked alongside the wagons, and it allowed them to visit and get to know each other. When they stopped to eat, the ladies concentrated on fixing a meal while the men took care of the animals, unhooking them and taking them to a river or creek they camped near so they could drink.

They were lucky that they had good weather to start off. They were able to travel without incident for the first four days. On the fifth day it started to rain and travel slowed some as things got muddy. It continued to rain off and on, and on the seventh day one of the wagons at the back of the train got stuck in the mud. It took some time for the men to free it. Several men tried getting behind and pushing as the horses were pulling, but they had no luck. As they pushed and pulled it was putting a strain on one of the wheels, and they stopped, afraid of breaking the wheel.

After some discussion, they decided their best hope would be with more horses pulling, while some of the men tried holding the wheel in question stable. Another family had an extra team of horses, as well as Franklin, and they decided to hook both teams up to the wagon to help the original oxen pull. Hopefully that would allow them to get the wagon out of the deep mud without breaking a wheel in the process.

They knew this would take some time to accomplish, so the wagon master sent a couple of men out to hunt while the rest worked on getting the wagon out. Hopefully they could get something large enough for everyone to share, like a deer. Some fresh meat for everyone would not only be very welcome, but it would make everyone's supply of dried meat last longer.

The men worked tirelessly, and eventually they were able to get the wagon free, without breaking a wheel. Just as they successfully pulled it free, the hunters returned with large quarters of venison from a deer they'd shot. They cut the meat into family-size pieces and distributed some to every wagon.

They pushed on for another couple of hours before stopping for the day. After Franklin and Martha had taken care of their animals, eaten their evening meal and cleaned up after it, they talked a few minutes. "We're not far from where we used to live, Martha. Do you have any thoughts on that?"

"I think I would like to go a bit beyond where we lived before. Enough people have come this way over the past couple of years that I fear this area will be quite full."

"I agree with you," Franklin said. "I feel we will have a better chance of finding a suitable farm if we continue on. In two or three days we can revisit the idea of going to the nearest town and seeing if there is anything available, but I believe we need to go a little further west first." The two of them went to sleep that night in agreement on that subject.

The next day went better for the wagon train. The rain finally stopped and a steady breeze helped dry up some of the mud they'd been fighting. The change in weather, together with everyone having enjoyed some fresh venison the evening before, seemed to put everyone in a better mood. Martha walked with a couple of ladies she'd made friends with as the wagon train made its way west.

The next day was good, as well. The sun was shining, which was helping the breeze dry things up. They made good progress both days. The ladies Martha had been walking with were all in a good mood, as well. Martha smiled to herself as she thought how much nicer it was seeing sun and having a nice breeze, than it had been trudging through the mud. By the third day after the rain the mud was gone and many of the children were back to walking barefoot.

When they stopped for their noon break that third day to water and rest the animals and fix a meal for everyone, Martha went back to their wagon, and was concerned. Franklin looked flushed and seemed to be struggling a bit with the animals. He insisted he was fine, maybe just a little tired, but Martha was worried. He didn't look good in her opinion. He said he wasn't hungry, either, which deepened her concern.

She offered to drive the wagon that afternoon, but he insisted he was good to drive, just a little tired. By mid afternoon, however, when she offered again, he agreed, finally admitting he was indeed feeling a bit off and thought a short nap might help. She climbed up onto the seat and took over the reins, while he immediately lay down in the bed they'd made in the back of the wagon. He was asleep within minutes.

Martha didn't have any trouble driving the wagon the remainder of the day. She'd done it on a regular basis before her father had died, so although that wasn't a concern to her, she was worried about her uncle. As soon as they stopped for the night she went to check on him. She reached up to touch his forehead and was shocked to find he was burning up. She tried to wake him, but he was unresponsive.

She knew she hadn't unfastened the oxen or cared for them yet, but they weren't her first concern. Leaving them still fastened to the wagon, she quickly got a towel and dipped it in their water barrel and placed it on his forehead. She started rubbing his arms in an attempt to get him to wake up.

She was doing this and calling his name when Anita, the wife of the couple in the wagon ahead of hers, came to check on them. "Martha, is everything okay? I noticed the oxen are still – oh, my goodness," she said, looking at her unresponsive uncle. "Keep working on him, I'll try to get some help."

She ran back to their wagon and told her husband, William, what was going on. He sent her to get Sam Hartley, the wagon master right away, then rushed back to talk to Martha. "I don't know much about medicine or how to help, but Anita went to get Sam. I'll take care of your team of oxen so they don't get restless while still hooked up to the wagon."

"Thank you, William." Martha opened her uncle's shirt and got another wet towel and used it on his chest in an attempt to cool him down. She was wringing the warm cloth out and rinsing it in cooler water to replace on his forehead when Mr. Hartley came rushing back, with a woman next to him. "Miss Welch, Sarah worked with a doctor in Pennsylvania before joining the wagon train. She's the closest thing we have to a doctor, if you'd like her to look at your uncle."

"Please," Martha said, moving to the side. "Thank you. I'm Martha Welch, and this is my uncle, Franklin."

"Sarah Tilton," she responded as she allowed the wagon master to lift her onto the wagon and moved close to Franklin. Martha watched as Sarah did the same things she'd been doing, feeling his forehead and face, and replacing the cloths with cooler, wet ones. She then started checking his arms and legs for rashes as she began asking questions. "How long has he been feeling ill?"

"He seemed fine this morning. I didn't think he looked good when we stopped earlier today, but he said he was just a little tired and insisted he was fine to drive the team again. Later this afternoon I thought he looked worse and asked again if I could drive a while, and he agreed, saying he was tired, but was sure a nap would help. He climbed in the back and fell asleep quickly. This is how I found him when we stopped."

"Has he been injured lately; any cuts or animal bites or scratches?"

"No, not that I know of."

"So it came on quickly," Sarah said as much as asked, pinching his arm and watching for any kind of response. She looked in his eyes carefully, and in his mouth, before turning to face Martha. "I'm sorry, I'm not a doctor so I can't say for sure, but it seems to me like it's a very high fever. I don't see anything causing it, like an injury that's become infected, though, so I don't know what's causing the fever. If there was an injury that had become infected we could make a poultice, but without that, all you can do is treat the fever. You're doing the only thing I know of to do, which is try to cool him off and hope the fever breaks. I'm sorry I can't help you any more than that."

Sam looked from Martha to Sarah before asking, "If you don't see a reason for the fever, are you saying it's some sort of illness, like the influenza?"

Sarah glanced quickly at Martha, but was quiet. Martha looked at the worried look on Sam's face, and turned to Sarah. "He's asking if this could be something contagious because he's worried it could spread through the wagon train, and by your silence I'm assuming you think it could be. I'll be the one caring for him, but can you give me any advice?"

Sam looked uncomfortable, but didn't deny what she'd said. Sarah also looked uneasy, but answered her question. "Martha, I'm sorry, but unless we can find a reason for the fever, it's a distinct possibility."

"Do you have any idea what disease or illness he might have?"

Sarah seemed very sincere when she shook her head. "No, I really don't. Normally with most diseases, like the influenza, or even cholera, it doesn't come on this quickly. A person is generally not feeling well for at least a couple of days, with a fever that gets worse gradually before it gets this high, where they don't respond. That's why I said I'm sorry, I just don't know what's causing his fever."

"Thank you for checking him and your advice," Martha said. She went back to dipping the cloth in water again and spreading it out on his chest, as Sarah and Sam left.

Anita came back with a dish of food. "Martha, you have to eat something. Let me take care of your uncle while you eat."

"I'm not sure you should. Sarah said whatever is giving Uncle Franklin this fever could be contagious. I'd hate for you to get it from him."

"Oh, nonsense. We've all been around Franklin the last couple of days, and if he's this sick now, I have to think he might have had it before and just didn't know it. If what he has is contagious I'd say we've already been exposed. Now, you go eat some dinner."

"If you're sure, I would like to stretch my legs a bit."

"Go ahead, but please eat something, too, Martha. If you don't eat you'll be weak and more apt to get sick, as well."

"I suppose you're probably right there. Thank you. You and William have been such good friends to us."

"We've been friends to each other, and we've enjoyed it, as well." She climbed up into the wagon next to Franklin and rinsed out a cloth to cool it off as she watched Martha take the plate of food and walk off.

Martha went first to thank William for taking care of their oxen and horses. She ate her meal, and was going to retrieve water to replenish their water barrel, when she saw two men heading toward her with buckets of water. "We got some more water for you, Miss Welch," one of them said. "We heard about your uncle. I'm sorry, and hope he makes a quick recovery. We filled your water bucket, and these are a couple of extra buckets you can use to rinse your towels you've been using to try to break the fever."

Martha felt tears come to her eyes. "I don't know how to thank you both. I so appreciate it."

"Ma'am, some of the kids you've been helping to entertain on this trip are ours, and we appreciate what you've done. Your uncle used his extra team of horses when we needed it to get the wagon out of the mud. We all hated to hear about him not feeling well, and we want to help. If there's anything we can do, I hope you let us know."

"Thank you again," Martha said, fighting back tears. This reminded her of when they lived in Missouri and people helped each other all they could. She'd missed that living in New York, but she hadn't realized quite how much until now.

Martha thought about that as she finished eating, and made her way off to some bushes to find a private spot to relieve herself. When she got back to her wagon she felt better and was ready to resume caring for her uncle. She thanked Anita once again, as she switched places with her.

She nodded off now and then during the night, but kept switching the warmer towels for cooler ones, hoping his fever would soon break, but it didn't. The next morning several people stopped by to ask how he was doing. Several people brought food for her, which again spoke to her about how good these people were.

Sam came by to check on Franklin, as well. "How is he doing this morning?"

"There's not really any change," Martha said sadly. She looked at him anxiously, wondering what would happen. She could drive the wagon if need be, but she wasn't sure her uncle could take the rough ride all day, and she would have to find some ladies, maybe Anita and one or two others that would be willing to ride with him and care for him.

Before she had a chance to ask the wagon master what would

happen, Sarah walked up to the wagon. "I heard you say there's no change?"

"No, not really. His fever hasn't broken, and he hasn't seemed to wake up at all. He has spells where he seems restless, and other times where he seems to rest more comfortably."

Sarah nodded and proceeded to check on him herself. After seeing no change in him, she asked a few more questions. "I've been thinking about him a lot, but I can't figure out what it might be. You haven't heard him mention anything at all about being sore anywhere, or even a slight injury?"

"Not that I can recall, no." Martha's head flew up and her eyes met Sarah's. "He did say he thought he might have pulled a muscle or twisted wrong when they were working to get the wagon out of the mud the other day."

Sarah obviously took a few moments to consider Martha's words. "Where did he say he twisted wrong? What did he say hurt?"

"He said he must have twisted funny because he felt sore in the lower right side of his abdomen. That was a few days ago, though. Surely twisting wrong couldn't have caused this, could it?"

Sarah's eyes widened, and she turned back to Franklin. She opened his shirt further, and loosened his pants. She carefully pushed and prodded in the area of his stomach and gradually moved lower and to the right. She barely touched one spot and he jerked, while his face winced. "Martha, I'm sorry, but I believe your uncle is having an attack of appendicitis."

"Is there anything you can do for him?" Martha asked with a worried expression.

"No. I'm afraid the only thing that will help is to find a doctor who can operate. His appendix needs to come out. It gets infected and could burst, spreading the infection all through his body." She paused, and took Martha's hands. "I'm so sorry, but it might already be too late. This has probably been sore since that day, but he hasn't mentioned it again, thinking it just needs a few days to get better. That means the infection has had several days to fester and spread through his body."

Martha looked to Sam. "Do you know of any doctor in this area? I have to try to find one. Even if it's too late and he can't help," Martha said as a few tears escaped her eyes, "I have to at least try. I can't just sit here and watch him die."

The wagon master nodded in understanding. "The closest doctor that I know of is further west a ways. It's not too far from where the wagon train passes. We can go on in that direction and stop when we're close to the town, but I have to find someone that can drive your wagon. I don't have an extra man. I have a couple of scouts that go ahead of the train to make sure there are no problems ahead. I can have one of them go into town and summon the doctor when we get close, but I can't really tie one of them up all day driving your wagon."

"I can drive the wagon myself," Martha said, "if I can find a lady that will care for Uncle Franklin while we're traveling."

Anita was standing off to the side and stepped forward. "I can do that, Martha." Another lady stepped forward and offered to help, as well.

Sam studied Martha, his eyes narrowed. "I appreciate your willingness to try to drive the wagon, Miss Welch, but driving a wagon is harder than it looks."

"I agree, sir, but I've done it several times. Not in a wagon train, but on a farm. I drove this wagon yesterday, from about mid afternoon on while Uncle Franklin laid down for a nap. I might need a little help getting the oxen in the yoke and hooked up, since I've never worked with oxen before, but if I could get some help with that –"

Before she could finish, three men stepped forward, assuring her they would take care of that. Another man offered to run his wagon next to hers in case she had any problems.

"It sounds like we have a plan then," Sam said. "Men, let's get all our wagons ready to go, including the Welch wagon, and we'll get going as soon as we can. It sounds like time is of the essence for Franklin."

Everyone agreed and left, leaving Martha and Sam. "Thank you, sir," Martha said sincerely.

"Unfortunately, I can't guarantee much," he said, patting her arm, "but I agree with you. We have to at least try. I do need to talk to you, though, and I might as well do it now. When we get close to Green Falls I'll send one of my scouts into town to find Dr. Campbell and try to get him out to the wagon train."

"Thank you."

He nodded. "I have to warn you now, though, I'm afraid I won't be able to hold the wagon train up long. We'll see what Dr. Campbell says, but if he has to operate on him, I'll have to take the train on west. There is another one in three weeks and hopefully Franklin will be healed enough by then and you can join that one and continue on with your trip. I'm sorry, but I just can't –"

"I understand," Martha assured him. "I understand you have a time line and you can't hold everyone else up, waiting for my uncle to recover from an operation, and I'm not upset about it. I want you to know that I very much appreciate what you're doing for us, finding a doctor for him."

Sam studied Martha again, this time with a smile on his face. "You're a rare find, Miss Welch. Good luck to both of you." With that, he turned and ran off, obviously with plenty to do. His words were unexpected, and Martha took a few moments to consider them and what he'd meant. She only allowed herself a few moments to ponder before turning to get busy. She had to get them ready to move out.

Word had already gotten out and people were hurrying to pack things up and get the horses and oxen fastened to the yokes and in place. Two men came toward Martha's wagon, one leading the oxen, the other with their extra set of big work horses, which he tied to the back of the wagon.

She got everything packed and ready to go, and when Anita came, ready to take over Franklin's care, they discussed what would be best to set close by to hold water for the trip and how to try to secure it so it wouldn't slide around and dump over.

Once they had that ready, she made her way to the front of the wagon, sat down on the bench seat and took the reins from Clyde, the gentleman that had just finished getting the oxen ready to go. He quickly ran to his wagon, which had been brought to the side of Martha's, and one of the scouts came back to ask if they were ready to start. Martha assured him she was ready, Sam nodded his readiness and William, whose wagon was on the other side of Martha's, nodded as well. The scout ran forward, yelling "Wagon Ho!" and soon the wagon train was on their way.

One of the scouts that generally rode alongside the wagon train stayed fairly close to Martha's wagon, and she was sure it was to ensure himself she could in fact handle the wagon. She didn't have any problem with it, but kept looking back to see if Anita was doing okay. She made herself focus on driving the wagon and not on her uncle.

After almost three hours of traveling, the wagon train slowed and stopped. Sam appeared at her wagon as she pulled the oxen to a stop. "I've sent one of my men into Green Falls to summon Dr. Campbell. This is about as close as we can get, so we'll wait here. It's a little early, but I'll tell everyone to fix something for the noon meal, and we'll wait for the doctor. Hopefully he's in his office when Matthew gets to town and he can come on out. If he's out on a call it might take a little time to find him and get him out here. All we can do now is wait for Matthew to return, and the doctor to get here."

"Thank you again, Mr. Hartley," Martha said. "I appreciate

what you've done to help us." She hurried back to check on her uncle. "Any change, Anita?"

"Not really, no," Anita answered with a depressing sigh. "He got a little restless over the rough ground, but the fever hasn't broken yet and he hasn't woken."

"Okay. Thank you for staying with him."

"I'll go fix us something to eat and I'll bring some for you, too. I'll be back soon. If you need anything before I get back, yell, and William or I will come."

Martha thanked her again and turned to concentrate on her uncle. As she was taking care of him she noticed the wagons around her were gathering firewood, getting fires started and cooking a meal. Anita brought her a meal, which she gratefully ate while caring for Franklin. Quite some time had gone by and she hadn't seen the doctor.

Eventually the wagon master came by and said he hadn't seen Matthew yet, either. He was guessing the doctor must have been out of his office and Matthew was looking for him, trying to track him down. He didn't address the situation directly, but Martha was getting the impression he couldn't wait much longer before having to get the wagon train moving again. She spent some time pondering that thought as she continued to keep cool cloths on Franklin.

After what must have been another hour, the wagon master was at her wagon again, with the man she assumed was Matthew, the scout that had gone for the doctor. Their expressions looked grim.

CHAPTER 4

*M*artha looked from Matthew to Sam, and locked eyes with him. "Mr. Hartley, what has happened?"

"Miss Welch, Matthew made it back with some news. Unfortunately, a roof collapsed on one of the buildings in Green Falls, leaving several people there injured. Dr. Campbell has been extremely busy caring for those people. He is aware of your uncle and has promised he will come out here to do what he can for him as soon as he's able, but he's not sure how long that will take."

"Is it far from here? Would it help if I drove the wagon closer to town so when he has a chance to look at him he doesn't have to travel as far?"

"Ma'am," Matthew said, "it's not far from Green Falls. Wyatt brought the wagon train about as close to the town as he could. It's only a half hour ride or less by horse, but it would take longer with the wagon. Dr. Campbell said it would probably be harder on him to travel than to wait the extra twenty to thirty minutes. He asked me to please apologize for the delay, and let you know he will be here as quickly as he can."

"Okay, thank you," Martha said with a long sigh.

"I'm so sorry, Miss Welch," Sam said, and Martha could tell by the look in his eyes he meant those words.

"Thank you for what you've done for us, Mr. Hartley. It sounds like the doctor has his hands more than full right now." The wagon master looked troubled and upset as he paused, and she could tell he had more to say. She knew he truly had done all he could do, and she hated to make his job any tougher. "Sir, if you need to get the wagon train moving again, I understand. We'll be okay while we wait for the doctor."

"I hate to do that, but I have a responsibility to all of these people."

"I understand."

"Before we leave, there isn't normally too much of a problem with predators, wild animals in this area, but I have seen an occasional cougar or coyote. Does your uncle have some type of gun and ammunition?"

"He does, and I know how to use it."

Both men's eyebrows rose. "You do know how to use it?" Mr. Hartley asked.

"Yes. I grew up on a farm and my father taught me how to use a gun. I've been hunting with him. If an animal approaches our wagon, I will shoot first to scare it off, but if need be, I can shoot it."

Martha saw the wagon master relax a bit, but she also saw a look of surprise in his eyes. "Okay, I'm glad to hear that," he said. "I'm sorry, but I will have to get the train moving again so we can get to an acceptable location with available water to spend the night. I'll have the men that took care of your animals bring them back to your wagon for you, and make sure your water barrel is full before we leave. I wish you and your uncle the best of luck, Miss Welch. I hope the doctor arrives soon and the operation is successful."

"Thank you, Mr. Hartley, and thank you, Matthew, for going for the doctor."

"Yes, ma'am," Matthew said as he turned his horse and rode off.

"Is there anything else any of us can do for you before we leave?" Sam asked.

"I don't think so, Mr. Hartley, but thank you for asking."

Several minutes later Anita came hurrying back to Martha's wagon. "Martha, I can't believe he's ordered the wagon train to continue. Will you be okay? Where is the doctor?"

Martha explained everything to Anita and tried to assure her she and her uncle would be fine. She certainly wasn't happy that the train would be moving on and leaving them, but she understood it. She didn't want the people who had been so kind to her on this trip worrying, so she tried to sound more positive than she felt.

William and Anita offered to stay with her, saying they could catch the next train, but she shook her head. "No, you can't do that," she objected. "Your family is expecting you and they will be concerned if you don't arrive. Besides, there will be a cost involved, and I know you wanted to get to the area they're calling Wyoming before bad weather so you can get a house built."

"But how will I know you're okay?" Anita asked.

"Write down the town you're going to, and I promise I'll write a letter and let you know where I've settled. I'd love to stay in contact through letters, so when I have an address I'll send you a post so you know where I am residing. Now you two go on and get ready so you can leave with the rest of them."

Several other families stopped by to say how bad they felt leaving, to wish her the best of luck, and ask if there was anything they could do to help her before they left. Those offers by the wonderful people they'd come to know meant a great deal to her. She thought about them as she watched the last of the wagons travel out of sight. She glanced over at the rifle setting close by and took another look around her area. Once she was assured there were no animals stalking their wagon, she turned back to her uncle. Surely the doctor would be here shortly.

As she cared for him, he was turning more restless, which worried her. She rubbed his arms and talked to him, hoping he would wake up. To her surprise, his eyes fluttered open. "Uncle Franklin? I'm here and you're going to be okay. Just rest."

He tried to speak, but nothing came out. She helped him get a few sips of water, and he smiled, and tried speaking again. His voice was very quiet, and she had to lean down close to hear him. "Martha, my dear, you've meant so much to me. My days are done, but –"

"No, Uncle Franklin, a doctor is coming, you'll be fine."

"No, I won't. Something inside burst and I'm filled with infection. But listen to me. You are a strong person. I want you to go on and find a place that makes you happy. Don't turn your back on all men you meet, but give them a chance. If you find the right man, you'll know it, and don't chase him away. Your father and mother were so very happy, as were Helen and me. That's what we all want for you. We've all loved you dearly." Franklin closed his eyes, and Martha watched helplessly as her beloved uncle died in her arms.

She tried to bring him back, rubbing his arms and calling his name again, but she knew he was gone. She held him silently for several minutes, looking into the eyes of the man who had meant so much to her. She thought back on his words, and realized he was right; she was a strong person. She was certainly going to miss her uncle, just as she still missed her father, her aunt and her mother, whom she never knew. But Uncle Franklin was right; she was strong, and she was still alive and she had to make some plans. Matthew had told her where Green Falls was, and she would go there and find a room in a hotel or boarding house for a few days while she gave this situation some serious thought.

First, though, she had to bury her uncle. He was a good man and had been wonderful to her. Giving him a decent burial was the least she could do for him. She allowed herself a good cry while she held him a few more minutes, then covered him with a blanket. She rummaged around on their wagon and found their shovel, hopped down from the wagon, and squared her shoulders. She could do this.

She looked around, and found a tree not too far away that offered a good shade. The area looked very peaceful, so she went to it. When she got there she realized the area was on a bit of a hill and had a good view of the valley below. It looked very similar to the area in Missouri where her papa and uncle had their farms, where she'd grown up.

Without giving it any more thought, she put the shovel in the ground and started digging. It was hard work, but she didn't really mind. Her mind was filled with memories of her uncle, and the others she'd lost. Digging became an unconscious act as she thought back on all the good times, and the bad, when they had passed. Tears streamed from her eyes as she worked, but she didn't care. She was so engrossed in her work and her memories that she never heard the hoof beats of a horse approaching until it had stopped close to her.

"Ma'am?" a deep baritone voice from behind her said, startling her.

She jumped and turned around. Seeing a stranger on a large horse, she looked toward her wagon, holding her rifle. Before she could respond, he held his hands up. "Whoa, ma'am, I'm sorry, I didn't mean to scare you. I'm not going to hurt you. My name is Wyatt Peterson. I own a ranch not too far from here, and I'm on my way into Green Falls. I'm guessing you were part of the wagon train that just passed through here, but something must be wrong. A young lady shouldn't be out here alone. Is there something I can help you with?"

"Thank you, sir, but I'll be fine. When I finish here I plan to go into Green Falls, too, and get a hotel room. Thank you for your offer."

"You say when you finish. May I ask what it is you're doing? Maybe I can help, and then we can ride to Green Falls together. I don't much like the idea of leaving a young lady out here by herself."

"Thank you for your concern, but –" She looked down at what she was doing, and she couldn't seem to stop the tears from flowing from her eyes again. That irritated her. She was a strong lady, and she didn't want a stranger to see her crying. She quickly wiped her eyes with the sleeve of her dress and tried to hold her head up and square her shoulders, but the man had already jumped down from his horse and was taking her in his arms.

He pulled her to his chest, rubbing her back. "Ma'am, it's okay. Something has obviously happened. I'm not sure what it is, but I'd like to help if I can. Why did you leave the wagon train?"

Martha wasn't sure why she trusted this man, but she did. That was very unlike her. Maybe it was because she'd just lost her uncle, she wasn't sure, but she felt safe in his arms. He didn't push for an answer, but continued to hold her, seeming to know somehow that it was exactly what she needed right at that moment. He rubbed her back, which helped her get control of her tears. After a couple minutes she was able to pull herself together and look up into his eyes, which seemed to be full of warmth and caring. "My uncle was sick and they couldn't wait any longer for the doctor to get here, so the wagon train left an hour or two ago. My uncle passed away before Dr. Campbell could get here. He was a good man."

"And you're trying to give him a burial, which he deserves," the deep voice said, not asked. He rubbed her back again and guided her head back to his chest. "I'm so sorry, ma'am. Dr. Campbell is a good man. I'm sure if he was delayed, there was a reason."

"A scout went to town to fetch him and when he returned he said a building had collapsed in Green Falls, leaving several people hurt. He promised to come out as soon as he could."

Wyatt's eyebrows rose. "A building collapsed? Oh, my." He took a deep breath, and patted her on the back gently. "Ma'am, please allow me to help with this. I don't have a shovel, but if you'll let me use yours, I'll help. We'll give your uncle a proper burial, and then I'll escort you to town."

"I can't ask you to –"

"You didn't ask me to do a thing, ma'am, I offered. I was serious about it, too. Please allow me to help."

She considered him, and looked down at how much, or how little she'd actually accomplished, and sighed. "I would appreciate some help," she said as she handed him the shovel. "I guess I'm not making much progress. My name is Martha Welch, by the way."

"Nice to meet you, Martha." He took his jacket off and laid it over his horse's saddle as he started shoveling dirt. "How far were you and your uncle planning to travel? Are you meeting family?"

"No, I have no family left," Martha said as she sniffled, but was determined not to cry again.

"Where are you coming from?"

"From New York. We decided we would rather live in the country than the city, but have no family anywhere, so we joined the wagon train. When we found an area we liked, we were going to stop and try to find a home."

His eyebrows jumped up again as he considered her words. It surprised him that a man and his niece from a large city on the east coast would decide they wanted to leave the city and go west. He wondered if they had any idea how different life was out here, and what made them think they would like living out here. He would never want to go east, where it was full of large cities and too many people for his liking. Living out here was hard work, but it also gave him a sense of peace and accomplishment. He wondered what about living out here they thought they would like. He also wondered if either of them had ever done a hard day's work in their life.

"So you didn't really have any specific area in mind?"

"Not really, no. We've been told Kansas is nice, so we were thinking about breaking away from the wagon train soon and looking around at the area. Then my uncle got sick."

"Well, if you're looking for Kansas, you've found it," Wyatt said.

"We're in Kansas now?"

"Yes, ma'am, you are. After we finish here we'll get you into Green Falls and see if we can get you a room at the hotel. You can think things over and decide what you want to do. You might decide you want to go back to New York."

Martha answered with no hesitation, but she spoke softly and he didn't hear what she'd said. He had to wonder why they decided to move. Perhaps something had happened there to make them want to leave, and if so, she might not want to go back. He couldn't help but think that once she was here and saw how different life here was, she might reconsider. "Once I find a room and get settled I'll take a few days to think, but I don't think I'll be going back to New York."

Wyatt didn't say anything, thinking it would be better to let her experience life here for a few days, and reach a decision on her own as to what she wanted to do. She asked him a few questions about what this area was like, and how big the town of Green Falls was, as he worked. He found she was very easy to talk with, and hoped things worked out for her, whatever she decided to do.

After they had buried her uncle, Martha was surprised when

Wyatt said a few words about how he knew he had been a good man, based on his niece. He quoted a couple of scriptures from the Bible, which also surprised Martha, but made her feel better. "I'll give you a few minutes here alone, Martha. When you're ready, come back to the wagon and we'll go into Green Falls."

She nodded, thankful for this opportunity to say her farewell in private. When she was done, she turned and saw Wyatt waiting patiently for her on the far side of her wagon, giving her plenty of space to be alone. "Thank you for all your help, and the kind words," she said as she approached him. "I appreciate all of it."

"You're welcome. Now, I've fastened my horse onto the back of your wagon. I'll drive it into town, if you're ready."

"I am, but I can drive the wagon. You don't need to –"

"Nonsense," he said, lifting her into the wagon. "We're both going the same place, you've just lost your uncle and I'm familiar with this area. The least I can do is drive the wagon for you."

"All right. Again, thank you."

They talked some, but not a lot on the way to Green Falls. She occasionally asked a question or two, which he readily answered, but he tried to avoid asking her too many questions. He was sure she had a lot to think about after what she'd just been through, and he wanted to give her time to do just that.

Not only that, but he was trying to come to terms with the feelings he was having for this lady. She was a small lady, petite in stature, and in his mind she needed to put a little more meat on her bones, yet she wasn't too thin, like a few ladies he'd met. They always looked sickly to him. She was polite, but not meek. For some reason, he had equated smaller ladies with being meek, not willing to voice an opinion or stand up for herself. That wasn't very appealing to him. This lady was small, but even right after losing her uncle she certainly wasn't meek. He liked that.

She was also a very pretty lady, with auburn hair she had in a knot of some sort at the back of her head. He normally didn't pay a lot of attention to ladies, feeling he had his hands full trying to run his ranch. He wasn't interested in finding a lady to complicate his life at the moment. He was having a difficult time remembering that at the moment, though. Her gorgeous green eyes seemed to pierce right through him, going right to his soul. He had this over-whelming feeling that she needed someone to protect her, and he found himself thinking maybe he should be the one to do it. He shook his head in an attempt to clear it. What was he thinking? He didn't have time in his life right now for a woman. He better get her settled in a room at the hotel, get his business done in town, and get home before he did anything he would regret later.

As they were about to the small town they saw a horse and small buggy approaching them. Wyatt watched the buggy as it approached. "There's Dr. Campbell now," he said. He stopped the wagon and waited as the doctor got closer. "Dr. Campbell," he said.

"Good afternoon, Wyatt. I can't really talk right now, I'm on my way to a bad situation, someone with the wagon train."

"I have her right here, Doctor. That's why I wanted to stop you. There's no need for you to go out there."

The doctor looked from Wyatt to Martha, with sadness in his eyes. "Does this mean I was too late?"

"I'm afraid so, Doctor," Wyatt confirmed, feeling bad for the doctor. "Dr. Campbell, this is Martha Welch. It was her uncle that passed."

"Ma'am, I'm very sorry."

"There's nothing for you to feel sorry about," Martha said, surprising Wyatt. "I understand you had your hands quite full here. Besides, I don't think you would have been able to help him. A lady on the wagon train that had been working with a doctor said she thought he was having an attack of appendicitis. It started several days ago, so she warned me that it might already be too late. As much as I hated to hear that and hoped she was wrong, I believe she was right."

"You say it was several days he suffered?"

"Yes, sir. The men all worked together to get a wagon free that had been stuck in the mud. Later that evening he said he felt he twisted wrong, and his lower right side of his abdomen was sore. He didn't say anything else about being in pain, but he wasn't the type to complain. So I think it bothered him for two or three days. Then when he got sick enough that I knew something was wrong, he lay down to take a nap and I couldn't wake him. He was burning up with a fever."

"Ah," the doctor said, nodding his head. "Then yes, I'm afraid you may be right. By the time you found out what was wrong, he was probably too sick to survive the operation."

"I'm actually rather glad that he wasn't awake the last two or three days. As much as I loved him and would have loved to have a few more days with him, I fear he would have been in a lot of pain, and I wouldn't have wanted that."

"Again, I think you're probably right. It's probably a blessing he wasn't awake to feel that pain." He paused a few moments before asking, "I'm sorry to have to ask this, but would you like me to send one of the men out, or do you have him in your wagon?"

"We gave him a proper burial," Wyatt said, speaking up. "Miss Welch found a very nice, peaceful spot, and she said her good-byes to him."

"Oh, good."

"We're on our way into town now to see about getting her a room at the hotel while she decides what she would like to do."

"Thank you for stopping me, Wyatt. I'll turn around and follow you back into town. There are several people there I should check on."

"I heard a building collapsed. Was anyone killed?"

"No, but there are four people that were hurt fairly badly.

There were a few others with injuries, but nothing as serious. There was a broken arm and several cuts, a bump on the head, but they'll all be okay with time. There are four that will take longer to heal, but I'm hopeful they all will in fact heal. I wasn't too sure about two of them for a while, but they both seem to be doing a little better now."

"Good, I'm glad to hear that," Wyatt said. They continued on their way, with the doctor following behind. Once the wagon was moving again, he reached over and patted Martha's hand. "Ma'am, that was very nice, what you said to the doctor."

She looked up at him, a little surprised. "I told him the truth."

"Yes, but as much as I'm sure you were wishing he would have gotten there sooner, you made sure he didn't feel bad about how long it took."

"Sarah had warned me it might already be too late to be able to save him, and now I believe that it was. I'm sure Dr. Campbell would have been there sooner if he could have, so what purpose would it serve to allow him to feel bad about something he couldn't control?"

Wyatt looked over at her and held her gaze for a few moments. His smile met his warm eyes as he said, "You are a rare lady, Martha Welch. I'm glad I met you."

Martha didn't respond, too busy thinking about his words. The wagon master had said something similar to her just a day or two ago. Before she had much chance to consider what that meant, they reached Green Falls. She looked around, seeing what all businesses were available. Several people were looking at them, but Wyatt explained that as he waived to a couple of people. "I'm sure people are wondering who you are, and why I'm driving a wagon with you and an extra set of horses into town. Don't let them scare you, though. They're curious, I'm sure, but once they know who you are, I'm sure they'll welcome you to town."

"Do you think?"

"Yes, I do. The people of Green Falls might be curious, but they're also very friendly and welcoming. Let's go first to the hotel and see if we can get you a room. Then I'll see if we can store your wagon and horses at the livery, and show you around a bit so you know where to find anything you might be looking for."

"Thank you, Mr. Peterson."

"Please call me Wyatt, Miss Welch."

"Okay, if you'll call me Martha."

"That sounds fair," he said with a smile as he pulled up in front of the hotel.

CHAPTER 5

*W*yatt escorted Martha into the hotel, but ten minutes later they were back out and he was helping her up into the wagon again. "I've never heard of there not being a room at the hotel. Let's go talk to Hank, Sheriff Miles. Maybe he'll have an idea, or at least know why the hotel is full."

Fifteen minutes later they were seated at the sheriff's office. Well, she was seated. Wyatt was up pacing back and forth, talking with Sheriff Hank Miles. "Hank, I don't understand. I know the Hendersons have a small home, but just because his family is visiting, why do they have to have four rooms in the hotel? I understand they need one for his parents and one for his sister, but couldn't his brothers sleep in the same room, or even in the barn? Where is Miss Welch supposed to stay?"

The sheriff had a bit of a smile on his face as he patted Wyatt's shoulder. "Wyatt, calm down. I know if it were you or me, or about anyone else around here, we'd just sleep in the hay in the barn, but they're from back east. They're used to nice things and fancy feather beds. Henry said they're already commenting about how they don't know how he can be happy out here in the middle of nowhere, with no nice restaurants or theaters. They've been there three days, and have booked the hotel for eight more days. They can't just kick them out."

Wyatt ran his hand through his hair, and for the first time Martha noticed his hair. In fact, she noticed the whole man that had been so kind as to stop and help her. She hadn't noticed before, but now that she looked at him while he was arguing with the sheriff, he really was quite a handsome man. He was tall, with broad shoulders, she assumed from working on his ranch.

He'd had a cowboy hat on before, but he took it off when he went inside, and she now noticed he had thick, dark brown, almost black hair that had just enough of a wave to it that it made her want to run her fingers through it, although she had no idea where that thought came from. She'd certainly never had any such thoughts with any other man she'd met.

The thing about this man that had caught her attention earlier was his eyes. He had beautiful brown eyes that were very warm. When he spoke to her he looked right at her, and those beautiful eyes stayed trained on her, as he listened to what she was saying. Not many men had done that with her in the past, but it was something that meant a lot to her. She'd met too many men who felt a lady only knew about cooking or needlepoint, and weren't interested in what she felt or had to say.

Her attention was drawn back to the room when she heard the sheriff speaking to Wyatt. "Wyatt, I know it might not be what you want to hear, but I don't see another solution at the moment. Several of the people that were hurt today live out of town, on neighboring small farms. Doc was worried about one of them getting worse and needing him, so several families in town are keeping one of the injured at their house so they're close to the doctor's house. You're the only one around here that has the extra room right now."

"Me? You know how people around here talk. What would

they say if I took a single young lady home with me? I can't, and won't do that to her reputation."

"My friend, you have to calm down. Everyone around here knows Rosy. She's been with your family since shortly after your parents moved here. She's a wonderful cook and house-keeper, but she knows everything that goes on in that house, and won't hesitate to speak up if something doesn't meet with her approval. More importantly, everyone here in town knows that."

Wyatt paused a moment and smiled. "Yes, I guess you're right there."

"Of course I am. When your aunt stayed with you for several months after her husband died, everyone in town heard about how she sat out on the porch in the evening if a suitor came to call, chaperoning the couple. She wasn't about to let her spend any time with a man, no matter how nice he seemed to be, without someone with her. People still laugh about how she chased Henry Wilson off with a broom when she saw him getting ready to kiss her."

Martha had to laugh at that story. Wyatt stopped pacing and laughed, as well. "Rosy does have strong morals," Wyatt agreed.

"Yes, she does, and she insists everyone around her does, as well, including you. Everyone around here knows that. On top of that, everyone knows there were people injured today and the hotel is already full with the Hendersons. Doc checked on that, thinking he could put a couple of the injured men in a room together, and stop in every chance he got to check on them since it's so close to his home and office."

"I didn't know he'd checked on that."

"He did. That's why he asked local people if they could open their homes to the injured men." He paused a few moments before going to Wyatt and putting his hand on Wyatt's shoulder. "Listen, I care a great deal about what happens in this area, and I wouldn't let you take her to your home if I didn't know for a fact that she and her reputation will be perfectly safe with Rosy in your home."

The sheriff turned to Martha and spoke directly to her. "Miss Welch, I mean every word of that. Our hotel is full right now, as are several other homes that would otherwise be willing to have you as a guest. But Wyatt here has a cook and housekeeper that's one of the nicest ladies you'll meet, as long as you don't cross her. I know you'll love her, but I can also pretty much guarantee she won't allow you and Wyatt here to be alone for more than a minute or so. You can trust me when I say your virtue will be fine out there. It will also be a good place for you to spend some time dealing with what's happened and will allow you to think clearly as you plan what you want to do next."

"Thank you, Sheriff, but I don't think Mr. Peterson wants me at his ranch, and I can understand that. I don't want to be a hardship for anyone. I have everything I need in our wagon and I can stay there. If there is another town anywhere close by, perhaps you could give me directions for it and I can leave in the morning."

Both men objected simultaneously. "Nonsense," the sheriff said.

"That is not going to happen," Wyatt said.

"I certainly don't like the idea of a lady leaving for another town, traveling alone," the sheriff added.

"You were mistaken if you thought I didn't want you at my ranch," Wyatt said, "and I'm sorry if I gave you that impression. My concern was for your reputation. Hank's right, though; we don't have anything to worry about as long as Rosy is there. I have a large house for just Rosy, and myself so there's plenty of room. Rosy will love having another lady to talk to. I have to stop at the mercantile and place an order, but after that I'll be ready to leave. Is there anything you'd like to do in town before we head out?"

Martha was confused by Wyatt's sudden change of attitude.

She had to work hard at not laughing when she saw the sheriff's eyebrows soar up to his forehead, so she had to assume he was taken back a bit, as well. "I hate to be a burden, Mr. Peterson. You've already done so much to help me, and I'm grateful."

"I thought we had agreed to Wyatt, and you will not be a burden. As I said, Rosy will be delighted to have you stay with us. Hank was right when he said the ranch would be a good, quiet place to get some thinking and planning done. Is there anything you'd like to do in town before we leave?"

"No, I don't think so."

"Why don't I take you with me to the mercantile. I'm sure people are wondering who you are, so I'll introduce you to anyone that's over there, and I'll tell them at Hank's suggestion I'm taking you to the ranch to keep Rosy company while you decide what you want to do."

"That should take care of any questions anyone might have," the sheriff said. "I'll tell anyone who mentions Miss Welch the same thing, that you took her there at my suggestion. Miss Welch, again, I'm sorry for your loss, and I hope you enjoy your stay with Wyatt and Rosy. Green Falls is a friendly little town and we'd be glad to have you as a new resident."

"Thank you, Sheriff."

Wyatt led her out of the office with a gentle hand on her back, which she noticed. Again, somehow that simple act made her feel safe, like she wasn't alone in an unfamiliar place. He led her down the boardwalk a little ways, then checked both ways carefully before leading her across the road to what appeared to be the largest store in the small town. She'd been pretty sure people had been watching them since they left the sheriff's office, but when they entered the mercantile people stopped talking and didn't even try to hide the fact they were all watching them.

Without even a pause Wyatt walked to the counter. "Good afternoon, Joseph."

"Hello to you, Wyatt, ma'am. Can I get something for you?"

"Yes, I need to place an order for next week, but first, Joseph and Eloise Hall, I'd like you to meet Miss Martha Welch. She and her uncle were part of the wagon train that passed by. Her uncle became ill and they were unable to continue on."

"Oh, I heard there was someone that rode in this morning looking for Dr. Campbell," Eloise said. "He said he was with the wagon train and there was a man that needed a doctor. I know Dr. Campbell felt terrible because he was so busy with the people that were hurt here that he couldn't get out there right away. Was that your uncle?"

"Yes, ma'am."

"Is he getting better now?"

Martha looked down, and Wyatt reached over and patted her hand as he looked at Mrs. Hall. "I'm afraid Mr. Welch passed on before Dr. Campbell was able to get to him."

Mrs. Hall's face went pale. "Oh, my. I'm so sorry, Miss Welch. You poor thing. You not only lost your uncle, but here you are, all alone now. Is there anything we can do to help you? Is there some family we can help you contact?"

Martha looked up, and Wyatt could tell she was surprised. "Thank you, ma'am," Martha said.

Wyatt took the opportunity to explain a little further, when he saw Martha was having trouble fighting tears and trying to speak. "I came across Miss Welch and her wagon as I was coming in this morning. I stopped to see if I could help. Once I saw what had happened, I helped her give her uncle a proper burial, then helped her bring her wagon into town, hoping she could secure a room at the hotel for a few days. She doesn't have any family, so she needs to give some thought to what she wants to do now."

"Oh, no," Joseph said. "The Hendersons are here visiting, and didn't Hank and Dr. Campbell say they'd taken all the rooms at the hotel?"

"Yes, that's what we found out," Wyatt confirmed.

"Oh, my goodness," another lady said as she stepped forward. "I know they were asking all of us that have an extra room in our homes here in town if we could let one of the injured people stay with us a few days while they recover, as well. The doctor wanted them all to be in town so he could get to them quickly if they got worse." She put a finger to her lips and tapped them a few times. "My dear, we'll come up with something. This town helps people who need help, and you've been through a terrible time already. Maybe we could open the church and –"

Wyatt broke in before the lady finished her thought. "Martha, this is Thelma Mellinger. Her husband, Jed Mellinger is our pastor in town."

"Nice to meet you," Martha said quietly.

"Oh, I'm sorry, my dear. There I went again, talking away and didn't even introduce myself," Thelma said. "It's so nice to meet you."

"To your concern, Mrs. Mellinger, Sheriff Hank had an idea, and I think it's a pretty good one. He suggested I take her to the ranch with me and let Rosy help her. She's so good at taking care of people and helping them heal and think things through. The ranch has enough space that she'll be able to find some solitude for thinking."

"If Rosy lets her out of her sight long enough," Thelma said with a little laugh. "Wyatt, I think that's a marvelous idea. Rosy is a wonderful lady, and you're right, she can make anyone feel better." She turned to Martha and put a hand on her arm. "Dear, I think, too, that's a very good idea. Rosy is about the nicest lady you'll ever meet, and she's very wise and thoughtful. Wyatt is a good man, as well, and you don't have to worry about him." She laughed, as did a few other people that were in the store and obviously listening to the whole conversation. "I doubt that Rosy will ever let you and Wyatt alone for more than a minute or two, but even if she would, you have nothing to worry about with our Wyatt."

"Thank you, ma'am," Martha said, looking from Thelma to Wyatt, who had a warm smile for her.

"I think it's an excellent idea, as well," Mrs. Hall said. "Rosy can help make anyone feel better, and she'll be so happy having another lady to visit with. It will be perfect for everyone. Welcome to this area, Miss Welch. I hope you decide to stay."

"Thank you," Martha said sincerely. "It was very thoughtful and kind of Mr. Peterson to invite me out there, and everyone has been very kind. I appreciate it more than I can say."

"I'm glad to hear that," Thelma said. "If any of us can do anything to help you, please let us know."

"I will, and thank you," Martha said.

"Wyatt, did you need something today?" Joseph asked.

Wyatt took care of his business quickly and led Martha back out of the mercantile and they returned to her wagon. Once they were out of town and headed toward his ranch, she turned to him. "Thank you for handling Mrs. Mellinger's question back there," she said.

"You're certainly welcome. I know it has to be hard for you to even think about that yet, let alone try to speak of it. I felt bad bringing up the fact that you were with the wagon train because I knew that question would be asked, but I wanted to be up front with them and be sure and remind them right from the start that Rosy will be there. I didn't want anyone thinking we were trying to hide you out there or give anyone a reason to talk."

"I appreciate that."

He reached over and squeezed her hand, something he'd done before, and although it wasn't something she was used to, she found she liked it. It helped calm her for some reason, made her think things would be okay. Before she had time to give that much thought, he was speaking. "So, you were in the wagon train. Did you say you were coming from the east coast?"

"We lived in New York."

"In the state of New York, or New York City?"

"New York City. My uncle had a manufacturing business. He sold his home and business and we decided to travel west. We hadn't decided on any specific place, but thought we might like Kansas. In fact, we were beginning to like the area we were passing through, and were thinking about stopping yesterday or today and going into town and look at the area. But then Uncle Franklin got sick."

"Well, you got to see a little bit of the town. The next couple of times I go back into town you can go along so you can get a better look at it and see what you think. Rosy and I can take you out for a ride in the county so you can see this area. You might like it here and decide to stay."

"I'll have to ask around in town and see if there is any kind of employment I might be able to obtain."

"Have you given any thought to what kind of employment you might be looking for?"

"No. That's one of the things I'll have to think about."

"What did you and your uncle plan on doing? Was he going to buy or start a business of some sort?"

"We were tired of living in the city and hoped to buy a farm. That's why we had the extra set of horses. We'd heard they're rather scarce out here, but necessary, so we brought an extra team with us."

Wyatt wasn't expecting her to say they'd planned on buying a farm. He had to wonder if people from a big city back east had any idea what living on a farm would be like. She was probably used to attending balls and fancy dinners and dances, wearing those fancy gowns ladies generally wore to them.

He'd seen a couple of other people from back east decide to come west and try farming, but none of them lasted long. Farming involved a lot of hard work, and working with animals. Most of the city folks who had come out had to learn how to drive a team of horses to pull their wagon out. They were barely able to do that, let alone use them to plow the fields and harvest in the fall. When people like that tried farming and failed, they generally moved back east. He was always torn between feeling sorry for them, since they generally invested all their savings into their farm, and laughing at them for thinking it would be easy.

In this case all he could feel was sorrow. Here was a young lady that was now alone, and had probably gone to a finishing school back east. That meant she was trained in doing needle-point, giving fancy parties, and running a staff of servants. He wasn't sure how any of that would help her out here. She could always go back east, but if she didn't have any family she could go back to, he wasn't sure that was much of an option, either.

Then he happened to think back on something she'd said. "Did you say you don't have any family?"

"No. My uncle and I were the last ones. We were the only family either of us had. He was my father's brother, and it was only the two of them. My mother was an only child, so she didn't have any family, either. She didn't have any cousins even."

"Was your uncle married?"

"He was, but she died just a little over two years ago, shortly before Papa died. She didn't have any family, either, so my uncle and I were all that were left."

"I don't mean to be intrusive, and if you don't want to answer, I understand and won't be hurt, but did you say your uncle sold his home and a business?"

"Yes."

"If you're the only family he had, I will assume you will be inheriting that? So if you wanted to return to New York you would have the funds to purchase a house?"

"I hadn't even thought of that," she said, turning to face him. "My uncle had a will. He made sure I knew where it was before we left. Do I need to take it to a lawyer?"

"Did he have any holdings?"

"No, not really. Like I said, he sold his home and business. He brought some in cash, and there is a bank check for the rest."

"Then yes, you will have to take his will to a lawyer so they can get his bank check put into a bank in your name. There's a good lawyer in town that I'm sure will be happy to help you with that. Once you have that taken care of, you'll have some funds, which might help you decide what you want to do. If you want to return to New York, you will have that option."

"I don't know yet what I want to do, but I do know I don't wish to return to New York. I'll have to give it some thought, but that option won't even be part of my thinking process."

Her words stunned him. Not so much the words themselves, as the way she said them. She was adamant she was not returning to New York. He had to wonder why. Something must have happened that brought back bad memories for her there. As he thought about it, he decided it was probably where she'd lost her mother and father, as well as her aunt. It probably would bring back unpleasant memories. Maybe she would be better off starting fresh somewhere else.

He wasn't sure if she would feel comfortable here, without many of the conveniences he was sure she'd been accustomed to in New York, but his protective instincts were kicking in with this pretty young lady. He was determined to give her a safe place to consider what she wanted for her future, and to make her comfortable and happy while she did her thinking. Staying with Rosy would help with both those efforts. Rosy was used to living on the ranch and knew where she could and couldn't allow her to wander as she took her time to contemplate her future. Beyond that, the ladies in town were right; Rosy did have a way of making everyone feel better.

He would certainly do whatever he could to help in the endeavor, as well. He could take her for trips into town so she could get to know some of the other ladies. Taking her with them to church services on Sundays would help with that, as well. He would also make sure they took a few trips to see the area. He found himself smiling as he thought of taking her riding in the country. Although that was something he seldom took time from running the ranch to do, the thought of taking her riding sounded nice. He was also looking forward to visiting with her in the evenings, getting to know her a bit. From the small amount of time they'd spent together, he felt there was more to this lady than he'd seen so far, and was eager to see what else this pretty lady surprised him with.

CHAPTER 6

osy was waiting on the front porch of the house when Wyatt pulled up to the house. "Rosy, I want you to meet Martha Welch. She and her uncle were part of a wagon train that went through, but her uncle became ill, so they stopped and went into Green Falls for Dr. Campbell. Unfortunately, her uncle passed on and she has no other family to go to."

"Oh, my dear, I'm so sorry," Rosy said, coming down from the porch and wrapping her in her arms as soon as Wyatt lifted her down from the wagon. "You poor thing, alone now."

"Hank suggested I bring her home with me so –"

"Oh, that's a wonderful idea," Rosy said. "We can provide a good place for you to grieve for your uncle, then contemplate what you want to do next. We have plenty of room here, so you can feel free to take your time and let your head tell you what will be best for you. If you don't hurry things and are willing to listen, your head and heart will tell you what you need to do."

Wyatt smiled as Rosy's hug and words seemed to be just what Martha needed. He asked which trunk was hers, and if she wanted anything else taken in the house. She directed him to her trunk and assured him that was all she would need. He let Rosy lead her inside and heard her instruct their new guest to have a seat while she made her some nice tea. He lifted the trunk down and carried it to the house. As he went past the kitchen he saw the two ladies were sitting at the table drinking tea, with a plate of cookies between them. He smiled as he took her things to their largest guest room.

Later that evening he took his horse into the barn, brushed him down and was ready to go into the house for supper, when he heard what sounded like a voice coming from the other end of the barn. His ranch hands had already gone to the bunkhouse to wash up for supper, so he went to see who or what he was hearing.

He rounded the corner and stopped when he saw Martha at the stalls he'd had his hands put her horses and oxen in. She was petting them and talking to them soothingly. As he approached he heard her telling them she was sorry she'd forgotten to feed them, but assured them she had oats on their wagon and she would indeed feed them. She praised Wyatt for being kind enough to put them in these nice stalls and giving them water. She gave the horses one last pat on their neck and told them she'd be back as soon as she found their wagon and the oats.

"Martha, I'm sorry, I should have told you not to worry about your animals. I took your wagon to the shed I use to store hay and machinery. It's next to the barn over here," he said, pointing, "and since there's not a lot of hay in that building now there's plenty of room for the wagon. That will keep it, with all of your belongings, out of the weather. My men and I brought your animals over here and got them settled in these stalls. They brushed them all out good and fed and watered them."

"Oh, well, thank you," she said, obviously not expecting him to have done that. "Did you find the oats we had on our wagon for them?"

"We didn't look at the things on your wagon, but we have plenty of oats and corn on hand for our animals. As long as you're staying with us my men will see to caring for them when they're feeding and watering our animals in this barn." Before she could respond, he added, "Those are some nice animals. When you decide what you want to do, if you decide to sell them, I'm sure you won't have any trouble getting a good amount for them. If you do sell them, I would be interested in making you an offer myself."

"Oh," she said quietly.

"Please understand I'm not trying to push you or influence you in any way, Martha. This is a very important decision for you, so take all the time you want to decide. I just want to say now that if you do decide you're interested in selling either or both teams of animals, they're nice animals and I would be interested in making an offer."

"Okay, I'll remember that. Thank you."

"Certainly. Now, I'm getting hungry. Are you ready to go in and have some supper?"

He escorted her to the house, and when they entered the kitchen Rosy's eyes widened. "Martha, I thought you were upstairs resting."

"I went up to rest a bit, but there were so many things on my mind I couldn't shut my mind down long enough to go to sleep. As I was thinking about all the things I'll have to do myself now that Uncle Franklin is gone, I happened to think of the animals. I went out to the barn to find them and feed them."

"Oh, I'm sure the men are taking good care of them," Rosy said.

"Of course they are," Wyatt confirmed, "but she had no way of knowing that. I should have told her we would do that. She shouldn't have had to worry about them."

"Well, you know now anyway. That's one less thing for you to be concerned about while you're here with us. Now, if you two want to go get cleaned up, I'll get supper on the table."

Fifteen minutes later they were eating their supper, and

Martha moaned after taking a bite of the beef roast Rosy had prepared. "This is delicious. I haven't had any beef since before the wagon train started out, and I've missed it. This is very good, though. I'd love to know what seasonings you used."

"Well, thank you, my dear. My mother taught me to make a mix of spices and rub it on the meat before you roast it. I'd be happy to show you what I use and how I do it the next time I make a roast, if you want to watch."

"I'd love to. This is the best beef I've ever tasted. You cooked the potatoes and carrots with the roast, I can tell, because they have that same wonderful flavor, as well."

Rosy looked at Martha, a big smile on her face. "Do you cook?"

"I enjoy cooking, yes, but I'll readily admit I've never cooked any beef that tasted this good."

"If you like to cook, I'm sure we'll get along splendidly."

Wyatt had a grin on his face. "Rosy is an excellent cook and I'm fortunate to always have a delicious meal waiting for me when I come in every evening. It sounds like I might be having some extra special meals for a while as you two ladies compare and share your cooking skills."

"No two ladies cook the same," Rosy explained, "and I'm always eager to see what other women cook and how they do it. There's always something new to learn."

"I feel the same way," Martha said, nodding with a smile.

"Bring on the food," Wyatt said, rubbing his stomach. Both ladies laughed, and the three of them seemed more at ease, like they were eating with friends.

The two ladies formed a quick friendship. When he came in for supper the next evening they were in the kitchen, talking and laughing as they worked. "Something sure smells good," he said as he inhaled deeply.

"We're sharing recipes," Rosy said. "Some of our meal I'm

sure you'll recognize, but some are things she showed me how to prepare. I'm eager to try them."

"I hope you like them," Martha said.

"They smell so good, I don't see how we won't. Now, Wyatt, go get cleaned up while we get the food on the table."

After the tasting and complimenting was over, they settled into comfortable conversation. As they were finishing their meal, Martha turned to Wyatt. "Would you mind if I take a walk tomorrow? There are so many things going through my head right now it feels clouded. I often find I can clear my mind and think clearer if I take a walk. Often I find a spot I like and sit down and simply take in the sights. That seems to somehow clear my mind and I can focus better."

Wyatt paused a moment before answering. "I understand what you're saying. I often find a quiet spot on the ranch when I need to do some thinking, as well. In fact, there are a few places I find myself going to specifically to be alone to think."

"It always helps me clear my mind," Martha said with a hopeful smile.

"However, a ranch can be a dangerous place, Martha, and as much as I wish I could, I can't say yes to your request." Her smile disappeared, her shoulder slumped and she looked dejected. She was about to say something, when Wyatt continued. "I understand why you're asking, I really do, but as long as you're on my ranch I feel responsible for your safety, and there are parts of this ranch that simply aren't safe for me to allow you to go to think. When you're thinking, you're not paying close attention to your surroundings, and there are wild critters around that would take advantage of that."

"Maybe you could show me around the ranch a bit and point those dangerous places out to me? Then I could avoid them when I'm walking."

Wyatt tried to think quickly. A ranch here in Kansas was no place for a young lady from New York to be wandering alone. It was much too dangerous, and he certainly was feeling very protective toward this pretty lady. The problem was, he was beginning to feel something for Miss Welch, and it wasn't just protectiveness. The more time he spent with her talking while they shared their meals, or in the evening afterward, the more he found himself wanting to spend time with her.

This was a new feeing for him, and frankly, it scared him. Not only had he told himself he was too busy with the ranch to have time to court a lady, but if he were to decide to find a lady to become his wife, his mind told him a lady from New York City was not a good choice. He certainly didn't have time to babysit a city lady on a dangerous ranch. Besides, chances were she would grow tired of living here, without servants and theaters and seemingly endless shopping possibilities.

Green Falls had a mercantile. Beyond that, the shopping experience was pretty much limited to something specific he might need from the blacksmith's shop, or the leather shop if he needed a new piece for his harness or saddle, or a new piece of furniture from the furniture shop, which was also the lumber-yard if he needed some lumber. If he needed anything else he had to travel to a bigger city unless he could find it in one of the catalogs Mr. Hall had at the mercantile. Then he could order it and in roughly a month it would come in. Somehow he doubted that was the type of shopping Miss Welch had been accustomed to doing.

Wyatt caught the look on Rosy's face, whose eyebrows were high on her forehead and she was already giving him a look he knew well. "Wyatt, maybe you could take all three of us in a buggy on a little tour of part of your ranch," she suggested. "Martha would probably enjoy seeing some of it, and I know there are some places a buggy can go."

Rosy's question, or maybe it was the look she was giving him, but one of them brought his mind back to the question. What he would like to do was take her out on horseback to show her his ranch. That was by far the best and easiest way to see it. He doubted she knew how to ride a horse, but that didn't matter. In fact, it would give him a good reason to put her in front of him on his horse. The idea of having her in front of him, with his arm wrapped firmly around her waist to keep her safe, appealed to him.

Before he let his mind wander too far, he glanced up at Rosy's sobering look. "You're right, Rosy, there are places on this ranch that a buggy can go, and Martha, if you'd like to, I'd be happy to take you. You can at least see part of the ranch."

"I would truly love that, Wyatt. The only part of this area I've had a chance to see is what we traveled through with the wagon train, and I was too worried about my uncle to pay much attention to it."

"That's settled then. Tomorrow after breakfast let me get my men working, then I'll hitch up the buggy and we'll go out for a ride."

"I don't want to take you from your work if you don't have time for it, Wyatt."

"I'll get my men working, and then I'll be able to take some time to do that. You're my guest here and I want you to be happy and enjoy your stay. I want you to feel at home and comfortable so you can open your mind to do your thinking. I would think knowing a little about where it is you're staying would assist in that endeavor."

"If you're sure you have the time, that's wonderful. I'll be looking forward to it." She gave him a smile that suddenly made him not care a bit about all the work they had to do this time of year. Spring was the busiest season for them, but nothing was as important to him as seeing that smile on her face. She hadn't had much to smile about lately, and if he could do something to bring it back, he would certainly try his best.

$\approx$

MARTHA WENT to sleep that night thinking about Wyatt. She was beginning to have feelings for him, but she wasn't sure if that was a good thing. He'd been kind from the moment he'd stopped to see if she needed help, but it was more than simply his kindness that had been drawing her attention. She'd learned a lot about the man as they'd talked every evening.

It was obvious he genuinely cared not only about the men working for him, but about his animals, as well. That was important to her. She'd met many farmers and ranchers who saw the animals as their means of support, necessary parts of the farm or ranch. But she had always seen them as living things. She had always cared a great deal for the animals on their farm, and had seen several times over that if they were treated well, they would treat her the same. Wyatt was like that, as well.

She could tell he felt that way about his ranch hands, too. They weren't merely his workers. Every one of them was a man with a life. The first day she was here she'd heard him talking to his men while she was out with her horses. They were coming in at the end of the day, and he was talking with them, not at them. He asked one if he'd seen his mother lately, since she'd slipped and fallen. He said not for a few days, but she'd been doing better the last time he saw her. Wyatt suggested he take enough time off in the next day or two to run into town and check on her. He assured him they could get along without him for a few hours and he wouldn't dock his pay any.

That conversation had touched her heart. Shortly after overhearing that conversation, he'd told her not to worry about her animals, that he and his men would take care of them while they fed and watered his. It wasn't that he'd told her they would care for them that had meant so much to her, but more the way he'd said it. It was as if there should have been no question about it, that naturally they would care for the animals, and take good care of them.

When she'd asked if he could show her around his ranch, she

was hoping they could go on horseback. In her opinion that was the best way to see the ranch. She remembered what everyone had said about Rosy, and her reluctance to leave a young man and lady alone, so it didn't surprise her when she suggested they all go in a buggy. Maybe in a couple of days she could ask if she could borrow one of his horses and go out on her own to look at it better. If he was concerned about predators in the area, she could take their rifle with them. She didn't want to push him, though, or appear ungrateful, so she would be happy with a trip in a buggy. She really was eager to see as much of this area as she could.

She was also looking forward to getting to know Wyatt better. That was a thought she wasn't prepared for, as she'd never felt that way about a man before. Most of the young men she knew were from Missouri and laughed at her for being a tomboy and having an opinion on things. They all seemed to think ladies were meant to cook and clean a house, have babies, and that was about it. They weren't supposed to think for themselves or care what crops were grown or what happened on a farm. On the contrary, in New York the men all seemed like city dandies, and not anyone she was at all interested in.

As she thought about that comparison, she wondered about Wyatt. He didn't know her, so he didn't know she'd grown up on a farm and would prefer being in the barn working with horses than in the house cooking. If he knew that, what would he think? In fact, the more she thought about this, she started to wonder just exactly what he did know about her.

She tried to think back to the conversations they'd had. She was in a fog part of the time right after losing her uncle, so she wasn't exactly sure what all she'd told him. She couldn't remember mentioning that she'd grown up on a farm or how much she liked working with horses. If he didn't know that, should she tell him, or would that chase him off? Maybe it would be safer if she didn't mention it until they'd gotten to know each other better. Honesty was very important to her and it wasn't like her to hide anything, but would it be wrong to simply not mention it yet? She had trouble falling asleep, debating that thought over and over in her mind.

SHE WOKE up the next morning ready to go. She got dressed, happy with her choice of dresses to bring with her on this trip. Having never been further west than Missouri, she didn't know what to expect. She knew people wore nicer clothes in New York than they did in Missouri, so she wasn't sure what would be considered normal dress in Kansas, or possibly even further west.

She left her formal gowns behind, knowing she wouldn't have a need for them. She knew she would definitely want her split skirts for the farm or ranch they'd hoped to buy, so she brought all of those. Beyond that, she brought a couple of dresses she hoped would be good for church, and a few house, or work dresses she wore on a daily basis in New York. They were nice, much nicer than what she'd worn to work in daily in Missouri, but they didn't have much lace or fancy edgings. They were the type ladies in Missouri wore when they went to town or visiting. If it turned out ladies dressed even planer in Kansas than in Missouri, those dresses might be better for church. She'd also brought three older ones that would be good work dresses for when they bought their farm.

After the first day on the wagon train and seeing how much dust and mud they were dealing with daily, the ladies had all been wearing work dresses. Once Wyatt took her to his ranch, she put on one of what she considered the middle range dresses, as they looked similar to the type of dresses she'd seen on the ladies in town. They were the ones she was used to wearing on a daily basis the last couple of years in New York, so she felt comfortable in them.

She put another of those dresses on and hurried downstairs. She was helping Rosy finish breakfast when Wyatt walked in and hung his hat on the peg by the door. He turned to them and his face lit up when he saw Martha cooking eggs on the stove. "Good morning, ladies. You both look lovely today."

Rosy smiled at him with knowing eyes. "I look the same as I did yesterday, Wyatt, but thank you. Now Miss Welch, on the other hand, does look lovely this morning. That's such a pretty dress she's wearing, don't you think?"

"I certainly do. The green in your dress brings out your pretty eyes, Martha."

Martha felt her face turn red and she quickly turned back to the stove. "Thank you. I believe breakfast is ready. I'll put the eggs and ham on a plate, Rosy."

"Okay," Rosy said with a little grin she kept to herself, "and I'll be right in with the biscuits. I already put the jam and fried potatoes on the table."

"I washed up at the pump on the way in, so I'm ready. Let me take that for you," he said as he lifted the plate of eggs and ham from Martha's hands and carried it to the table. He set the plate down and pulled Martha's chair out for her, holding it while she sat, which surprised all three of them. None of them said anything about it, however, other than Martha quietly thanking him.

Hoping to eliminate the awkward feeling, once they had their plates full he asked, "Are we still on for a little tour of the ranch this morning?"

His heart clenched when she awarded him with another of her beautiful smiles. "Absolutely. I've been looking forward to it, unless you're too busy."

"I'm fine. I talked to Dallas this morning, my foreman, and he knows what the men are to do today. He'll get them going, so we're free to go after we finish eating."

Rosy looked from one of the young people to the other, noticing the looks in their eyes. She was glad to see Wyatt looking interested in a lady finally. There weren't a lot of single young ladies in the Green Falls area, and none of them had been able to grab his eye, although it hadn't been for lack of trying. All of the single ladies saw him as quite the catch, and made it their mission to be sure he noticed them.

None of them had caught his eye, until now. From what she'd been able to tell so far, Martha seemed like a very nice young lady and certainly could cook. In her mind the two of them would make a good match, but she would definitely have to keep an eye on them. She would have to figure out a way to give them enough time alone to let the feelings they obviously had for each other develop, without giving anyone in town a reason to talk.

CHAPTER 7

*R*osy and Martha cleaned the kitchen up after breakfast while Wyatt went out to hitch up a buggy. When he went back in the kitchen he was glad to see both ladies ready to go. Martha had such an excited look on her face, he couldn't help but smile. As they neared the buggy, Rosy hurried to it. "Why don't you two sit in the front, and I'll sit on the back bench. It will be much easier for her to see the area and things you point out to her if she's on the front bench with you. I've obviously seen it already."

"If you're sure you don't mind, Rosy, Martha will get a better view of the ranch from the front bench."

"I don't mind at all," she assured him as he helped her up and into the buggy. He lifted Martha up next, and climbed in next to her.

As they headed down the path behind the barn, Martha looked and listened closely to everything Wyatt pointed out. She was surprised at how many cattle were in some of the pastures, and asked several questions as to how and why the cattle were separated. She commented several times on how pretty the area was, which Wyatt agreed with. He took them up a hill and pulled the horse to a stop at the top. "What are we doing?" she asked.

"There's something I want to show you. You have to walk on up here to see it, but it's not far. Stay there, and I'll help you down." Once he had both ladies out of the buggy he led her to the top, with a hand on her lower back.

She turned to see where Rosy was, and saw her walking up the hill a few steps behind them. "Rosy, come on up here so you can see whatever it is he wants to show us, too."

"I've already seen it, and I'm glad he brought you here. It is beautiful."

She looked over at Wyatt, who was watching her. "Does it have anything to do with that sound I'm hearing?"

"It certainly does."

Martha turned back, looking ahead again, and after just a few more steps, she froze. They'd turned just a bit of a corner and a large waterfall came into view, which explained the thunderous noise she'd been hearing as they approached. "Oh, my," she said, holding her hand over her heart. "This is magnificent."

"It is pretty, isn't it?"

"It certainly is. I've only seen one other waterfall. It was smaller, and it was clearer. This one looks green, especially where the sun hits it."

Wyatt chuckled and nodded. "That's how Green Falls got its name."

"Is the town named after this waterfall on your ranch?"

"Not really, but kind of." He led them over to a rustic bench overlooking the falls. Once they were all seated so they could watch the falls for a few minutes, he explained. "There is another waterfalls further up, which is larger than this one. A town sprang up at the foot of it, and they named the town Green Falls. You can see it from the end of town. The next time we go to town I'll try to remember to take you to a spot where you can see it from town."

"I'd love to see it. I can't imagine a larger waterfalls than this one. I take it that one looks green, as well?"

"Yes."

"The one I saw one time was clear. What makes these look green?"

"Moss, or algae. If you go up closer you can see all the rocks are covered with what I thought was moss, but I'm told some of it's algae, which also looks green. It grows when the sun hits the rocks."

"So all the rocks are covered with the algae, and that's why the water is green?"

"The water's actually clear, but with all the algae and moss on the rocks, the water looks green."

"Thus the name Green Falls," she said, nodding her head. "This is so interesting, and beautiful. Thank you for bringing me here."

"I thought you might like this."

"Oh, I do. It's kind of like your own smaller Green Falls."

"I guess it is. I just know it's relaxing to watch the water falling over the rocks."

"Relaxing, yes," she agreed. "When we first turned the corner and saw it, the sound was so loud I thought of it as rather thunderous. But now that we've been here a little while it doesn't seem as loud. I guess as I think about it I shouldn't be so surprised. The sound of water is usually very calming, which is why I've always enjoyed sitting by a babbling brook. There's no better place to read a good book than under a good shade tree next to a brook with water running over rocks."

The happy, far away look in Martha's eyes affected Wyatt in a way he wasn't prepared for. This pretty little lady had not only taken up temporary residence in his home, but she'd taken up residence in his heart, as well. He truly hoped that residence wasn't temporary, however. He had to figure out how to make it permanent. He shook his head a bit and forced himself to answer, and pay attention. "You like to read?"

"I love to. I had several books in New York. When we joined the wagon train I knew I couldn't bring all of them with me, but I did bring a few of my favorites I just couldn't part with."

"I love to read, as well," Wyatt said. "The ranch keeps me too busy to read a lot, but like you, I have a few favorite books I've read several times, mostly in the winter. Maybe we can compare books. If I have any you haven't read and would like to, you're welcome to them."

"I'd love that. Maybe I'll have one or two you'd like to read." She turned to Rosy. "You're free to read any of my books you'd like, as well. This spot right here would be a wonderful place for a nice Sunday afternoon with a good book."

"Maybe we could bring some good books and a picnic up here some Sunday afternoon," Wyatt suggested.

"Oh, wouldn't that be fun?" Martha enthused.

They watched the falls a while longer before Wyatt helped the ladies back in the buggy and they went on their way. It was noon by the time they made it back to the house, and Martha's eyes were large, as was her smile. "Thank you, Wyatt, for that tour. I very much enjoyed seeing your ranch."

"You've only seen a fairly small part of the ranch. Much of it isn't accessible with a buggy."

"Oh, my goodness. Your ranch is that large? What I saw was beautiful. I would love to see more of it sometime."

"Maybe sometime I can take you out on a horse to see it." As he said it, he noticed the frown and warning look on Rosy's face. Rosy was not a horsewoman. She didn't like riding on one, by herself or with someone else, so her going along with them on horseback would be out of the question. He knew he would have to deal with her at a later date and see if he couldn't work something out. After seeing the look on Martha's face as she saw different parts of the ranch today, he would love to grant her wish and take her out to see more of it.

"I would very much like to do that sometime," she said with a dreamy look in her eyes. "In the meantime, thank you for taking the time today to show that much to me. Rosy and I can have a meal ready for you shortly so you can eat something before you go back to work." She turned to follow Rosy, who was already in the kitchen.

"I'll put the horse and buggy up and be in," he said as he watched her walk toward the house.

Inside, she and Rosy worked quickly to make some sandwiches from the roast beef Rosy had fixed for supper the night before. While Rosy heated the beef, Martha cooked a little bacon and added a jar of green beans Rosy had canned the summer before, and they opened a jar of pickled red beets. For desert they brought out the rest of the chocolate cake they'd had the day before, and they had everything out and on the table when Wyatt came inside. "It looks delicious. You ladies did some quick work," he said appreciatively.

"It's nice having a helper," Rosy said. "Let's sit down and eat while it's warm."

While they ate they talked about the tour they'd taken. "I didn't ask while we were out there, but are there some places it would be okay for me to take a walk? I really think it would help me clear my mind so I can decide what I want to do."

"Let me say a couple of things about that. I understand that you want to give it some serious thought, and I agree with that. But don't think you have to hurry and decide right away. We have plenty of room right here for you, and it isn't often Rosy has some female company. I've seen her smiling more lately, and I'm glad."

"I do like having you here, dear," Rosy said, reaching over to lay her hand on Martha's arm. "Wyatt's right, I don't often have company, and I've very much enjoyed visiting and sharing recipes. And he's right, we certainly have plenty of room in this big old house."

"Thank you both."

"But to answer your question," Wyatt continued, "I'm not sure how long a walk you were thinking of or where you like to walk, but I'm not opposed to it as long as you avoid certain things. I don't want you going into any of the woods alone because of some of the wildlife you might encounter. I probably don't need to say this, but stay out of all the pastures and don't open any gates. The cattle are not pets, and aren't used to being around people much. If a gate is left open they will eventually find it, even if you don't see any cows there at the moment. They will find an open gate and get out."

"But if I stay out of the woods and pastures, you wouldn't mind me taking a walk on your ranch?"

"I would prefer you not go too far from the house, but with those conditions in mind, no, I don't mind. I guess I should add one more proviso. Please tell Rosy or myself when you leave, which direction you're headed, and how long you plan to be gone."

Martha's eyes grew a bit, but after a few moments she nodded. "Okay. I think you're worrying about me more than you need to, but I'm a guest at your ranch, so I will do that."

"Thank you, Martha," Wyatt said. "I apologize if I'm being too stringent, but I tend to be protective of the people I care about. Rosy I'm sure would confirm that, or any of the men working for me."

"Or most anyone that knows Wyatt," Rosy added with a fond smile. "His father was much the same. Two of the best men I've ever known, but very protective of the people they care about, both of them."

"I believe that," Martha said, catching and meeting Wyatt's eyes for a moment. "Let me ask another question, after hearing that. If you would rather I not go too far from the house alone, which is the only way I'll be able to get some serious thinking done, would you mind if I go to the barn? I won't open any gates or anything like that. When I was out there the other day, intending to care for my animals, I couldn't help but notice there are a lot of animals in the barn. I very much enjoyed simply watching them, especially the interaction between a mother and her offspring. It's very calming, watching how she knows instinctively how to care for her little one."

"I watch that in awe every time I see a cow or horse give birth," Wyatt told her. "I understand exactly what you're saying. Somehow the mother always knows what to do for her newborn. I don't mind you going out to the barn for some quiet time and space to think, as long as you don't get the animals riled up. By that, some of the cattle in there have been injured, and that's why they're there. Like I said, they're not used to interaction with people. If you go in and sit down on a bale of hay or straw, I don't think they'll pay you any mind. If you try to get too close, try to pet them, some of them will not like that a bit and get anxious or scared. I can't have that happening."

"I understand," she assured him, "and thank you."

"You're welcome. I hope it gives you the calming and peaceful spot you're looking for. Let me remind you again, however, there's no rush. Take your time and let your thoughts come to you. If you feel rushed, you may be forcing your thoughts toward what you feel you should do, rather than what feels best for you. Do what will make you happy. Also, let me state, if you ever want to talk about your thoughts, I'm a good listener. If your thoughts become confusing or overwhelming, I may be able to help you sort them out."

"I bet you are a good listener. Thank you, Wyatt. I'll keep your offer in mind."

"Good. Now, thank you, ladies, for another fine meal, but I've got to get back to work."

Rosy, who had been watching and listening carefully while

the two talked and shared thoughts, didn't miss the look that crossed between them as their eyes met before he walked out the door. She smiled a bit when she thought her insides were probably just as happy and excited right now as theirs.

Wyatt's father had died two years ago rather unexpectedly. Ever since then he had thrown himself into the ranch, determined to prove he could run the ranch and make his parents proud. It was a lot for a twenty-three year old man to take on, but he never hesitated. He'd grown up learning ranching from his father and working side by side with the ranch hands. He'd earned their respect, which made for an easy transition when he took over the ranch.

As proud as Rosy was of him, stepping into his father's big shoes at such a young age, she also worried about him. Wyatt was a good man, and she knew he would make a good husband and father. Beyond that, he deserved to be happy in life. To Rosy's way of thinking that meant he needed to find a good lady to settle down with and have a family. Rosy might have been a bit disappointed, but she wasn't upset that none of the local ladies had grabbed his attention, as she hadn't seen any she thought would make him a good wife.

Martha was an exception to that, and Rosy was glad to see Wyatt taking an interest in her. Martha was a very nice young lady, easy to talk to and quick to help others, just like Wyatt. The only hesitation Rosy had was her background. Coming from New York, she was afraid after a time Martha would tire of life on a ranch, which was hard work and not much socializing; the opposite of what she imagined a lady from New York was used to. The more she was getting to know and watch Martha, though, the more she was beginning to question that notion. Martha had never once asked about going to town, or even what all Green Falls or any other towns in the area had to offer.

When she asked Wyatt about going to the barn, it added to her questions. She never would have expected a young lady from

New York to want to be around animals. In her experience, most ladies that hadn't grown up around large animals shied away from them. It was possible, she supposed, that while not being around them prior, Martha had simply gotten used to them while on the wagon train. While it was a possibility, Rosy didn't think it was likely. Whatever the reason, she was glad to see Martha's willingness to be around the animals. That boded well for a relationship between the two of them. She was eager to watch and see what the future would bring for them.

MARTHA HAD a lot on her mind when she went to bed that evening. She'd thoroughly enjoyed the tour of the ranch. Seeing the green waterfalls was breathtaking, and hearing the history of their little town was interesting. The parts of the ranch she'd seen were impressive. It was nice country. She thought for a few minutes of her uncle. This would have been an area they would have looked for a farm to purchase, or vacant land to start a farm. She was sure he would have liked the area, as well. She forced her mind away from that. Things were different now, and she had to stop thinking about what could have been and face the future as things are now.

Thinking back on the ranch tour, she smiled when she thought about Wyatt and the conversations they'd had. It was clear to her that Wyatt was a good man. Rosy's words came back to her. She had no trouble believing Wyatt would try to protect the people he cared about. Rosy seemed to think a lot of his father. In fact, she'd said his father had been like that, as well, and again, that was easy enough to believe. He'd learned kindness from his parents, or at least his father. She hadn't heard anyone mention his mother, which made her wonder about that. Had he possibly lost his mother at an early age, like she had?

The more she got to know Wyatt, the more she felt these

feeling she couldn't seem to shake. As she thought about her feelings further, she reluctantly admitted she was was falling for the handsome rancher. That thought frightened her. She'd never had feelings like this for a man before, but she was sure that's what it was. Aunt Helen had talked to her about what it was like to fall in love. She'd told her what it was like for her when she fell in love with Franklin, and assured her she would know it when she felt it.

She was sure that's what these feelings were, and although it was a bit alarming because she didn't know what to do about it, it didn't account for her fear. It took more thinking to come to terms with what was causing the fear. What if she was falling for Wyatt, but he didn't have reciprocating feelings for her? She'd just lost her uncle, and she wasn't sure her heart right now could stand to fall in love with a man, only to find out he didn't return the feelings. Not only would it hurt, but she would feel like a fool, especially staying at his house.

She fell asleep that night still worrying about that thought. She just wasn't sure she could allow herself to fall in love with Wyatt right now. But the more she thought about it, the more she realized it might be too late. If so, it was more a question of how could she protect her heart at this vulnerable time for her, and how could she put all that aside and come to a decision as to what to do with her life.

MARTHA WOKE the next morning after a fitful sleep. She still had a lot of unanswered questions in her mind, but one thing she had decided was that she needed to do some serious thinking about what she wanted to do with her life. She'd never been one to rely on other people or take advantage of them, and she didn't want to start now. She had a life to live, and she needed to decide how she intended to do that. Once she had a purpose in life again she could give more thought to Wyatt and her growing feelings for him.

The only way she knew to do that would be difficult. For the time being she had to put Wyatt out of her mind and think about her options. She wasn't sure what Wyatt's feelings for her were, or if he even had feelings for her. They seemed to get along well, and they'd gotten to know each other well enough to know she'd developed strong feelings for him, but that didn't mean he shared those same feelings. She did feel they owed it to themselves to find out, but she wasn't sure they could do that if she was staying there.

There was one other thing she felt she had to consider. As much as she loved staying on Wyatt's ranch, it wasn't fair to him. Although she hated to admit it, it wasn't really giving them or anything that could develop between them, a fair chance. As long as she was staying at his home they would see each other daily, but not by choice. For true feelings to develop, or see if they already had, they should see each other because they chose to.

With those thoughts in mind, after breakfast that morning, she talked to Rosy while they were cleaning the kitchen and washing the dishes. "Do you have anything special planned for today, Rosy?"

"No, but why are you asking? Do you have something planned?"

"If you don't have anything you'd like me to do, I think I'd like to take a short walk. I need to do some thinking."

"That's fine. Martha, you're here as a guest, and I don't expect you to help me do my work. Don't get me wrong, I've appreciated all your help. I especially have enjoyed getting to know you and exchanging some ideas for cooking. I don't want you to feel you need to help, though."

"I understand, and thank you. But to be honest, I've appreciated being able to help. It got my mind off things when that was exactly what I needed to do. I needed a few days to grieve for my uncle and come to terms with my situation now. You and Wyatt have given me the perfect place to do that, and I will be forever grateful for that. I can't keep taking advantage of his generosity and yours, though, and I need to find a purpose for my life. I don't think I'll truly be happy until I do."

Rosy paused and studied Martha several long moments. "I understand, my dear, and that tells me a lot about you as a person. Would you mind if I make one suggestion?"

"Of course not. I will cherish any suggestions or advice you could offer me. I will admit my mind is still confused, with a lot of things swimming around."

Rosy laughed, but laid her hand on Martha's arm. "I can certainly understand that, and it's part of what I want to say. I think it's a good idea for you to start giving some thought to what you want to do. But the one warning I would give you is the same thing Wyatt told you. Don't rush the process. Take your time and make sure you feel good with your decision. You said you can't keep taking advantage of us, but let me assure you, you are not taking advantage of us in any way."

"I'm another mouth to feed and –"

"Nonsense. Martha, I cook for Wyatt and myself. Cooking for three instead of two makes very little difference. This is a ranch. We have plenty of beef that we raise, we trade some with a farmer down the road for pork and chicken and we raise a large garden because I enjoy it. I can about all of our vegetables. So cooking for you along with us is a very small thing. What you have given us is a different story."

Martha looked at Rosy, confused. "A little help in the kitchen and a few new recipe ideas? That's hardly –"

"Trust me, Martha, you have given us much, much more than that. I can't tell you how much I've enjoyed having your company. But beyond that, I haven't seen Wyatt smile this much in the last two years, and it's something I've missed and he's needed." She took a moment to choose her words before continuing. "Wyatt has been running this ranch for the past two years, since his father died. I won't say anything more about that because it's his story to tell you when he's ready to. But what's important now is that while he's been out to prove to himself, the ranch hands, and everyone that he can do it, which he has, he's made the ranch his entire life."

"I'm sorry for him."

"Since you've been here I've seen him open up. He's not only smiled more, but his whole demeanor has changed. This is the old Wyatt, the one I've missed. It isn't just me that's noticed it, Martha. Dallas commented on it yesterday. He's noticed the difference, and he agrees it's good to see the old Wyatt returning. He wondered if it just took him time to come to terms with his loss, but I don't think that's it. I think it's having you here. He's enjoyed the time he's spent talking with you, getting to know you."

"I've enjoyed it, too," she said quietly. "Maybe too much."

Rosy sighed and reached out to take Martha's hand. "I don't think so, dear. I may be overstepping my bounds here, but I know you care for Wyatt." Martha tried to pull away, but Rosy held onto her hands. "Let me finish, please. I've seen that look in your eyes, and I've seen it enough over my life to know what that means. But before you get upset, I've seen a very similar look in Wyatt's. I haven't seen that look in his eyes before, but it's awfully nice to see. Both of you have a special place in my heart, and I couldn't be happier."

Rosy could tell Martha was listening, but she was also apprehensive. Rosy believed that was her way of guarding her heart, and she couldn't blame her. "Now, I apologize if I've made your decision even more confusing, but I didn't mean to. Wyatt told you if you want to talk he would be happy to listen, and from my point of view, that wouldn't be a mistake. Wyatt is a very good listener. But let me offer the same thing. If you would like to have another woman to talk to, please come to me. I'll be happy to talk, and I promise to do my best to listen and give an opinion only if asked. This has to be your decision. You've been through a lot recently, though, and I want the best for you, whether that includes Wyatt or not. Sometimes it's easier for other people to see things more clearly."

Martha's eyes met Rosy's. "My papa told me that one time."

"He sounds like a wise man."

"He was. Thank you, Rosy," she said as she gave her new friend a hug. "This talk has meant a lot to me."

"Good. Now, where are you planning on going for a walk, in case Wyatt asks?"

"I'm going to head down the path we followed with the buggy yesterday. I won't go too far, though. I'd also like to spend a little time in the barn."

"Okay. I know you have a lot to think about, but please remember to be patient. The harder you try to reach a decision, the more rushed it will be. Just let your mind wander where it goes."

"That sounds like very good advice. Now if I can just follow it." Both ladies chuckled a little as Martha went outside.

CHAPTER 8

"Wyatt, everything okay?"

"Sure, Dallas. Why do you ask?"

"Because you've just put about ten nails in that board to fix that fence. Two or three will generally do fine."

Wyatt looked over at his foreman and best friend, and found him laughing. He looked down to see that he had in fact just put way too many nails in the fence he was repairing. "Okay, maybe I am a wee bit preoccupied," he said with a chuckle of his own.

"Anything you want to talk about?"

"No. Well, not yet anyway. I'm still trying to figure a couple of things out."

"It wouldn't have anything to do with that pretty little lady staying with you, would it?" Dallas laughed when Wyatt's head snapped up quickly. "Well, I'd say that answered that question." Wyatt looked around to be sure none of the other men were close enough to hear them. "Relax. No one else is within hearing distance or I wouldn't have asked you that."

"How did you know? I haven't said a word about her to anybody," Dallas said.

"Not with words, but to someone who knows you as well as I

do, you've said plenty with your eyes and the way you watch her anytime she's around. Mind you, it's not a bad thing. I like seeing you have a little life in those eyes for something other than the ranch again. It's about time you start living again. But if I can ask, what seems to be the problem?"

Wyatt was quiet for a couple of minutes, then looked around again and sighed. "You do know me well, I guess."

"Of course I do. I've assumed you've gotten to know her and have grown fond of her. Again, I'm glad to see it. But now again I'll ask, what's the problem?"

"I don't know. She was awfully quiet during breakfast this morning."

"And you don't know why?"

"Exactly. If something's wrong I'd like to know what it is. Maybe I can help."

"If this is none of my business, I know you won't hesitate to tell me, which is fine with me, but what was the plan when you brought her here? I know her uncle died and they were part of the wagon train, but why did you bring her here?"

"There were no rooms available at the hotel. Hank suggested I bring her here since I have room. I had to admit I knew Rosy would like having the company and the ranch would give her a quiet place to decide what she wants to do."

"All very good ideas. The one thing you weren't counting on is having feelings for her, or her having similar feelings for you."

"No, I – wait, what did you say?"

Dallas grinned. "You didn't count on having feelings for her?"

"No, the other part."

"Oh, you mean about her having feelings for you?"

"What would make you say that?"

"Because I've watched both of you stealing glances at each other when the other wasn't looking. Every time she goes outside she looks toward the barn first, and her eyes survey the area. If you're out a smile appears on her face when she finds you. Maybe I'm reading more into that than I should, but I don't think so."

Wyatt was quiet, but slowly looked up at him with a grin on his face. "Really, she smiles when she sees me?"

"She certainly does, just like you smile when you see her. It seems to me you both have feelings for each other, and I'll say it again, I think that's a good thing. It doesn't surprise me at all that you want to help if something's wrong, so my suggestion would be that you do the obvious; ask her what's wrong. Have you considered that?"

"I can't just –" After a rather long pause, Wyatt continued. "No, I guess I hadn't considered that. Do you think it would work?"

Dallas laughed. "Boy, that pretty little lady sure has your brain addled, doesn't it? To answer that question, if you think something is upsetting her, yes, I think asking her if something is wrong would be a good start. She may be willing to talk to you about it. If she's hesitant, try and draw it out of her."

"If she won't tell me what's wrong I can't help her."

"Tell her that," Dallas said. "Let her know you care about her and would like to help."

"Do you think I should let her know I care about her already? I mean, I've only known her a week."

"It has only been a week, but since she's staying in your house you've spent much more time with her getting to know her than you would anyone else in that same week. You know her better than most people you've only known a week."

"Hmm, I guess you're right about that. I wondered why I felt like I knew her pretty well, when it's only been a week. Seeing her every morning, and talking with her every evening, it makes sense I would know her better."

"Of course you know her better. Add to that the fact that you both seem to care about each other, and that you helped her during a very difficult time, it's not hard for me to understand why you feel like you know her. I'm sure she's feeling the same thing."

"Maybe. Okay, that all makes sense, so I'll talk to her this evening and see if I can figure out what's bothering her. Thanks, Dallas, for the advice." He pounded another nail in before adding, "Thanks especially for telling me she looks for me when she comes outside. That's good to know."

"It's good to see, too. I hope it works out for you both."

"Me, too."

MARTHA WENT outside to take a walk, but a quick glance at the sky had her changing her mind. It was cloudy and overcast, and looked like a rainstorm was headed their way. She decided instead to spend a little time in the barn. If the storm passed over them she could take a walk later.

Inside the barn, her first stop was to see her horses and oxen. She greeted them and all four of them came over to see her, which she hadn't been expecting. She hadn't thought she'd had sufficient time for them to get to know her, but apparently she was wrong. In stroking their necks and watching them, she became a little concerned. Both teams of animals seemed restless, especially the oxen.

She hadn't been around oxen before, and relied on what she'd heard from other people. From what she'd heard, though, they weren't accustomed to staying in a stall. They were animals built for working; hauling wagons, or pulling plows or other equipment on a farm. She would have to talk to Wyatt about that. Maybe he could use them on his ranch. If not, maybe he would have a suggestion.

After petting them she roamed on down the aisle to see what all animals were kept in the barn. She was used to living on a farm, but a ranch was different. She wasn't exactly sure what to expect. It was a big barn, and there were several stalls. There were two rows of stalls the whole way down the length of the barn, with an aisle between the rows. The barn also included a good-sized tack room, and an open space that was open to a fenced in pasture. She saw a few horses in the pasture.

Curious as to why some animals were in the barn in stalls and not outside, she started down the aisle, looking in the stalls. A few were empty, but one had a young colt. She went to the gate, hoping to pet the small animal, but it didn't move. It was lying down and although it turned its head in her direction and seemed anxious, it didn't move. She moved over to the side so she could see it from a different angle, and gasped. The poor little thing was injured. She wasn't sure what had happened, but there was a bandage on its leg, and some blood had leaked through the bandage.

She talked to the poor little horse, who seemed to enjoy the company. Afterward she went on down the aisle and found two other stalls with injured animals. There were two stalls that had a horse, but she didn't see any injury and wasn't sure why they were there, separated from the other horses. She would ask Wyatt that evening.

She sat down on a bench that was situated in a place to enable her to see the horses outside in the pasture, as well as the two horses in separate stalls. Being back in the barn brought back memories for her, and she let her mind wander a bit. While she was thinking back on her life on the farm, it started raining. The horses that were in the pasture came inside, and she got up to go closer to look at them. Like all the other horses she'd seen on Wyatt's ranch, they were nice looking. They had raised horses on their farm, and people came from all around that area to buy them, knowing they would be good horses and trained well. It certainly looked to her like Wyatt knew good horses, as well.

That thought brought Wyatt back to the forefront of her

thoughts. She needed to give her future some serious thought, and see if he held a place in it. As much as she'd enjoyed herself in the barn, walking generally helped her clear her mind better than anything. It had stopped raining and the horses had gone back outside to the pasture, and she decided to do likewise.

She was anxious to take a walk, and started off along the path they'd taken the day before with the horse and buggy. The weather was perfect for a walk in her opinion. It was late spring, and warm enough that she didn't need a shawl, but the sun wasn't so hot yet to be uncomfortably warm.

As she started down the path she thought about what Rosy had told her earlier that morning. She was finally able to admit to herself that she was beginning to have feelings for Wyatt, which was why she felt she needed to make some plans and leave the ranch. While she was certainly not opposed to seeing if there was anything between them, she had thought staying there wasn't a good idea. However, after talking with Rosy this morning, she felt she needed to think this through a little more.

Rosy seemed to think Wyatt might be having similar feelings for her, which was a pleasant surprise for her. However, Rosy seemed to be advising against leaving the ranch. The more she walked, the more things she thought of, and the more angles she was seeing to this dilemma. On one hand, Rosy said since she'd been there Wyatt had seemed happier and was smiling more. She didn't want to end that. She also said he hadn't done anything but run the ranch for the last two years, and it was good to see him interested in something other than the ranch again. She certainly didn't want that to end, either.

As much as she loved living on the ranch, and knowing Rosy thought it was a good thing, she couldn't get the concern out of her mind that staying there was forcing them to spend time together, which could be forcing a relationship between them. Her papa had always said if two people were meant to be together they would find a way, and it shouldn't be forced.

That thought brought back memories of her father. Oh, how she missed him, and wished he was here right now. He would know what to tell her. She stopped walking and found a rock to sit down on. Before she could stop them, tears streamed down her face, as the memories came unchecked. She couldn't stop them, which was not like her.

She was normally in control of her thoughts and emotions, but as she sat there, her mind wouldn't shut off. She tried thinking of Rosy instead, or of the days on the wagon train, but nothing worked. Her mind seemed to be bombarded with memory after memory of her father, and her Uncle Franklin, even some of her Aunt Helen. She sat on the rock and wept.

WYATT AND DALLAS finished fixing the fence they'd been working on and headed back to the barn, just in time for supper. Wyatt was feeling more confident after talking with Dallas, and had decided he would definitely find a way to talk to Martha tonight. He knew it would probably be easier to get her to open up to him if he could find a way to talk to her alone, but getting the two of them away from Rosy would be tricky. She had good intentions, but a little time alone to talk would be nice. He was contemplating how he might manage to do that, when he heard something.

"Did you hear that?" he asked Dallas, looking around.

"Yes, but I'm not sure what it was. It's awfully close to the house and barn for a wild critter, but it's possible. It didn't sound familiar, though. Did it to you?"

"No, not at all. We better be careful, though, as we go around this bend."

Dallas nodded as they both reached back for the rifle they always kept strapped to their horse when they left the barn. They rounded the curve and Wyatt immediately put his gun away and hurried his horse over to Martha, where she sat crying on a rock. Dallas was close behind.

Wyatt slid off his horse and went straight to her. He knelt down in front of her and put his hands gently on her knees. "Martha?" She had been crying so hard she hadn't even heard the horses approach. She jumped when he touched her, her eyes wide. "Oh, Martha, I'm sorry. I didn't mean to startle you. Are you okay?"

"Yes, I – oh, my goodness. I'm sorry."

"No, there's nothing you need to apologize for. I'm sorry I scared you. When I came around the curve and saw you sitting here, crying your eyes out, it scared me half to death. Are you sure you're not hurt anywhere?"

"No, nothing like that. I was thinking about what to do while I took a walk, and I thought of something my papa told me one time. That made me wish he were here to tell me what to do. Then I thought of my uncle, and my aunt, and the next thing I knew I was crying for all the people in my life I've lost." She sniffled, trying again to gain control. "I know that sounds silly, but –"

"No, it doesn't sound silly at all." He sat down next to her on the rock and before he realized what he was doing he'd pulled her over against him, guiding her head to rest against his chest. "You've been through so much, Martha. I know a little bit about what that's like, and it's not an easy time to go through. I wish I knew something I could say or do to help you."

"You have helped," she said quietly and lifting her head just enough to meet his eyes. "Saying you know what it's like and I'm not being silly has made me feel better. At least I know you don't think I've lost my mind." She laid her head back on his chest.

Dallas, who had been standing close, realized there was no emergency, and patted Wyatt on the shoulder. "Wyatt, with your experience you can probably help Martha more than most of us. Talking often helps more than anything. Take your time and I'll stop in at the house and tell Rosy you two will be along shortly for supper."

"Thank you, Dallas. Would you mind taking my horse with you? When Martha feels ready to go back, I'll walk in with her."

"Good idea. I'll brush him out and put him up, then I'll talk to Rosy."

Wyatt caught the glimmer in Dallas's eyes when he let Wyatt know in which order he would do that, giving him a little more time with Martha before Rosy would worry about them being together alone. "Thanks, Dallas," he said with a bit of a nod to know he appreciated it.

"Now," Wyatt said, rubbing her back with one hand while he held her tight against him with the other. "There's nothing silly about what you're feeling right now."

"Did you say you know a little bit about what it's like?"

"I know what it's like to lose someone you love, and it can seem overwhelming if you lose more than one person. If there's anything I can do for you, please tell me."

"Maybe I shouldn't ask, but —"

"No, Martha, if there's something I may be able to help you with, please ask. I'll do what I can to help you."

"Would you tell me what happened with you? You said you know how I feel, and I think maybe you might. Right now I do feel overwhelmed, just like you said, like I'm drowning. Maybe hearing another person's story will help me see I can get through this."

Wyatt took a deep breath and exhaled slowly. "I don't normally talk much about it, but you're right, it might help you see that things do get better."

"If it's hard for you to talk about it, I understand."

"No, I want to help if I can, and that makes a lot of sense." He took a moment, and sighed. "Besides, it might help me, as well."

"What do you mean?"

"Dallas and Rosy have both been telling me I should talk

95

about this and face it, instead of trying to pretend things didn't happen. I've pretty much ignored them, but they may be right. I probably haven't handled it the best, either. Maybe we can help each other."

"Maybe. We can at least try."

"Yes. I like that idea." He took another moment to gather his thoughts, and started his story. "I had a brother who was a year younger than me. His name was William, and we were very close. We pretty much did everything together. Then when I was thirteen and he was twelve he got sick. The doctor said it was the influenza that was going around and so many people were getting. It was awful. Mama took care of him, keeping Papa and I away as much as possible so we wouldn't get it. She tried to be careful, too, but it didn't help. He got worse, and no matter what Mama and the doctor did, it didn't help. He died, and the day after he died Mama got sick. She died two weeks later. Papa and I were left alone."

"Oh, I'm so sorry, Wyatt."

"Thank you. Papa got more land to grow the ranch, and we kept ourselves busy taking care of it. Then two years ago I lost him." Neither said anything, but seemed to cling to each other.

"I know that was hard, but thank you for sharing it with me. What you went through was worse than my experience, and I see you made your way through it."

"Martha, give yourself time, plenty of time, and let others help you."

"But I don't have any family left."

"Neither do I. Rosy and Dallas stepped in and helped me, and we'll all be more than happy to help you. Rosy is already so happy to have you here, if you ever try to leave she'll be upset. She's got a lot of love in her and she's more than willing to share it. You just have to let her. Like I told you before, I want to do anything I can to help you."

"That means a lot to me."

She hesitated several long moments, and he rubbed the back of her hand with his thumb. "Martha, I know you want to say something. Please do. If you have a question, ask it."

"Why do you think that?"

"I guess I know you well enough now to know when something is on your mind, or you want to say something. This morning at breakfast I could tell your mind was elsewhere. I decided I would give you until tonight, but if you were still quiet, I planned on trying to get you to talk to me. Now again, I can tell you want to say or ask something. I was serious when I said I want to help, so please let me. I talked to you, told you my story. Will you please trust me now and tell me what's on your mind?"

"I believe you do want to help, and as much as I appreciate it, can I ask why? Why do you want to help me? You've only known me a week or so."

He looked down at her, debating how he should answer her question. She was looking into his eyes, and the lost, hurt look in them told him what he needed to do. "Martha, honesty has always been very important to me. Papa always insisted on it when we were smaller, but as I grew up I saw why. Honesty and trust go hand in hand. If you want someone to trust you, you have to be honest with them. By that, I don't just mean honest, but totally honest."

"I agree."

"Good. I want you to trust me, so I'm going to be totally honest with you now. I don't want to scare you, and let me assure you I won't put any pressure on you at all, but to be honest with you I have to tell you it seems I'm starting to have feelings for you, Martha Welch."

Martha inhaled a bit, but then was quiet, so he went on. "I will admit I'm surprised by this, and I've never felt this way for a woman before. But the more we talk, the more I want to talk. I want to know everything about you. Like I said, I won't push, and if you tell me to leave you alone, I swear I will. I may not like it, but I will. I can go out and eat my meals with the men in the bunkhouse."

"No, please don't do that." She pulled back from his chest far enough to look up into his face. "I, too, believe in being totally honest, and Wyatt, I'm starting to have feelings for you, as well."

He was quiet, but slowly smiled and guided her head back to his chest. "Is that what was on your mind this morning?"

"Yes," she admitted quietly. "I didn't plan for that to happen. I've never felt this way about a man before, either, so I wasn't sure at first what the feelings were. Last night I realized that's what's happening, and I didn't feel it was fair for me to stay here. I went walking today to decide what I should do, where I should go. Then I started having memories of my papa."

He rubbed her back to try to calm her and let her know he cared. "Martha, if you're having similar feelings as I am, why did you think you had to leave? Was it because you didn't think I felt the same way?"

"Partly, yes. But also, Papa told me one time that relationships shouldn't be forced. If I'm living in your home I'm forcing you to see and speak with me on a daily basis."

"So you're not against a relationship between us developing, you just didn't want to force it?"

"Yes."

He pulled her shoulders away and shifted a bit so they were facing each other. "I'm glad to hear you're not against it, because I would very much like to see where this leads. I think your papa was a smart man; I don't think it should be forced. I don't think you staying here is forcing anything, though."

"You don't?"

"No. We've spoken every morning and evening since you've been staying here, and I haven't felt forced to do that at all. In fact, quite the contrary. I find myself looking forward to seeing you. I've been happier than I can remember being in quite some time." He was quiet several moments before adding, "Since my papa passed on. That's what I meant when I said I think maybe we can both help each other. If we're both forming feelings for the other, then I think you should stay right here, where we can prove to each other we can be happy again."

"But what if you lose interest and decide –"

"Then we'll talk about it. The same with you. We've both said we believe in being totally honest, so let's just agree if either of us starts feeling this isn't what we were looking for in life, we'll talk about it. I think I know you well enough already to know that if that were to happen, I'd still like to have you as a friend. If that should happen, I'll help you find something else you want to try, whether it be here in the Green Falls area, or somewhere else."

"Do you think that would work?"

"I give you my word that I will tell you if my feelings change. Will you give me your word that you will, as well?"

"Yes," she said seriously.

"Then you'll stay and we can see what happens between us?"

"Yes."

"Good. Rosy will be very happy, I'm sure. So will I."

"And me."

He smiled and stood, offering her his hand. "I'm glad we had a chance to talk privately, but if you're ready, we better head back to the house. If Rosy doesn't see us walking back pretty soon, she'll come looking for us."

Martha giggled as she accepted his hand and allowed him to help her up. "Then we best be going. We don't want her upset with us right away."

He offered his arm, and she slipped her hand through his elbow. He patted her hand gently before he headed them toward the house. They talked along the way about where and how they both grew up, determined to learn more about each other.

CHAPTER 9

*R*osy looked out her kitchen window and saw Dallas riding toward the house and barn, down the path she'd seen Martha walk down a little while ago. She watched him as he got closer, concerned when he saw he was leading Wyatt's horse behind him. Her first thought was what if something had happened to Wyatt. Or maybe something happened to Martha and Dallas and Wyatt stopped to help her. As soon as that thought entered her mind she dismissed it. If that were the case Dallas would be heading to the barn at a gallop. He'd harness the horses to a wagon and he and some men would head back to help them, while someone else went straight to town on the fastest horse they had to fetch the doctor. One of the men would be sure to tell her, so she could ready a bed.

No, she was sure nothing like that had happened. Dallas was taking his time, so there was no emergency. Several thoughts and ideas floated through her mind, but only one made much sense. The men had come across Martha. Wyatt was not only a good listener, but he was also very astute and knew when someone needed to talk. Her guess was the two of them were talking, and Dallas was giving them some privacy.

Her first instinct was to go meet them, to be sure nothing happened that people could talk about later. As she thought a bit more, though, she decided against that, at least for now. Rosy knew Dallas was a good man, with morals similar to her own. He wouldn't have left them alone unless he had a good reason to. Wyatt was a good man and would never take advantage of a woman, and Dallas knew that. If they were alone on his ranch, no one would see them together, so no tongues would wag.

Not only that, if Martha was upset, as she was when she'd left this morning, Wyatt would be a good person for her to talk with. He had a gentle, understanding way of getting people to open up to him, and once they talked, they felt better.

No, even if they might be alone, unchaperoned, Rosy knew Martha was perfectly safe. Wyatt, being very protective of people he cared about, would never hurt her, or allow anyone else to hurt her. In this case, she chose to trust Dallas. If he thought they needed some time alone, she would allow it. She knew they both had feelings for the other, and they were both special to her, as well. She would love to see them realize how good they were for each other. They both deserved to be happy. Maybe a heart to heart talk would help them along their way. She would give the situation some time, and if she didn't hear anything from Dallas she would go talk to him.

Over half an hour after she saw Dallas disappear into the barn with the two horses, just as she was thinking she was going to have to go talk to him, she saw him walking toward the house. She met him at the door. "Did you finally decide it was time to tell me what's going on?" she asked with a smile.

Seeing her smile, he knew he'd been found out, but that she wasn't upset, so he decided to play along. "What are you talking about?"

"I saw you bring Wyatt's horse back to the barn over half an hour ago. I also know Martha walked down that lane not too terribly long before that. Would you care to tell me why you thought it was a good idea to give them this much time alone, unchaperoned?"

He came in the kitchen as she held the door for him, and sat at the table where she indicated. "Let's talk a few minutes," she said. "I'll get some cookies for you. Would you prefer coffee or milk?"

"If you've got cookies, I'll have some milk, please." He started explaining before she got back to the table with his treats. "Now, before you chew me out, there was a good reason I gave them a little privacy."

"I assumed so."

"So you saw me come back a while ago, but you let it go?"

"I trust you, Dallas, or I would have been out asking about them. I assume Wyatt and Martha are together."

He furrowed his brows together a bit as he looked at her momentarily. "You're right about that. Tell me, what else have you been assuming? Why did you allow this to go on?"

Rosy sighed and her shoulders slumped. "Like I said, I trust you. I know those two have eyes for each other, and I personally think it's a good thing."

"Agreed."

"They're both good people, and from what I've come to know about Martha so far, they're a good match, with similar thoughts and feelings."

"I don't know Martha yet, but I agree she seems to be having a good affect on Wyatt. Go on."

"They've both been through some hard times, and I think they can help each other."

"Again, agreed."

"So I'm in favor of them getting to know each other. I also know sometimes that's easier to do without an audience. I trust both of them."

"Agreed yet again."

"I'm okay with giving them some time alone once in a while.

I still don't think it's a good idea for long periods, or often enough to tempt them. They're both good people with good morals and upbringing, but they're still human."

"Again, we're thinking alike."

"Good. So why did you decide to give them this much time alone, this soon into their getting to know each other?"

Dallas picked up another cookie. "Rosy, when we came upon Martha she was sitting on a rock, crying her eyes out."

"Oh, my dear."

"She was crying so hard she didn't even hear our horses approach."

Rosy looked concerned. "That's not safe."

"Exactly. I could tell how much Wyatt already cares about her by how quickly he made it to her and held her to him while he checked to see if she was hurt. It turns out she was walking and had a memory of her father, and I think that's all it took for her to break down."

"Oh, the poor girl. She's been through so much."

"How long ago did she lose her father?"

"Only a couple of years. She lost her mother a long time ago, and was raised by her father and her aunt and uncle, who used to live close to them. They moved away, leaving just her and her father. Now within just over two years she's lost her aunt, her father, and now her uncle."

"Oh. I didn't realize she'd lost so much."

"She has no other family."

"So she's alone, on her own in an unfamiliar place. It's no wonder she broke down crying."

"So were you able to calm her down?"

"Wyatt was doing a good job of that in the slow, gentle way he has. They were starting to talk, which I thought was probably the only thing that might help her at this point, so I left them alone to talk. I got the impression she needed to confide in someone, talk to him about what she's been through, and he's the best person I know that might be able to help her do that. But I also thought he would have a better chance of it if they were alone."

"You're probably right. If she was so upset she didn't hear you coming, she was most definitely in need of someone to talk to. Maybe if he's the one she confides in it will help their budding relationship. This could be a good thing."

Dallas was smiling, watching Rosy. "Why, Miss Rosy, I believe you're playing the role of matchmaker here. I never would have thought that would happen."

"Oh, nonsense," she insisted, trying to brush him off. "I'm simply saying it might be acceptable for them to have a little privacy if he's helping her cope with what she's been through by encouraging her to talk through it."

He laughed as he winked at her. "I heard you say it was good for their budding relationship." He watched as her face turned red, before placing his hand gently on her arm. "But all teasing aside, I have to admit I agree with you. I, too, hope this works out for both of them. It's certainly good to see him smiling and have more on his mind than just the ranch again."

"Yes, it is, and I'm glad we agree on this. Now, how long do you plan on giving them together?"

"I trust Wyatt, and because of that I expect they'll be showing up here before long. If not, I'll ride out and check on them."

Rosy got up to get some more cookies for Dallas, and after setting them down on the table she went to the window. "You were right again, Dallas. I see something down the lane a ways that looks like two people walking."

"Well, I hope they're arm in arm or he has her hand, or at least he has a hand on her back. That would tell me they had a good talk." He stood and went to the window with Rosy, and they watched as they got closer. "She has her hand at his elbow. That's real good to see, at least from my point." He turned to look at Rosy. "Are you okay with them showing that much affection?"

"I certainly am. To be honest, I agree with you. If they were walking separately, no contact at all, I would be worried. That's a gentlemanly way of keeping a little contact. I see nothing wrong with that at all. After all, they are both adults."

Dallas had to smile at Rosy's insistence that things remain proper. As they got closer he smiled again. "He has his hand over hers at his elbow. That's my boy!"

"Dallas!" She nudged his shoulder playfully. He laughed, knowing she might think that was a little forward and not appreciate his glowing remarks about it. "But good for him!" Now she was the one smiling as his jaw dropped open. She gave him a moment to recover, then faced him, her hands on her hips. "So, what are we going to tell them about why you're in here? We were talking about how to get them together, or do you have a better idea?"

Dallas laughed again. "Miss Rosy, I'm seeing a different, sneaky side of you I haven't seen before. But I like it." He paused a moment before coming up with an idea. "Let's just tell them pretty much the truth. I came in to tell you they would be along in a little while, as he was planning on walking her back here, and you offered me some cookies. Everyone knows I can't turn down delicious warm cookies, so I took you up on your generous offer."

She nodded, thinking about what he'd said. "Of course. That is the truth, after all, and that's always best."

"Of course it is." They watched at the window as the two talked and laughed as they made their way back toward the house. "I'm going back out to the barn. Thanks for the cookies and the talk, Rosy."

"Yes, thank you."

He talked to them momentarily as he returned to the barn. Rosy hurried to the stove to finish up supper, and turned to face them when they came through the door. "There you two are. Dallas said you would be along shortly. I hope you had a nice walk. Supper is almost ready, so when you're both washed up we can eat."

Fifteen minutes later they were eating their meal, and Rosy asked about their walk. "Martha, were you able to get any thinking done on your walk?"

"Yes, I did, especially once Wyatt came along."

"Wyatt has a way of helping people talk through situations. Was he able to do that with you?"

"Yes, he did, and I'm so thankful for it."

"Sometimes it's easier for someone else to see through things that seem very clouded through your own eyes," he said simply, then changed the subject. "Rosy, I think I'm going to take Martha to town tomorrow to talk to Jed Hawkins, the lawyer. Her uncle had a will, and I think it would be best if Jed looks at it and decides what they need to do. He sold his house and business before he left and had that money put in a bank note so he could use it to buy a place and get them started out here. I'm not sure what, but I'm sure he'll have to do something so she can deposit that bank note so it doesn't get lost or stolen."

"That sounds like a good idea. It would be awful if something untoward happened to it."

"Do you want to go along with us? There are probably a few things you could use from the mercantile."

"Yes, there are a few things I could use. I'll make up a list this evening after I wash the dishes."

"You can make the list while I wash the dishes," Martha said. "I stayed out walking so long today I didn't help you prepare the meal. The least I can do is wash the dishes."

"You don't need to do that, Martha. You're a guest here."

"Please, I want to feel I'm doing at least a little bit to earn my keep. I won't take no for an answer this time, so start thinking about what will go on your list."

Wyatt smiled, liking the feisty little lady sitting across from him more all the time. "After you do that, would you sit out on the front porch with me a while? I've thought about what you said about your oxen and horses, and I have an idea. Maybe we can talk about it and see what you think."

"Yes, I will definitely do that. I'm worried about the animals."

"Are they not well?" Rosy asked.

"No, they're healthy," Wyatt said, answering for Martha. "She's concerned that when she went out to the barn today they seemed restless. She's right, they are, and I thought of a possible solution."

They finished their meal and Rosy insisted on helping with the dishes and cleaning the kitchen. "I'll make my list while you two talk about the animals," she insisted. "I don't know much about animals, so I'll enjoy the evening breeze with you, but I'll make my list while you two decide what to do with the beasts."

With both of them working together it didn't take long. Martha fixed a tray with glasses of iced tea, and the two ladies went out to join Wyatt on the porch. He immediately stood and took the tray from Martha, placing it on the small table between two of the chairs. Rosy took a seat in the last chair. "You two go ahead and talk all you want. I'm going to make my list of things we can pick up tomorrow in town, while I enjoy this evening breeze."

"It is nice out here this evening," Martha agreed, before turning to Wyatt. "So, you have an idea about the animals?"

"Yes, I do, but it's your choice. You have an extremely nice set of oxen. They're big, strong, and I'm guessing they're used to working together, judging by the way they act."

"The man Uncle Franklin bought them from said they'd been a team for three years, and they worked well together. I know they pulled our wagon every day, and we never had any problem with them. Uncle Franklin said they were the easiest team of oxen to work with he'd ever seen."

"I don't doubt that. I'd say they're used to working, too, because you're right, they've been restless the last few days."

"I don't know a lot about ranches, but do you use oxen for anything? Could you or your men use them for anything you do?"

Her question caught him by surprise, and he thought a few minutes. "We don't have any oxen, but we have three teams of large work horses that we use to pull wagons full of fence posts when we're fixing fences, and things like that. If you're not opposed to us using them some, it might be a good idea. My suggestion was unless you're planning on buying a farm to run yourself, which I'm assuming you're not," he said with a smile for her and a wink, "you may want to consider selling them. They are nice animals to be keeping in a barn. There are a number of farms and ranches around that would love to have a pair of oxen like that. Your suggestion that we use them may be a good idea, though. If you decide to sell them, it might help if we use them some so we can attest to how they work as a team."

"Wyatt, if you can use them, I'd like to give them to you. You've been so kind to me, helping me when you saw me along the road, and everything you've done since, including letting me stay here. I didn't know how to thank you, but if you can use those animals, I'd love to be able to give them to you."

He reached over and patted her hand she had on the arm of her chair, leaving his hand on top of hers. "Martha, thank you for that offer, but you don't need to do that. You've returned any kindness I've given you, and we enjoy having you here. But more importantly," he went on before she could argue, "we don't use oxen as much as the local farmers do. They do well pulling their plows and other equipment, and a good team can be very benefi-cial on a farm. Like I said, we have three teams of work horses we use for pulling wagons full of wood, feed, or whatever we're hauling, but we don't use them often enough to keep a team of hard-working oxen happy."

"Would you help me find someone who wants them and would take good care of them?"

He quickly nodded. "Some farmers take better care of their work animals, so I think I understand your concern. I don't think we'll have any trouble finding a good farm who would appreciate them and take good care of them."

"Good. That would probably be the best. I know they looked antsy and restless."

"I agree. Now, your team of horses, that's a different matter."

"Do ranches use them much?"

"We do use large horses on this ranch. We have the horses the hands ride every day, and we have three teams of larger horses like those that we use for hauling things, like I said. One of our teams is getting older and I don't know how much longer they're going to be able to work."

"Could you use them and see how they are? The only time we used them was when a wagon got stuck in the mud. They hooked them up to the wagon along with the team that was pulling the wagon when it got stuck, and several men worked with the two teams. Together they were able to pull the wagon out. Uncle Franklin said they did a good job, but he's never tried working them. He bought them to bring along as an extra set, in case one of the oxen got hurt or something. He said they would also be handy if he found a farm. He'd heard they're harder to find out here."

"The more I hear about your uncle, the more respect I have for him," Wyatt said. "That was a very smart thing to do, and he's right; they are hard to come across out here. That's why I don't think you'll have any problem selling either the horses or the oxen."

"Would you use the horses on your ranch and see how they are as a team?"

"If you will allow that, I would very much like to. The truth is, if they work well as a team, if you decide to sell them I would like to make you an offer. To be fair, I'd like to get an offer from someone else, but I might very well be willing to better that offer."

Martha heard a noise and looked in the direction of Rosy, where she thought the noise had come from. When Wyatt said he would like to make her a higher offer than someone else made, Rosy smiled, but didn't appear to be surprised. She looked out at the horses in the pasture, where the noise had actually come from, before looking back to Wyatt. "Wyatt, why don't you use the horses for a few days and see if they work well. If they do and you like them, I will gladly give them to you."

"But Martha –"

"If, however," she continued, holding her hand up to stop him momentarily, "you don't feel comfortable accepting them, I trust you. Anything you offer will be fair and acceptable to me."

"I think we will get along fine and be able to work something out with your team of horses," he said with a smile.

"So do I," Rosy said quietly, without looking up from the list she'd been making.

Wyatt and Martha both looked toward her, but she didn't say anything further and didn't look at them.

Wyatt smiled at the lady furiously making her list, before turning back toward Martha. "We will talk to Jed tomorrow and do whatever we need to do to get things taken care of so there will be no question as to your ownership of the oxen. Once that is complete, I will be glad to help you find a good man who wants to purchase them and will appreciate and care for them."

"Thank you, Wyatt. I appreciate your help."

Things were quiet for a couple of minutes, until a coyote howled somewhere in the distance and Martha sat up straighter. "That sounded awfully close."

"It's closer than I would like, but not as close as you would think. They seldom come close to the house or barn, but they are definitely out there. That's part of the reason I don't want you walking too far from the house."

"What's the other part?"

Martha seemed to be good at asking questions Wyatt wasn't expecting, and this was another one. It took him a moment to answer. "There are several other reasons, actually. Coyotes aren't the only animals out there you don't want to tangle with. But besides the various animals you have to be careful of, a ranch can be a dangerous place. It's easy to get turned around and become lost."

"That's why until I know the area better I stayed on the path."

"That's a good idea and I appreciate that you did that. There are other things, as well. If you slip and fall you can twist an ankle, or something similar that would make it difficult to get back to the house. I hate to think of you being far from the house and injured, unable to get back here so we can help you. That's why I asked that you let someone know when you go for a walk and which direction you are headed. If you're not back at mealtime we can go out looking for you. This ranch is large, about a thousand acres, but if we know which way you went when you left, we at least have an idea where to start looking for you."

"This ranch is a thousand acres?"

"Roughly, yes. Looking for someone on that large of an area is a little like looking for a needle in a haystack."

"I can understand that, and I see why you asked that I tell someone when I go walking and which direction I'm headed. I don't have any problem doing that."

"I'm glad to hear it. I want you safe while you're here."

Rosy stood, her paper clutched to her chest. "Well, I've got everything on my list I can think of. I'm going to let you two talk more while I go into the kitchen and look at my shelves to see if there's anything else I need."

"Okay," Martha said. "If it's okay with both of you, I think I'd like to stay out here a few more minutes. I'm enjoying both this breeze and the sounds of the crickets and horses and cattle in the pastures. The evening sounds so different than it did in the city."

"If you don't mind," Wyatt said, "I'd like to stay out here a few more minutes, as well. Although I've visited a city a few times, I don't remember much about what evening sounds like there. I have always enjoyed sitting out here in the evening, but I guess maybe I have to admit I've come to take the sounds here for granted. Now that you pointed it out to me, again, I have to say I'm enjoying it a little more."

All three of them laughed as Rosy went to the door. "Sometimes it's good to have people bring our attention to things we take for granted," she said. "You two enjoy the evening. I'll be right inside, in the kitchen if you need me."

"Okay, thank you, Rosy," Wyatt said with a grin as she went inside. Once he heard her on the other side of the kitchen he leaned over close to Martha so he could whisper. "That was her way of telling us she'll give us a little time alone, but she's still close enough to watch and listen."

They both laughed quietly. "I like her a great deal," Martha said softly."

"As do I. She's a true gem."

A horse nickered, which started a conversation between them. They spoke in normal tones, certain Rosy was listening inside. Conversation flowed easily, and before they knew it they'd been visiting, learning more about each other and things they enjoyed doing, for over half an hour. "Well, as much as I've enjoyed our visit, Martha, I best get to bed. Morning comes early on a ranch."

"I don't know how early you get up, but I know you've already been at the barn when you come in for breakfast," she answered.

"The men and I get up and do the morning chores, feeding

and caring for the animals before breakfast. By the time we're done Rosy has my breakfast and Will has breakfast ready for the men in the bunkhouse."

"Will is their cook?"

"Yes, Will Blakely. He does all the cooking for the hands."

"I wondered where they ate their meals."

"I didn't show you inside the bunkhouse, but it's got the bunks for the men, but there's also a kitchen and dining hall. Will cooks their meals and they eat in the mess hall."

"That's interesting. I'm learning a lot about how a ranch works. I don't want to keep you here any longer, so go ahead. Do you mind if I stay another couple of minutes?"

"No, of course not, as long as you stay here on the porch. Even in the dark you'll be safe."

"I'm not going anywhere, but this breeze is helping me clear my head."

"I do a lot of my important thinking right here, as well, after the day is over and it's dark out. Once the sun goes down it's a different feeling, one that seems to allow a person to think. Enjoy your time here, Martha, and I hope you're able to do some clear thinking. Good night."

"Good night, Wyatt, and thank you for our talk this evening. I enjoyed it."

"I did, as well. We'll make sure we do it again. I'll see you for breakfast, and then we'll go talk to Jed Hawkins in town."

CHAPTER 10

*M*artha was helping Rosy finish breakfast the next morning when Wyatt came in. He hung his hat on the peg, and when he turned toward the ladies he met Martha's eyes, and saw her smiling at him. His smile in return was immediate and sincere. It was also not missed by Rosy, who looked down quickly with a smile of her own.

As they finished their breakfast, Wyatt leaned back in his chair. "While you ladies do whatever you need to do in the kitchen I'll get the rig ready. Rosy, are we getting much at the mercantile? Should we take the buggy or a wagon?"

"The buggy should be sufficient. I'm not getting any large bags of flour or sugar. Smaller things will fit in the back of the buggy."

"Okay, buggy it is. I'll harness the horses and bring the buggy around front. You ladies may want to grab a shawl. It's not as warm as it has been the last few days."

"Thank you for telling me that, Wyatt. I thought the spring heat had finally arrived for good," Rosy said.

"It's not cold, but it isn't as warm as it has been. If the sun comes out more it will probably warm up, but it's pretty cloudy right now and the breeze has a chill to it. I had a jacket on all morning doing chores."

He left and the ladies got busy cleaning the kitchen. They were just finishing when he walked back inside. "We were just ready to grab a shawl," Rosy said. "We'll be right out."

"Good timing," Wyatt said. "I want to grab that contract for the Lingle place. Since we're going in to see Jed, I'd like him to look it over and make sure it says what I think it says. He had a relative of his that's a lawyer write it up, and he used a lot of those big fancy words. I think I understand it all, but I'd feel better if Jed looked at it, too."

"That's a smart move," Rosy said. "Your father would be proud of you."

Wyatt paused a moment, but turned to face Rosy. "Thank you," he said, and Martha could tell he meant it completely. He then went to his office, while the ladies went to retrieve their shawls. Wyatt was walking back toward the kitchen when Martha was at the door of her room with her shawl. He took the shawl and held it out for her. She moved into place and he wrapped it around her shoulders. "This is a very pretty color on you, Martha. It brings out your shining green eyes."

"Thank you," she said in a whisper as she felt her face heat.

"Did you remember to bring your uncle's will?"

"Yes, I have it. Thank you again for taking me to our wagon and helping me find it. I knew he had put it with his papers, but I hadn't seen where exactly it was. I appreciate your help."

"You're welcome."

"That's something else I'm going to have to do something with. I had forgotten about the wagon and all the things in it. I need to do something with that so you can have the space back in your shed. I appreciate you storing it inside, out of the weather, but I need to get it out of there."

"It's not hurting anything in there. We got the food items off it the first day so they don't go bad, and everything else will be okay until you're ready to go through it. You don't need to be in any hurry."

"Thank you. I think after I speak with this lawyer and he gets everything settled, I would like to go through it. Every time I see it I get a chill up my back. I think it's time I deal with it so I can move on."

"Again, I understand what you're going through, Martha. Take whatever time you need, but when you're ready, please tell me what I can do to help. I'm here and I'll do whatever I can."

"Thank you, Wyatt. I can't tell you how much that means to me, because I know you mean that."

He smiled and nodded, then led her to the kitchen with his hand on her lower back again, something she was starting to like real well.

The three of them started an easy conversation before they were even out to the road. "I wonder if this is going to be very involved, or take long," Martha said.

"Did your uncle have much property?" Rosy asked. "I've heard that's what takes a while, is getting it to where an heir can sign the paperwork to sell property."

"He already sold his house and business. He had that put into a bank check, which he was going to deposit in a bank when we got settled. Then he planned to use it to purchase a farm or whatever property he decided to buy. I have that bank check with me, also."

"Good," Wyatt said. "I think he should be able to start what-ever papers he has to do, and in the meantime he should be able to take the bank check and those papers to the bank. Even if they can't deposit it in your name yet, they should be able to store it in the bank vault. That way you don't have to worry about the check being lost or stolen."

"That would be a big relief. I didn't like having it. I was afraid I might misplace it."

"I was afraid of it being stolen. I don't think any of my men would have taken anything from the wagon, but word gets around. I was afraid if the wrong people heard your wagon was in our shed, they might go through it looking for whatever they could find. When people join a wagon train they take all their belongings with them. If they have much they can't take with them they generally sell it before they leave and take the money. Some people on wagon trains have very little, but some have things worth taking."

"I hadn't thought of that before," Martha said, "but you're right. It would be safer for everyone if I do something with those things. If I empty it out, can you use the wagon on your ranch?"

"We have a wagon we use to haul fence posts and other things we need for repairs, and injured animals we bring back to the barn, but it's not as big as this. Yours is not only large, but very sturdy. It's a good wagon. There have been a few times that I've wished we had two wagons so two crews could go out to fix fences or line shacks at the same time. If we buy the Lingle property we'll have even more land to cover. I've been thinking that if you decide you want to sell it, I'd like to make an offer on it."

"Once again, yes, I don't have need of it any longer so I would like to sell it, and any offer you make I'm sure will be fair. I have no idea how much he paid for it or how much it's worth, but I trust you. I would rather give it to you for all the kindness and hospitality you've shown me, but I will accept anything you offer."

"I'll make you a fair offer, Martha."

"I don't doubt that for a minute," she said.

Rosy asked what kind of business her uncle had in New York, and they spent the rest of their trip to town talking about New York. Rosy had never been there, but she'd heard various stories about it and was curious.

When they arrived in Green Falls Wyatt parked the rig close to the mercantile. "Rosy, if you want to go on in and give Joseph and Eloise your order, go ahead. You'll have a little time to visit with Eloise or browse through the store."

"That sounds nice."

He turned then to Martha. "I'll take you over to Jed's office. I'll give him my contract to look over, and introduce the two of you. While you're talking I'll go talk to the blacksmith about shoeing a horse. When I'm done there I'll go back to Jed's, and wait in his outer office for you to finish. If you finish before I get back, wait there for me."

"I can meet you back here if I finish before you get back. You don't have to go clear back to get me."

Wyatt laughed, and when she looked at him with questioning eyes, he explained. "Martha, you said I don't have to go clear back there, but you don't know where it is. You also don't know where the blacksmith shop is."

He was impressed with Martha's reaction. Rather than argue, as many people would when challenged like that, she thought a few moments, then smiled. "That is true. In my mind I was picturing it being clear across town, but you're right, I don't know that to be the case at all." She looked a bit sheepish as she asked, "Are they close to each other?"

"Pretty much next door," he said with a grin.

"Oh, my, I've made myself look like a ninny."

"No, you haven't," he assured her. "You were being thoughtful and I appreciate that. I didn't want you to leave without me because there's something I want to show you before we leave that end of town."

"Oh, okay."

"If you're ready, let's go see Jed." Again, she found his hand on her back comforting as they went across town. He introduced her to Jed Hawkins, the lawyer in town. "Martha and her uncle were on the wagon train that went by, when her uncle became ill."

"Yes, I heard about that unfortunate situation. Dr. Campbell was busy here and couldn't get out to see him right away. He felt bad about that." After a short pause, he added, "We all did when we heard about it. I'm sorry for your loss, Miss Welch."

"Thank you. I don't want Dr. Campbell to feel bad about what happened, because I don't believe he could have helped. I believe my uncle was already too sick. It was an unfortunate situation, but I don't believe Dr. Campbell being there several hours earlier would have made a difference."

"That's kind of you to say, Miss Welch. I assume there's something I can do for you?"

"There's something you can do for both of us, actually," Wyatt said. "I have a contract for purchasing the Lingle place I'd like you to look at for me if you would, please. Miss Welch has her uncle's will and a bank check in his name. She's the only family he had left, but I assume you need to do something so that she can deposit the bank check."

"Yes, I can help with that. With a will and no other family it shouldn't be too involved or take long. Wyatt, how much of a hurry are you in for this contract?"

"Help Martha first. I have a couple of weeks yet to give them an answer on the place I want to buy. I read it and I think it's okay, but there are several terms I'm not familiar with, so I'd feel better if you can just read it over and make sure you're happy with it. I can stop in sometime next week."

"That will be fine. Miss Welch, if you'd like to come on into my office, we can get started."

"Thanks, Jed. I've got a quick errand to run, then I'll wait in the other office," Wyatt said before leaving.

Jed led Martha into his office and closed the door. Once they were seated she handed him her uncle's will, and the bank check. He glanced at the bank check, and his eyes grew. He looked at it again a bit closer before looking back at Martha. "This is quite a substantial amount, Miss Welch."

"He sold his house and business, and cashed out his bank

accounts before we left. He took some in cash and put the rest in this check. Will the amount of it be a problem?"

"No, not a problem, but we will have to make sure everything is done properly before the bank will be able to deposit it in your name."

"I understand. I'm hoping they will be able to keep it there, possibly in their vault, until everything that needs to be done has been completed."

"I think that's a good idea, and I'm sure Mr. Taylor, who runs the bank, will be happy to do that." He took a few minutes to read the will, before addressing her again. "Your uncle left his entire estate to you, as his only heir. I will need a list of all family members your uncle had. Because of the amount we will also need to put a notice in the newspaper in New York, as well as the area he is from, just in case there is anyone else there that claims to be family."

"I understand. I can give you the list, but it really isn't very long. My uncle only had one sibling. That was my father, Frederick Welch." She continued, explaining he was married one time, and his wife was an only child. She gave him all the names and dates he needed, and the town her father and uncle were from. They were just finishing up when Wyatt got back to Jed's office.

"Wyatt, I need to take Martha down to see Mr. Taylor at the bank. I'm sure he'll want to keep this bank check in his safe while we wait to get the paperwork back from New York. Would you like to walk along with us?"

"I'll do that. If you're done here, I have something I want to show Martha afterward, and we can go there when we leave the bank."

"That would be fine. I have everything I need from Miss Welch for now. It will probably take a few weeks for me to hear back so I can get this completed, but if you're in town in a few weeks you can stop in and see if I've received anything yet."

"I'll make sure she gets back to town in a couple of weeks and we'll stop in. I'll stop in sometime next week for my contract. Thank you, Jed, for your help."

"Yes, thank you, Mr. Hawkins."

"Certainly. It was nice to meet you, Miss Welch. I take it Wyatt and Rosy are treating you well out there?"

"They've both been so kind and generous to me."

"I'm sure Rosy's happy to have another lady to talk with," Jed said.

"Oh, she certainly is," Wyatt said.

When they finished their introductions at the bank and Mr. Taylor had Martha sign a few papers, Wyatt led her back out to the boardwalk. "Now, if you're ready, I can finally show you something I've been eager for you to see."

"What is it?"

"It's right down this way," he said, directing her past the bank. They came to the edge of town, and he turned her sideways, and Martha gasped. "Here is the green falls this town is named for."

"Oh, my. It's gorgeous. I thought the waterfalls on your land were impressive. It's the largest waterfalls I've seen, but this one has to be three times the size of it. I heard a lot of noise, but I thought it was from the lumber mill, sawing the logs."

"Much of it is from that. If you come down here in the evening when the mill is shut down you can hear the falls better and it sounds more like running water, even from this far away."

"This is amazing." She stood watching for several minutes before leaning over toward him and speaking rather softly. "I have to say, as impressive as this is, I prefer the one on your land."

"You do?"

"Yes. This one is bigger and with all the moss it's green, which is very different, but pretty, but yours is green, as well, and we can get closer to it. I love the sound of the water running over the rocks it hits at the bottom. You can also feel a bit of spray from it, which is very unique. I guess being up closer to it, you can experience it more, rather than just see it."

"You know, I always liked watching ours better, too, but I could never put a finger on why. I thought maybe it was simply because it was on our land. But I think you're right; up closer you not only see it, but you hear it and feel it. Thank you for clearing that up for me."

She giggled, but cuddled a little closer to him, which he noticed and liked, very much. "I'm glad I could help. Thank you for bringing me here so I could see it."

"I thought you would like it. If you're ready, we probably should get to the mercantile. Rosy likes to visit with Eloise, but she'll think we forgot about her."

Wyatt took the ladies to the restaurant in town for their noon meal. He introduced Martha to several people, all of whom came to their table asking who his guest was. Martha wasn't at all surprised at how curious everyone in the small town was. The small town they lived close to in Missouri was the same way. After living in New York a couple of years, though, she was touched at how friendly and welcoming everyone was. So far she liked Green Falls a great deal, and that included her host.

The ride back to the ranch was full of conversation and laughter, and all three of them were happy and felt refreshed when they got back. Wyatt went to help with the evening chores while the ladies got busy in the kitchen so they could get some supper ready for Wyatt when he came in for the evening.

That evening Wyatt and Martha spent a little more time talking on the front porch. They didn't stay outside as long, though, as it was getting pretty chilly. They called it an early night.

Martha went to bed, but her mind wouldn't settle down. She had enjoyed her day with Wyatt, which was good. She was glad she'd talked to a lawyer and got that process started. One thing Jed said kept coming back to her, taking front and center in her mind. He'd commented on the amount of the bank check. She hadn't really thought of that before, because she'd never looked at it as being hers. In her mind it was her uncle's. When he commented on the amount, for the first time she thought of it as becoming hers. As she thought about that, she didn't know what she should do with it.

Right now she didn't need any money. Wyatt refused to take anything for her staying there. She didn't want to leave, but even if she decided it would be better if she stayed in town, she could buy a home of her own in town for a small portion of that money. If she did decide to stay in town she would prefer staying at the hotel or a boarding house until she made permanent plans. She knew she and Wyatt had feelings for each other, and it didn't make sense in her mind to buy a home in town. Wyatt seemed like a man that knew his mind, and so was she. If they decided they were right for each other, she didn't think it would be a long time before they would be together.

That thought was exciting to her, but just as quickly, she warned herself not to get ahead of herself. They might decide they weren't meant to be together. She started questioning again whether it was right for her to stay at the ranch. Her papa might be right, and it might be forcing their relationship. Her conversation with Wyatt came back to mind, and the more she thought about it the more confused she became. She eventually went to sleep, but she tossed and turned so much she was still tired and confused the next morning. She decided to take another walk. Maybe it would clear her mind.

MARTHA WENT to the kitchen the next morning and greeted Rosy. "Good morning, Rosy."

Rosy turned to face her with a smile, but her look turned to concern. "Are you feeling okay, Martha? You look a little pale."

"I feel okay, but I didn't sleep well last night."

"Something on your mind?"

"Yes. I think maybe I'll take another walk today and see if I can clear my head."

"I hope it helps. Maybe you can take a bit of a nap this afternoon. You do look tired."

Martha nodded, and the two started making breakfast. When Wyatt came in he hung his hat up and turned to the ladies. "Good morning, ladies." Martha turned and smiled at him, but he tilted his head as he studied her a bit. "Are you feeling okay?"

Martha had to smile, but explained, "Rosy said the same thing. I must look terrible."

"Not terrible, but –"

"Tired?" Rosy asked.

"Yes, that could be. Did you not sleep well last night?"

"No, I didn't. I told Rosy I plan to take a walk today and clear my head."

"If there's anything I can do, let me know. My offer to listen and help you make decisions still stands."

"Thank you."

She was quiet during breakfast, and Rosy and Wyatt both allowed that, not pushing her much to participate in the conversation. After they had the kitchen cleaned up she told Rosy she planned to walk along the path she'd followed the last time she went walking. Rosy nodded and Martha left.

She did as she said, and followed the path. She walked for a while and simply let herself feel the nice breeze, which was warmer again, and hear the birds singing and the horses in the pastures. She started feeling better and her mind cleared. She started thinking about what her papa said, trying to decide if she should move into town a while and see if Wyatt would actually court her. It wouldn't be forced then, but it would require him to ride into town to see her, and she was sure they wouldn't get to see each other as often, or as long. It would be harder on him, as well, because spring was a busy time on the ranch.

She didn't want to do that. She loved staying at the ranch and hated the thought of leaving. If she did go into Green Falls, she wondered what she would do. With the money she had from selling her father's farm, plus the money she would get from her uncle, she wouldn't need to worry about having enough money to live. She could buy a home and live comfortably.

However, she knew that would never work for her. She would be miserable not having something to do, something that would make her feel productive. Along the same line, she worried about how that would look. If she didn't find some kind of employment, people would assume she must have a lot of money. That might be dangerous. A single lady with money, living alone would be an easy target. If she moved to town she would have to find some type of employment. She wasn't sure what might be available for a woman, but she would ask Rosy and Wyatt. Maybe she could help cook at a restaurant, or maybe clean the rooms at the hotel. Surely she could find something she could do that would earn her a paycheck, so others wouldn't consider her an easy target.

CHAPTER 11

$\mathcal{M}$artha kept walking, trying to think of places she might be able to find employment, until she heard some horses. Glancing over at the pasture on her left, she saw two horses trotting over toward her. She looked at them closer and recognized them as the two horses she and her uncle had on the wagon train. She went to the fence and they came to her. She patted their necks as she talked to them. Some other horses came close to the fence down a little way, so she slowly walked in their direction. She was glad to see they stayed there and allowed her to scratch their necks, as well, as she talked to all of them.

While she was talking to them some others came to the fence. She laughed and kept walking on down along the fence line, scratching the horses' heads or necks. She had always liked horses and loved seeing them come to her while she talked with them. Wyatt had some very nice looking horses.

The horses started running back the other direction, and she stopped and looked around. This really was nice country. Wyatt had various pastures, with various animals in them. There was a walkway of sorts between the pasture the horses were in and another pasture. On first glance she thought it was empty, but as she looked further down, she saw animals in it, as well, although she couldn't make out what kind. She walked a little further in that direction until she could see them better, and saw that it was cattle. She was used to having a few cows they milked on their farm, but this was a whole pasture of beef cattle.

She wished she could see more of the layout of the ranch, and decided to climb up onto the first rung or two of the fence. Perhaps from that added height she could see if there were more pastures, or if there were any fields. She climbed up on the first rung, but it didn't help much, so she climbed up onto the second rung. She could see much better, and turned to see in all directions. She saw a smaller pasture not too much further up the walkway that had two white animals in it. They were large, and it looked to her like it was her oxen.

She climbed back down and went toward the pasture, anxious to see if they were indeed out in a pasture, and how they were getting along. Unfortunately, as she got closer to them she could see them better, and it wasn't her oxen. It was cattle, large cattle. She knew cattle on a ranch weren't tame, like the cows they had on the ranch, so she didn't figure it was any use getting closer.

Glancing around her, she realized she was now at the top of a small hill, and this would be a good place to climb back up on the fence rail for another look around. She did that, turning in all directions so she could see more of the ranch. It really was a pretty area. There was a woods off a ways on two opposite sides, and a valley with a stream flowing through in one direction. She could see several pastures, most of them with cattle. Some had large cattle, some were smaller, so she assumed Wyatt must separate them out by age, at least somewhat. As she looked again, she saw a couple different kinds of cattle apparently. The coloring was different on them.

She climbed down from her perch on the railing and moved

over to a different pasture and climbed up on the railing there. It afforded her a different view of the area. Now she could see a little more of the countryside, and a couple more pastures. She loved it out here, and loved being in the country again. She moved from one spot on a fence rail to another, relishing all the interesting countryside and types and sizes of cattle she saw.

As much as she was enjoying herself, it occurred to her she'd been out longer than she'd planned on being. A quick glance at the sun told her it had to be close to lunchtime. She jumped down from the railing and turned to head back, hoping if she hurried she would be back before Wyatt came in for his noonday dinner. She turned in one direction, then the other, and quickly realized she had no idea which way she'd come from. She had never been good with directions, but relied on landmarks to remember where she'd been. At this moment as she looked from one side to the other, they looked the same.

She berated herself mentally for not paying more attention. Normally she was very good at watching her surroundings and committing them to memory. This time she was more interested in deciding what she should do with her life, and Wyatt. She was so busy debating whether to move to town or stay on the ranch that she had paid very little attention to where she was going. She was simply following the trail, which she could no longer see.

She looked around the area at the footprints. Maybe she could tell by them, which direction they were headed. Unfortunately, she'd been walking in that area so much that she couldn't tell anything from them. There were footprints coming to that area from both sides, where she'd gone back and forth and all over in the area. That wasn't any help. She climbed back up on the railing and looked for a trail. If she could find the trail she'd followed, she should be able to follow it back to the house. She had to look from several different points on the fence rails, but did finally find a trail.

She was happy to see a pasture of horses next to the trail. She remembered she got off the trail when she saw her two horses in the pasture close by the trail, so that had to be the spot. She held her skirt up so she could run back to the trail. She had to hurry back to the house before anyone started to worry about her. When she reached the trail, she remembered the horses were to her left, so she turned to the right to head back toward the house.

She felt much better now that she was on the trail back. Even if Wyatt did become concerned and go looking for her, she would be on the trail and easy to find. She had to chuckle a bit when she thought of it as being a trail. A trail to her was a well-worn route. Looking down, this was more of a path than a trail. It was mostly grass, and basically just a strip of land between pastures. It was, however, as she'd remembered it previously; a piece of ground between fences on both sides, and had a mixture of grass, weeds, and dirt. She kept walking briskly, hoping to get to the small knoll she remembered going over that blocked her view of the house and barns.

When she did finally get to the small knoll, she gasped. There were no buildings in sight. If the house and barns weren't just over this knoll, where were they? She stopped and looked around, but everything looked pretty much the same. This area was basically flat. There were small knolls and valleys, but nothing spectacular or note worthy. There were woods on both sides of her, as she remembered from earlier when she set out on her walk, but she really couldn't tell one from the other.

A horrible thought crossed her mind. What if she went the wrong way when she started back? She knew for sure the horses were on her left as she was walking earlier, so that would mean she had to turn right to go back. She hadn't seen her horses in the pasture when she got to the path and turned right, but she had assumed they were on the other side of the pasture, out of sight. Now she had to wonder, was that somehow the wrong pasture? She had been turned around, so could she have somehow gotten herself lost? Maybe this wasn't the same path.

She'd never been on a large ranch before, but she supposed it wouldn't be out of the question for a ranch to have two, or even several trails leading from the house and barns. After all, Wyatt mentioned taking horses and a wagon out to fix fences or bring an injured animal back to the barn. The more she thought about that, it would make sense that there would be several trails. How else could they take wagons to all the pastures to fix fences?

If there were several trails on a ranch, that meant she could have found a trail, but not the same trail she'd been on earlier. Her heart raced. If that was the case, she had no idea where she was, or how to find the house and barns.

Rosy kept watching the trail Martha had gone down, hoping to see her returning. She'd been gone all morning. She didn't begrudge Martha being gone that long. In fact, she hoped that meant she'd been able to clear her head. In her mind, Martha didn't need to worry about deciding what to do with her life so much yet, but she had to clear her mind. The poor girl had been through a lot, and Rosy knew she needed to come to grips with everything that had happened so she was ready to face the future.

If she was able to do that, Rosy was fine with her being gone this long. The reason she kept checking the window to see if she was coming back yet was because she was worried about her. There were a lot of things that could happen on a ranch, and Rosy hated to think of Martha out there needing help.

Moreover, she was certain what Wyatt's reaction would be. She'd thought several times about going out to the barn to see if he was out there, or if he'd gone off to some other section of the ranch. If he was at the barn she could tell him Martha had been gone all morning, and she felt pretty certain he would head out on Thunder, his horse, in search of her. She hesitated doing that, however. Maybe Martha was perfectly safe, just over the knoll, sitting on a rock or downed tree, watching the brook splashing over the rocks while she was thinking.

She also knew Wyatt could be very protective of people close to him, and that very definitely included Miss Martha. She wasn't sure if he'd admitted that to himself or not yet, but she was sure Martha had found a way to sneak in and had invaded his heart. In fact, she was pretty certain that was a two-way thing; he had become lodged in her heart, as well.

But there was no need for him to be worried about her if she was simply sitting somewhere and enjoying her time alone. He was like his father in a lot of ways, and being worried about a loved one could bring out rather strong feelings they would act on before thinking it through completely. It would be better for Martha not to meet those tendencies yet, and not in that manner. So she didn't go to the barn looking for him, but continued to wait, hoping to see her come walking over that ridge any minute now.

Unfortunately, that didn't happen. She had dinner ready, but kept it on the back burner. When she saw Wyatt and some of his men riding in, she headed to the barn. He saw her and let the others head to the bunkhouse, while he met her. "Rosy, everything okay?"

"I don't know. Martha went for a walk after breakfast, but she isn't back yet."

"She knew I expected her to tell one of us when she left and when she planned to be back. Did she tell you that?"

"She told me when she left, and she planned to be back for lunch. You don't suppose she got hurt or lost, do you?"

"I don't know, but I'll go look for her. Which did she go?"

"The trail over here," Rosy said, pointing.

"The other time I found her she was right along the trail. Hopefully I'll find her easily again this time."

Dallas had also seen Rosy heading to the barn, and went to meet the two of them. "Boss, any problems?" Wyatt explained the situation to Dallas, who quickly asked, "Do you want me to go with you, or should I start off in another direction? Should I get a few of the men looking?"

"Let's hope she's right along the trail, and on her way back. I'll go out along the trail, and if I find her and she's okay I'll fire one shot in the air. If I find her and she's hurt or I need some help, I'll fire three shots."

"Okay, so if I hear more than one shot, I'll get a couple of the men and we'll head out."

"I'll fire three shots at a time, a few minutes or so apart so you'll be able to find us."

"Okay, good luck. Hopefully I'll hear a single shot and you'll be back with her shortly."

"Let's all hope that happens," Wyatt said as he turned Thunder and wasted no time starting down the path she'd taken. Once he passed over the knoll he slowed down so he could search, and began calling for her. If she had tripped and fallen, perhaps twisted an ankle, hopefully she could hear him calling and would answer. He called, then listened carefully, but wasn't seeing or hearing anything.

He looked for footprints, but there weren't many patches of dirt along the trail. It was mostly weeds and grass, and although he would probably see footprints from a man walking through, she was so small, he wasn't sure he would even notice any. Still, he continued to look for any signs of her, and continued to call. Eventually he came across a place where he did see small footprints. They led off from the path to a nearby pasture.

He got down from Thunder to look closer. There were numerous footprints, leading to the pasture and in that area, like she'd walked around some right there. He looked up at the animals grazing in the pasture, and noticed her two workhorses were in among his larger horses. That made sense. Maybe she saw them and went to the pasture to watch them.

He looked around at the footprints until he saw them leading off in another direction, away from the trail. He stayed on foot, leading Thunder behind him as he followed the footprints. They were hard to follow through the weeds in places, but every time he lost them, he was able to pick them up again further down. He found another place where she apparently had spent some time, since there were not only lots of footprints, but the weeds and grass were pushed down a little from all the walking she'd done.

He scoured the area for footprints leading away from there, but wasn't seeing any. Finally he went on further in that direction, and just as he was ready to give up and turn around and go back, he came across what he thought might have been some grass knocked down by a footprint. He continued on, and sure enough, he came across a couple more similar spots. He continued calling, but never heard a response.

Further down he came to another trail, and studied the area carefully. The more he walked in an area, the more the grass was knocked down from his boots, and the harder it was for him to see any signs of a much smaller, much lighter person having been there. He went back to the fence and got up on the first rail, so he was up a bit higher. Now when he looked at the area he was able to make out a few places that were slightly pushed down. They appeared to be following the trail, but heading away from the house and barn.

Not seeing anything else that looked to be footprints, he followed the trail and headed deeper into the ranch. The further he went, the more concerned he became. This was too far from the house for a lady to be walking alone, without a gun for protection, or even a horse. Not only were there wild animals to contend with this far out, but like other ranches and farms in the area, they occasionally had a drifter or two pass across their property. Occasionally they would even make camp for an evening and catch a fish in one of the streams or kill a rabbit for their supper. He wouldn't even allow himself to think of what some of the drifters would do if they found a pretty little lady walking alone without a gun.

He shook his head to get that thought out of his mind. He had to concentrate on finding her. He called yet again, and thought he heard something. He waited a moment, and yelled again. This time he was sure he heard something, and it came from further up in the direction he was headed. He spurred Thunder on and kept looking side to side as he hurried forward. He called again, and this time he was sure he heard a response. "Martha, is that you?"

He listened carefully and heard what he was pretty sure was, "Yes. Wyatt?"

He hurried on in the same direction as he yelled, "Martha, this is Wyatt. Can you hear me?"

He heaved a sigh of relief when he was sure he heard, "Yes."

"Hang on, honey," he yelled, "I hear you and I'm coming. Keep answering so I can find you. Are you okay?"

"Yes," he heard, and released the breath he'd been holding.

"Okay, I'm coming. Can you still hear me okay?"

"Yes."

"Are you close to the trail?"

"Yes, I'm on the trail."

"Okay, good. Stay on the trail and I'll be able to find you."

"Okay."

He spurred Thunder on a little faster now, since he knew she was on the trail. He should see her shortly. Now that he knew she was okay, a different feeling started settling in. He was not happy that she took a walk and wasn't back for lunch. He'd told her to be sure she was there for meals, or he would become worried. That was exactly what had happened. He had been scared to death when he heard she wasn't back yet. There are so many things that could have happened to her, and they all kept running through his mind.

By the time he saw her up ahead, he had worked up a lot of emotion. It was partially relief, partially worry, partially anger, and partially disappointment that she would do something to cause him that much worry. One thing he was sure of, he needed to make sure she knew it was not acceptable and would not happen again.

He stopped his horse next to her, and as he climbed down he was trying to decipher her expression. He saw joy, relief, but also he was pretty sure there was some fear. He would have to sort them out later. First he had to hold her, assure himself she was indeed okay. He had barely turned toward her before she ran into his arms. He caught her, holding her tight against him. "You're sure you're okay?"

"Yes, I'm fine now," she said, though he noticed a few tears escaping her eyes. "Thank you for coming for me."

"You may not want to thank me quite yet," he said, causing her to look up at him with a confused look in her eyes. "I have to let Dallas know I found you and you're okay. Hang on just a minute." He kept her in his arms, but moved them back to his horse. He unhooked his rifle from where he kept it and held it up and fired off a single shot.

He held the rifle in one hand as he turned back toward her. "Now, you're sure you're okay?"

"Yes. I didn't get hurt at all."

"Then we need to have a little talk." He looked around, then took her hand and led her to a large rock not too far away.

MARTHA WAS SO glad to see Wyatt, she couldn't stop the tears that escaped. Once she'd realized she was lost, it hadn't taken long for fear to set in. When they lived on the farm she enjoyed going off by herself now and then. She was way more familiar with the land then, and knew where their property ended and their neighbor's property started. More importantly, though, she generally rode her horse, and always took a gun, generally a rifle along with her in case she had a problem. There had been a few times she'd had to use the rifle to scare off a coyote or wolf that started tracking her.

Having her horse meant she had a means of escape if necessary. Out here she wasn't familiar with the land at all, and if she encountered any wolf or bobcat, or anything else that could pose a possible danger, she had nothing to protect herself. With no gun and no horse, she was very vulnerable. Hearing Wyatt's voice had been such a relief.

She was shaking like a leaf, and as soon as he got down from his horse she couldn't stop herself from running to him. His open arms were exactly what she needed. When he wrapped his arms around her she felt safe again. Such a relief. It didn't surprise her much when he fired a shot in the air to let Dallas know he'd found her and she was safe. That's what her father and uncle often did if they were missing a cow or calf. They would both go out hunting for it, and fire a shot off when they found it. If they needed help they fired off two or three, and the other man would be there to help. She hated that she'd worried Wyatt and Dallas, but she hadn't meant to get lost. She would explain that to him so he understood what had happened.

Before she had a chance to do that, however, he was taking her by her hand and leading her to a stone. It seemed his demeanor had changed, which was confusing. Unsure what he was doing, she was taken totally by surprise when he sat down on a rock, and she found herself quickly pulled over his lap. She was lying across his knees, staring at the ground. What had happened? What was he doing?

Before she even had a chance to catch her breath, she felt his hand on her bottom. What was he doing? She was about to ask, when his hand smacked down on her bottom again. At the same time, he started talking. "Martha, what were you thinking? You scared me half to death. I told you not to go too far from the house and barn because it wasn't safe. Do you know how many ways you could have gotten hurt out here this far? There are bobcats, coyotes, wolves, even a few bears out in this area. That's not mentioning smaller animals like raccoons and groundhogs that will attack a person if they're sick."

Martha might have been momentarily confused, but it didn't take long for her to realize he was spanking her! What— did he think she was a child? He hadn't even let her explain what had happened, but simply started spanking, and it hurt. She was a grown woman. How dare he do this to her, without even letting her say a word on her behalf first. How could she think she had feelings for this man? She never would have guessed he would do this to a woman without even asking a single question first.

This was not the kind of man she wanted to even consider spending her life with. She was just about to tell him exactly that, when she felt him lifting her skirt up over her back. What was he doing? He had no right! Before she could get a word out, his hand came down again, but this time it really hurt! He had lifted not only her skirt, but all of her underthings. His hand came crashing down directly on her pantaloons, and it hurt something awful!

It took four or five more powerful swats before she managed to take in enough of a breath to object. "Ow! Stop that right now! Wyatt, that hurts! What do you think you're doing?"

"What I'm doing is giving a well-deserved spanking, young lady, and I know it hurts, as it should. Don't you ever scare me like that again." He kept spanking, and it hurt terribly. "You could have been hurt seriously out here, and we wouldn't have known where you were. It was lucky that I was able to find you as quickly as I did today. We might not always be that lucky, though, so don't ever go walking alone this far, with nothing to protect you, and not be back in time for a meal. Dallas was ready to get all the men saddled up and out hunting for you. Rosy was beside herself when she came out to tell me you hadn't come back yet."

As angry as Martha was at Wyatt for doing this to her, hearing Rosy was worried tore at her heart. Tears started flowing heavier, for a different reason. She loved Rosy and hated hearing she was worried enough to get Wyatt. Once her heart was filled with thoughts of worrying Rosy, those thoughts and that feeling seemed to replace the anger she had in her heart for Wyatt. Unable to do anything else, she collapsed over his knees, sobbing her heart out. "I'm sorry," she said, feeling terrible for making Rosy upset.

WYATT WAS WATCHING Martha as he was spanking her. So far she hadn't looked a bit sorry for the worry she'd put him through. In fact, he thought a couple of times she was about to yell at him, chew his head off. If they were going to spend their life together as man and wife, which he truly hoped they would, he couldn't allow her to scare him like that again. She needed to know he was serious about this. His head jerked up when he realized what he'd just been thinking. He wanted to spend his life with this little lady. He kept spanking, although not as harshly, as he considered that thought.

When he'd heard Martha was missing, his heart instantly tightened in his chest. The thought of her being out here some-where hurt was almost more then he could bear. That had to mean his feelings for her were stronger than he'd realized. It took such a fright to point that out to him. Before he could give it any more thought, he watched as she went limp over his knees, and she was sobbing hard. She spoke so softly he almost missed it, but he was sure she said she was sorry.

He stopped the spanking completely and rubbed her back lightly. He would give her a minute to catch her breath, then pull her up on his lap and wrap his arms around her so they could talk. After his new discovery, they had more to talk about than he realized. As he was taking a moment to gather his thoughts so he knew where to start, she seemed to come back to life. She tried getting up, and he could tell she was not at all happy with him. Not wanting to let her run off before they had a chance to talk, he helped her up and pulled her directly onto his lap, keeping a tight hold on her.

"Wyatt, let go of me right this minute. I don't know who you think you are, but you had no right to do that." She struggled, trying to get loose. When she had absolutely no success, she turned to face him and started crying again. "Why did you do that?"

Of all the questions he expected, or thought she might ask, that was not one of them. It was pretty obvious to him why he'd done it, so the question took him totally by surprise, and he struggled with how to answer that, while his prior thoughts were still weaving their way through his foggy mind. His answer was ultimately a result of all those rambling thoughts. "I, because I, I – I guess I love you."

His jumbled thoughts and words succeeded in doing one thing, anyway. Martha stopped struggling. When she did, he actually heard what had just come out of his mouth. Oh, my goodness, what had he just said and done? That comment certainly wasn't going to sweep her off her feet.

CHAPTER 12

Wyatt was beyond nervous now. Martha sat perfectly still on his lap, staring down at the ground, for a full minute before looking up. She momentarily seemed to focus on her hands in her lap. Her sobbing had stopped, but she was still sniffling as she looked further up, searching for his eyes. "You guess you what?"

In his mind he once more heard the words that had fallen from his lips, and he shook his head. "No, that's not what I meant. I mean, yes, I did mean it, and still do, but not the way I said it. Or not the way it came out. I mean –"

"What exactly do you mean?"

"Oh, boy," he said with a long sigh. "Let me try and explain this."

"Please do, and then please explain how you can tell me one day you're developing feelings for me, and then just a few days later do this to me. Do you have any idea how much that hurt? I was developing strong feelings for you, Wyatt, and they were real. This really hurts, but at least I guess I'm glad I know now what kind of man you really are, before my feelings got any stronger." She starting crying again and tried once more to get up.

Wyatt held her tight, not letting her budge a bit. "Settle down, Martha. Please, hear me out. Hopefully I can make you understand what's going through my heart and head right now."

"Wyatt, please let me up. I know I asked you some questions, but honestly, after what you just did to me, the only thing I want to hear from you right now is an apology. I'm not really interested in hearing anything else you have to say, at least right now."

"Then let me start with an apology. Maybe once you hear that you'll listen to more of what I have to say."

"I'm not promising anything else, but I'll listen to your apology."

"Thank you." He took a moment to gather his thoughts quickly before speaking from his heart. "Martha, I am very sorry for the way I spanked you. That is not the proper way to spank a lady, especially if it's the first one. For that I'm truly sorry. In the future I promise to –"

"Wait a minute," she interrupted. You're apologizing for the way you did it; not that you did it at all?"

Once again she tried to get up and run, but he tightened his hold on her again, ensuring she would stay where she was. "Martha, settle down. You're not going anywhere until we have a talk. As I think back to what you told me about your history, I'm thinking we may have more to talk through than I realized. It also makes me see how wrong I was to spank you the way I did. I need to explain that to you, though, because it's important that you understand why I acted the way I did. I promise you, after you hear what I have to say, if you want to leave, I understand. I will not try to stop you."

She looked up at him and studied his eyes a few moments before slowly nodding her head. "Apparently you aren't going to let me up until you say what you have to say anyway, so okay, I'll listen. But you better not try anything else, and as soon as you're done speaking –"

"I give you my word I will let you up." She nodded and he started. "Okay. Now, I hope I can say everything in a way that makes sense to you. If it doesn't, please stop me. Let me start with the apology. You are upset that I apologized for the way I spanked you and not the mere fact that I spanked you. Kansas can be a dangerous place, especially for women and children. It's the man's responsibility to keep his family safe. The way most men do that is with spanking."

"A father spanks a child in New York, as well. What does that have to do with me, a grown woman?"

"I'm getting to that. Men spank their wives out here, as well. They have to make sure the lady they care so much about knows what they did was dangerous and that they won't do it again. Often times if a man tells his wife not to do it again, they get into an argument. They say things they don't mean, often hurtful things that are hard to take back or get beyond. Often they stop speaking and can go days or weeks without speaking, and hurt feelings can fester. Once it gets to a certain point, the marriage can't be fixed.

"Other times a man can tell his wife not to do something, but she may not see the harm in it and simply ignore his instruction and do it again. Or he may tell her not to do something again and she may forget. Either way, if she does something dangerous again, not knowing how dangerous it can be, she can be hurt badly, or even killed. Out here, to avoid those things husbands spank their wives. It's something that is painful at the time, but it causes no permanent damage. Generally in an hour or so she's fine again. But it gets her attention and she is much more apt to remember not to do it again."

Wyatt could tell she was listening, but he could also see she wasn't totally convinced. "This happens a lot more often than you apparently think, Martha, but as I think about it, I think I know why it seems so odd to you."

"And why is that?"

"You said your mother died when you were little, didn't you?"

"Yes. I hardly remember what she even looked like."

"See, I lost my mother, as well, but I wasn't as young as you were. The one thing I remember about Mama and Papa together is how you could tell they truly loved each other. But I also remember Mama doing something every once in a while, not often, but every now and then that Papa took offense to. They never argued much about it, but after supper that evening they would go for a walk outside. Sometimes when they came back Mama's eyes were red like she'd been crying, but regardless, every time they came back they were holding hands and smiling at each other."

"And you're saying he took her outside and spanked her, then she held his hand and smiled?"

"Yes, that's exactly what I'm saying, Martha. Let me finish. I didn't understand that when I was young, but as I got older I asked Papa about it. I was very fortunate because I always felt like I could talk to my father about anything. He always took the time to explain things to me. One time when we were in town a lady got upset and turned to her husband. She yelled at him, right there in the middle of town where everyone else could see and hear, and then stomped off, aiming to cross the road. A wagon was coming down the road and that man had one heck of a time getting that team of horses stopped without hitting that fool lady. She was upset and had stomped right out into the road in front of them."

"Oh, my. Was she hurt?"

"The horses got stopped, but just barely. She hurried away, but the horses were spooked and reared up. The man had an awful time getting them under control again. Papa went to try to help the man calm the horses down. I stayed on the boardwalk, but I could hear them and a couple other men working with the horses and talking. One of the men told the lady's husband if she were their wife they'd take her home and straight to the wood-shed. Another man said she needed to have her bottom blistered but good for that stunt. Later that night when we got home I asked Pa about that, and why the men said those things."

"And he answered?"

"Of course he did. He told me one of the best ways a man can show a woman he loves her is by giving her a spanking if she deserves one. He said it shows he cares enough to do that, when ignoring it would be much easier for him. But if he loves her enough he'll take her over his knee and see that she doesn't do that again, thus keeping her safe. I said it looks like it would make her awful mad, and he chuckled a bit and said it some-times does, especially the first time or two. But he said after the spanking is over it's up to the man to take her in his arms and make sure she knows he did that because he loves her and couldn't bear to see her hurt."

Martha had been looking down again, but she slowly lifted her head to his eyes again. "That pretty much takes me to what I meant when I said I guess I love you, Martha," he continued. "I did mean it. You may not want to hear this right now, but I do love you. The I guess part didn't come out as it should have, though. As I was spanking you I realized that the reason I was so scared when I heard you were missing is because I want to spend the rest of my life with you as my wife. I was scared because I love you and I hated the thought that you could be out here somewhere hurt."

"You really do love me then?"

"I absolutely do love you. I had just realized for myself that I don't just have feelings for you, but I've already fallen in love with you, so when you asked why I spanked you, I was dealing with that, and when I said I guess, that was my answer to myself as to why I spanked you. To be honest, I didn't plan the spanking, it just sort of happened."

She furrowed her eyebrows as she looked at him. "Are you trying to say it surprised you as much as it did me?"

"In a way, yes. I instinctively did that because it scared me so much and I didn't want you to get hurt. So I guess the why is that I did it because I love you. I think I'm just now understanding exactly what Pa meant when he said when you love a lady you instinctively do what you have to do to keep her safe. I guess I did that instinctively to keep you safe."

She was quiet, and alternated between looking at him and looking at the ground again. He was nervous and wished she would say something. Finally, what seemed like over half an hour but was probably two to three minutes later, she finally spoke. "Are you done saying what you wanted to say?"

Now he was really nervous. She didn't look convinced, but he'd given his word. "I guess, except to ask if you have any questions about anything I said?"

"I do have one question," she answered quickly.

"What is it? I'll answer it as honestly and completely as I can."

"Do you really love me?"

Once again, of the many things he thought she might ask, that was not one of them. He didn't hesitate, but answered quickly, and completely honestly. "With all my heart, yes. I didn't realize it before, but now I'm sure of it."

"Even knowing I could tell you I want to move away and never see you again, that is still your answer?"

"It is. I told you I would answer you honestly, and I did. I hope you don't tell me that, but it wouldn't matter. I still love you." When she didn't say anything, he continued. "I gave you my word and I have always stood by that. If that's what you want, I will take you to town to either find a place to stay or buy you a ticket on the next coach to wherever you want to go. I hope you don't tell me that, though, because even though I've never been in love before, I know it will take me a long time to recover if you leave."

He watched as a few tears escaped her eyes again and started streaming down her cheeks. Without thinking, he reached out and used his thumb to dry them. He loosened his hold on her and pulled her in next to his chest and wrapped his arms around her. He kept his hold on her gentle, letting her know she was free to run away if she wanted. He held his breath until she reached up with one small hand and laid it on his shoulder. After another few moments her other hand found its way to his other shoulder, and she held his shirt in both hands as she leaned her face against his chest.

After a few minutes of just holding onto his shirt, which for some reason felt really good to him, she lifted her head. "Is this the part where you're showing me that you love me? Because if it is, I have to admit I like this part."

"Does that mean you believe me now?"

"I do. 'I guess I love you' wasn't the most romantic way you could have told me, but then again, I wasn't in a very romantic mood at that point anyway. When you explained what you meant, I could tell you were speaking from your heart, and that's what I needed."

He gave her a hug, then kissed the top of her head. "Good. So now that you know what happened and why, are we okay, or do –"

She pulled back, away from him, but stayed on his lap as she looked into his eyes once more. "Absolutely not."

His smile left. "No?"

"I repeat, absolutely not, no. Not in the least."

"Okay, then we need to talk," he said. "What do we need to talk about?"

"Wyatt, I heard what you said about husbands spanking their wives. I can't say I agree or think it's fine, but I think I under-stand your reasoning. I cannot agree to what just happened, though. You grabbed my hand, and before I knew what was happening, you spanked me. You didn't even ask me what happened. Did you even notice that I was so happy to see you I was crying? Do you know why I was crying? No, of course you don't, because you didn't ask. All you did was spank me."

Wyatt was quiet. She was right. He took one of her hands in his and rubbed his thumb over her knuckles. "Martha, you're right, and I'm sorry. I told you this is the first time I've been in love, and apparently I have a lot to learn. I have to be honest with you, though, and warn you that this doesn't mean I'm ready to give up on spanking. I firmly believe it is indeed a way a man out here shows he loves his wife. Holding you in my arms just a few minutes ago after the spanking, knowing you're safe was about the best feeling I've ever had. I told you I feel a strong need to protect you, and at that moment I felt very close to you."

Martha was very quiet again, and Wyatt worried about what that might mean. Finally, he couldn't wait any longer. "I'm very nervous right now. Can you please talk to me, tell me what you're thinking? I hope it's good, but even if it's not, I have to know."

"Actually, I'm quiet mostly because I'm not sure what I'm thinking right now. I hated that spanking, especially since you didn't talk to me first and I didn't know what it was about."

"You're right about that, Martha, and again, I'm sorry. I reacted out of my fear, and that wasn't fair to you."

"No, it wasn't." She sighed. "Okay, I'll tell you my thoughts, and maybe you can help me figure this out, because I'm not really sure how I feel, other than sore. I understand you were scared, and I'm sorry about that. But I never set out to worry you. I would never do that. In fact, what happened was definitely not planned, and I was very frightened. I wasn't in a safe place and I knew it. I didn't know how to fix it, though I was trying to get back to the house."

"You were lost?"

"Yes, of course I was. Why else wouldn't I have been back at the house for dinner? But what upset me was that you never asked me why I was there and not at the house. I guess you just assumed I got lost on purpose or didn't care about you and Rosy, and that's not true." A few tears started streaming down her cheeks again, and she turned away.

Wyatt guided her face back toward him and wiped her tears with his handkerchief he pulled from his pocket. "Martha, I never would have thought that. I acted simply out of my fear, and I now see how much that hurt you. Would you please give me another chance? I meant it when I said I love you, and I think you have feelings for me. I hope you do, even after I disrespected you by not talking to you about it first."

She was quiet a few moments again, before looking up at him once more with a look of resolve. "Wyatt, I do still have feelings for you, which frankly, surprises me a little. I was very upset when that was happening. I absolutely hated that you were doing that without even talking to me, telling me why. But I have to admit one thing."

"What's that?"

"As much as I hated it, you said you liked holding me in your arms and felt very close to me afterwards."

"I did."

"I had similar feelings. Once we talked enough that I had an idea what had happened, and you apologized for not talking to me about it first, or asking why I was out here, I was able to understand what you were saying. Your arms around me felt good, and it made me feel safe, which is what I needed right then. I felt close to you, as well."

"Then can we please try this again?" Her eyes grew large, and he had to chuckle. "Not the spanking. Again, that didn't quite come out the way I meant it. What I mean is can we try getting to know each other better? I honesty do love you and hope you come to feel the same way and will become my wife some day. I think we would make a good couple. I promise I won't act so quickly out of fear the next time something like this happens, and will talk to you first."

"That would mean a lot to me."

"I will always be honest with you, and part of that means I still believe spanking has a place in a marriage, especially out here where it can be dangerous. I think I have my father's protective instincts and a need to protect you, but I know I can do better in the future."

"I will admit I believed you when you said you love me, partly because I could feel the love in your arms when you held me afterwards. And it made me feel safe, and that was a good feeling, as well." She took in a large breath, and sighed slowly. "Okay, I'm still willing to try, if you promise to talk to me first. I think I deserve that much."

"You do," he quickly agreed, and leaned down to place a tender kiss on her cheek. "Now, let me ask you something. I want to know what happened and how you got lost, but do you suppose we could talk about that as we head back? I sent a shot up to tell them I found you and you're okay, but they'll be worrying if we don't get back before too long."

"Of course we can talk as we go back. I'm glad you're willing to listen to me. I know I made a mistake somewhere or I wouldn't have gotten lost, but I would like a chance to explain what happened and why I did what I did. Maybe you can tell me how to avoid that same mistake again."

"I will certainly try. We can walk back, although it's quite a ways, or you can sit in front of me on my horse, if you think you would feel comfortable doing that."

"I'm fine on the horse if you are."

"Then let me lift you up onto the horse, and I'll get on behind you. We'll go slow so we can talk. I'm ready to hear what happened."

They had a good talk on the way back to the ranch. Wyatt

admitted he completely understood why she went to pet her horses, and agreed the cattle in the one pasture did look like her oxen. He understood why she climbed up on the railing to look at the area, and even agreed that her thinking made sense when she thought it was the same pasture with horses and turned the direction she'd turned.

They finished their talk as they were nearing the barn. "Thank you for explaining all that to me, Martha. I have to admit I feel better. I thought you carelessly roamed the area and got lost, and that concerned me. This is not a place to be complacent."

"I know it isn't, but I thought I was being careful. When I realized I was lost I was frightened because I knew it was not a good place to be lost and alone. I was so happy to see you." She paused before adding, "Well, at first, anyway."

"I plan to earn your respect back so you'll always be happy to see me." He saw Dallas, a few of the men, and Rosy waiting for them. He leaned closer to her ear. "Thank you for giving me a second chance." He jumped down and helped her down off the horse. Not surprisingly, Rosy ran to her and had her in a hug before Wyatt had a chance to thank one of his hands for offering to put Thunder up for him.

He turned back to Martha, to see tears streaming down her cheeks again. "Rosy, I'm so sorry I worried you. I got turned around out there, and was so happy to see Wyatt."

"Are you okay? You look like you've been crying. Are you hurt?"

Wyatt tensed, but she covered for him with no hesitation. "I was so frightened, but I'm fine now. I was lucky that Wyatt found me before any wild animals did."

"She must have been quite a ways out," Dallas said rather quietly to Wyatt, with a little grin or smirk on his face. "It's been a while since you fired the shot to tell us she's okay."

"She was frightened, like she said," Wyatt told his friend who could always see through him. "I helped her calm down before we came back."

"Well, I'm glad she's back safe and sound, and you two seem okay."

"I'm glad of that, too." He gave Dallas a little grin of his own before going to Martha. "I don't know about you two ladies, but I'm hungry."

"I imagine both of you are," Rosy said. "Let's go in and eat."

While they shared their meal, Rosy asked about her walk. "I know you wanted to get some thinking done. Did you have any luck with that before you lost your way?"

Wyatt studied Martha as she was answering Rosy's question. When they were done eating she got up to start helping Rosy wash the dishes and clean up, but he stopped her with a gentle hand on her arm. "Martha, you said you thought you saw your oxen in the pasture and went to look at them. If Rosy can do without you a few minutes, I'd like to take you out to the barn a minute where the oxen are."

"I already did much of the cleaning before we ate, so it won't take long to finish. You two go on ahead," Rosy insisted.

"Thank you, Rosy," Wyatt said, as he led Martha out the door, noting the inquisitive look on her face. Once they were out of hearing range of the house, he explained. "You're right, I really didn't need to show you the team of oxen. In fact, we've been using them the last couple of days, so I'm not even sure they're in the barn right now."

"I'm glad to hear you're using them. How are they?"

"The men say they're strong and real easy to work with. I'll more than likely be making you an offer on them, but I need to ask around a little and see what they're worth. I brought you out here to talk to you a minute, though."

"Okay. What about?"

"Rosy said you went walking today so you could think.

Maybe this isn't any of my business, but are you still thinking about leaving the ranch?"

"I've been trying to think a lot of things through, and that's one of them, yes," she said honestly.

"I wish you wouldn't, especially now. It's your choice and I will respect your wishes, but I would really rather you stay here."

"Why especially now?"

He glanced around to insure their privacy before answering, "Because now that I've realized I love you, I want to be able to prove that to you, and hopefully you'll come to feel the same about me."

"But what if I'm forcing this by staying here?"

"You're not," he assured her. "My feelings are so strong for you that if you move into town, I'll be forced to go in there every day to see you, just to ease my mind that you're safe. I'll worry about you when you're not here where I can see that for myself." He looked off into space several moments before continuing. "If you do feel like you need to move out, could I suggest you see if you can stay at the hotel? That way if I can prove to you I'm the right man for you, we won't have a house or anything to keep you from moving back in here."

She giggled as she slapped his arm. "You seem pretty sure of yourself."

"I'm hopeful, is what I am. I do think we're right for each other, though. That's why I'd rather you stay. I really would be making a trip to Green Falls every day to make sure you're okay."

"You couldn't do that, Wyatt. Spring is a busy time for you."

"It is, but it wouldn't matter. Now that I've fallen in love with you, I would be going to town daily."

"You're sure my being here isn't forcing us together?"

"I'm sure of it."

"Then I'll stay here, at least for now. I don't want to cause more work for you."

"Trust me, Martha, seeing you daily is pure pleasure for me, and something I genuinely appreciate. You being here will save me time and give us more time to spend together, though. Thank you for agreeing."

"Thank you for letting me know how you feel." After a quick look around again, he leaned down and gave her another quick kiss on her cheek. Again, she turned red, but he could tell she wasn't opposed to it, which made him feel good.

CHAPTER 13

hings started changing around the ranch over the next few weeks. Martha went out to the barn more often, as she very much enjoyed visiting with the animals. Dallas and several of the other men got to know her, and everyone got along well with her. Wyatt didn't hide his feelings, and when he found Rosy alone one evening he told her he had feelings for Martha.

"I know you do," she surprised him by answering calmly, "and I've been glad to see it. I think Martha is a fine lady, and more importantly, I think she is a good match for you." She turned him to look her in the eyes. "I trust you, Wyatt. You're a good man. I've been giving you two a little more privacy than I would other people, but only because I trust both of you and want to see you together. I will continue to do that, as long as you don't give me any reason not to."

"Thank you for your trust, Rosy. I value that, just as I treasure the trust Martha has been giving me. I assure you, my parents raised me to be a gentleman, and I will do that. I do not ever want to hurt her."

"Hearing you say that makes me think I'm doing the right

thing. Just don't disappoint me." She turned to leave, but stopped. She turned back and quietly said, "For what it's worth, I think your father would be proud of you. I also think your parents would love her and be happy to see you with her." Then without a word she turned back toward the house.

Wyatt noticed Martha had been spending more time in the barn, and made sure all the men were aware he had feelings for her. He didn't want any of them getting too friendly with her. He was happy to see they all seemed to like her and watched out for her. He wasn't even too surprised when he found out she'd gotten to know Will, the bunkhouse cook, and the two of them got along well. That was something to be proud of, as Will was a bit on the cantankerous side.

One evening he was going toward the house for supper a few minutes earlier than normal, and saw Martha coming out of the kitchen door, headed toward the barn. She had something in her hands, and he hurried over to find her carrying two good-looking pies. "Martha, where are you taking these pies," he asked as he took them from her hands.

"Thank you. I made them this afternoon and I'm taking them out so Will can let the men have them with their supper tonight. I hope they like them."

"You made pies for my men?"

"Yes. That isn't a problem, is it?"

"No, of course not. I'm sure the men will love them. Is there another one in the house for us?"

"Yes. I made one for us, and I thought the men might appreciate them, so I made a couple more. Will said he doesn't mind cooking, but he doesn't bake. I asked what they normally have for desert, and he said they don't normally have anything. Sometimes he makes pudding, but not too often."

"He always has said you don't need something sweet every day. I'm sure the men will love these, because Will may say that, but I don't know any man who would turn desert down."

"You don't think it will upset Will, do you? I hadn't thought of that until I was taking the pies out. If he would rather I not make things like this, I won't again. I don't want to upset him."

"I can't imagine why he'd care, but let's ask him." She opened the door to the bunkhouse and he walked in with the pies.

Will looked up and came over to meet them. "What are these?"

"Martha made some pies for you and the men. You don't mind, do you?"

Will looked from Wyatt, over to Martha, back to the pies, and finally out to the men, who were all watching with big, hopeful eyes. Finally he looked back to Martha. "You made these for the boys and me?"

"Yes, I thought you might like them. If you'd rather I didn't, I –"

"I may not be the brightest man around, but I'm certainly not crazy. The men would chase me off this ranch if I told you not to make us anything else. These look delicious. Thank you, Martha. Did you make them?"

"I did. Rosy was busy today and I told her I'd make something for us for desert, and I made a couple extras for you."

"Well, I appreciate it," Will said.

"I think it's safe to say we all do," Dallas said, coming up to look at the pies. "Thank you."

As they were walking back to the house, Wyatt took her hand in his. "You certainly have made friends with my men," he said, "even before baking them pies. I'd say now you'll have them eating out of your hand."

She stopped and looked at him. "Do you really think they like me, at least a little?"

Wyatt laughed out loud. "Honey, my men all think a lot of you. Like I said, even before you made them pies."

"I'm glad to hear that. I was afraid they thought I was just in the way out there."

"No. They're impressed with the way you talk and interact with the animals."

"I've always enjoyed animals. Hearing you say that, though, maybe this would be a good time to ask you if I could –"

She paused, and he squeezed her hand. "Ask me anything, Martha. What is it you want to do?"

"I've really enjoyed my walks, but I'd love to go further. Could I take one of your horses out sometime?"

"You know how to ride?"

"Yes, of course I do or I wouldn't want to take a horse out."

"You never said you could ride."

"You never asked. Papa always said men wanted a lady that acted like a lady, so I never volunteered that information. But yes, I love to ride."

The big smile on her face told him she was being honest. "Well, Sunday after church let's go riding. Once I see that you can ride well enough to go out alone, we can talk about where you can ride."

"Thank you, Wyatt," she said, bouncing on her toes.

He loved her enthusiasm. "We'll have to make sure Rosy doesn't object to us going out alone, but as long as she's okay with it, we'll go Sunday."

SUNDAY after they got back from church Wyatt had another surprise when he saw her coming down the stairs in a split skirt. "I changed into these so I can ride better," she explained, seeing the surprise written on his face.

"You're sure you're okay with this, Rosy?"

"I am. She's been talking about it the last couple of days, and I can tell she's eager to go riding. Besides, I trust you both. Go have a good afternoon."

Wyatt's next surprise was when he showed her several horses

and asked if she saw any she especially liked. It didn't take her long to pick out what he thought was the best of the ones he showed her. "She's got a lot of spirit. I like her."

"I do, too," he said as he opened the gate to lead her out. "I'll get her saddled up for you, then get Thunder saddled."

"I can do mine while you do yours," she said with a grin. "We can get going quicker that way."

"You can saddle a horse, too?"

"Of course. Once I was big enough, Papa said it was important to know how to saddle a horse, so he wouldn't let me go riding if I didn't saddle it first."

"Like I said, your papa sounds like a smart man."

"And like I said before, he was. Now, if you'll let me borrow a saddle, I'll get busy."

Wyatt tried not to be obvious, but he kept an eye on her as she saddled the horse. When she finished, she looked over at him. "So, did I pass the test? If you're convinced now that I can indeed saddle a horse, quit watching me and finish your own horse so we can get going."

She was trying to keep a straight face, but he saw her struggling. "Yes, ma'am," he said, and mumbled something about a feisty little lady as he cinched his saddle tight. He had a smile on his face as he looked up and said, "Let's go."

They led their horses out of the barn, and as soon as they were clear she put her foot in the stirrup and pulled herself up and flung her leg over the horse. She reached down to pet the horse's neck. "Good girl. Are you ready to go?"

He shook his head as he mounted and started them toward a trail she hadn't gone down before. "You've been keeping secrets from me," he said lightheartedly.

"No, I haven't," she said seriously. "I haven't tried to hide anything. If you would have asked I would have answered you honestly."

"Maybe I need to ask then. What other surprise talents does my little lady from New York possess?"

"I'm not sure how to answer that. You want me to tell you everything I know how to do? That could take a while. I can cook, I can saddle and ride a horse, I can read, I can write, I can –"

"Okay, fair enough," he said with a good chuckle. "Let's start with, how good of a rider are you?"

"I think I'm pretty good, but I'm willing to show you so you can see for yourself. How good is this horse? I mean, I can show you I can trot, gallop, let them have a full head, or jump over logs or anything like that, but I won't try any of that without asking about the horse first."

"That just told me you're good at all of them, and that you know how important the well being of the horse under you is," he said with a proud nod. "You're riding Lilly, and she's a strong horse, and well trained. She'll do any of the things you just mentioned. Will you be upset if I ask for a demonstration?"

"Of course not. That's the only way for you to feel confident, and without that I know you won't be allowing me to go out. Tell me what you want to see me do and Lilly and I will show you you can trust us."

An hour later Wyatt was satisfied that his New York lady was in fact a good horsewoman. They rode side by side as they were going back to the barn so they'd be on time for supper, and talked as they rode. "You've proven to me you're quite capable of riding, so I have no problem with you going out to ride, but I don't feel comfortable with you going too far alone yet, because of the wildlife and drifters. I'll be happy to go riding with you when I can, and I'll take my rifle so we can go further."

"How about if I take our rifle? Can I go a little further then? I'd love to see your ranch."

"Having a rifle with you and knowing how to use it are –"

"I'll be happy to go out and show you I can do that, too, so you'll feel comfortable with it."

His head swiveled so fast she was afraid he saw something behind them, and she turned, looking around them. "What? Did you see something?"

"No, but are you saying you're proficient with a rifle, too?"

"Yes."

"How does a lady from New York learn to shoot?"

She was about to tell him she wasn't actually from New York, but Dallas came out from the barn and waved them in. "Something must be wrong," he said, kicking his horse into a gallop.

She followed right beside him, and he slid off his horse as they reached Dallas. "That mare we were worried about is trying to foal, but it's not going well. I've been trying to help her, but you're better at that than I am. Let me take Thunder and you go see if you can help."

Wyatt sent Martha into the house with instructions to go ahead and eat supper with Rosy, and he would be in whenever he was done.

Three hours later Martha returned to the barn to check on the progress, and stood watching a very small, but healthy foal stumbling around as it took its first few steps. Wyatt looked happy, but exhausted. "Go get cleaned up and eat your supper," Dallas said. "I've got this. They seem to both be doing well, but I'll keep an eye on them a little longer."

"Thanks, Dallas," Wyatt said as he crawled over the side of the stall. He and Martha walked together to the house. She helped Rosy heat his supper up while he got some clean clothes and went to the creek behind the house to take a bath.

She sat with him while he ate, and they talked about the new foal, but she could tell he was exhausted. "Why don't we call it an early night, Wyatt. You're exhausted and tomorrow is another day. We can visit tomorrow evening."

"I am pretty tired," he said as he yawned. "If you're sure you don't mind, I think I will go to bed."

"I'll feel better knowing you got a good night's sleep before working another day."

He stood and pulled her up with him. "You're a pretty remarkable lady, Martha. I'm looking forward to our talk tomorrow night about where and how you learned to shoot. Thank you for understanding tonight."

"Of course I understand."

"Good night, Martha." He leaned down and gave her a quick kiss on her lips, and when she didn't object, he kissed her again, releasing some of the passion he'd been holding in. He forced himself to keep it to a short kiss, even though it wasn't what he wanted. He pulled back to look at her eyes and make sure she was okay with his kiss, and had to smile at the look in her eyes. It certainly looked to him like there was passion in those eyes.

"Good night, Wyatt," she whispered.

Rosy and Martha had the noonday meal ready the next day, and moved it to the back of the stove when Wyatt hadn't come in yet.

"He didn't say anything this morning at breakfast about doing anything special that would cause him to be late for dinner," Martha said.

"No, he didn't," Rosa agreed. "He must have gotten held up with something."

Forty minutes later he still hadn't shown up. "I'm going to slip out and see if Thunder is in his stall," Martha said. "If Dallas is out there I'll ask him if he knows where he is. If he got held up, maybe I can take something out to him so he has something to eat."

"That's not a bad idea," Rosy agreed. "Dallas may know something, if he's around. They may have eaten their meal and gone back out by now, though."

"That's true, but it won't hurt to check."

Martha was about to the barn when Dallas came out, leading a horse. "Good afternoon, Miss Martha," he said in greeting. "Going out to spend some time with the animals again?"

"I'm going out to see if Thunder is in his stall. Wyatt hasn't shown up yet for dinner. Do you know where he is or what he was doing this morning?"

Dallas stopped walking and he became instantly concerned. "Wyatt's not back yet? He was going to check on some young cattle in a pasture, then go check a couple line shacks to see if they need any fixing up before flood season gets here. He should have been back way before noon." He had fastened his horse to a hitching post and escorted Martha to Thunder's empty stall.

Martha could tell he was concerned, but trying not to let her see it. "I'll get the men gathered up and we'll pair off and go out looking for him. Why don't you run in and tell Rosy we'll be going out to make sure he's okay."

"I'll tell her and be right back. Count me in on the search party."

Dallas put his fingers in his mouth and gave a loud shrill whistle. She knew that was his way of gathering all the hands to him. Once he did that he swirled around to face her. "Uh, Wyatt said you ride a horse well, but I don't think he would approve of you going out with us to look for him."

"Why not?" Dallas stuttered a bit, so she tried to help. "Because it's work for men? Because you don't want me finding him if he's hurt? Because you think I'll slow you down and you'll have to keep your eyes on me? I assure you, Dallas, I won't slow you down or require any extra help. If he's out there somewhere hurt, I want to at least be out there helping to look for him."

While they argued a couple of minutes, the hands had gathered. Dallas turned toward them a moment. "Men, Wyatt hasn't returned yet so we're going out in pairs to look. He planned on checking the young steers in the small east pasture. Then he was going to go up north and check the two line shacks along the Sanderson property. Austin, you come along with me and we'll check the small east pasture. The rest of you pair off and go together. Remember, if you find him and he's okay, fire one shot and head back here. If you find him and need help, fire three shots."

"Three, or two?" Austin asked.

"Three. It's possible to miss one, and if you fire two and someone only hears one, he thinks it's all good. So if anyone hears more than one shot, head to that location. Repeat it again five minutes or so later until help arrives, in case we're having trouble pinpointing where the shots came from." He told each group of two men where he wanted them to look, and sent them all on their way. Finally he turned back to Martha. "I'm sorry, Martha, but I have to ask you to stay here with Rosy. We'll talk to Wyatt about it later today, but for now, wait here." Without giving her time to argue, he and Austin turned their horses and left quickly.

Martha watched them go, then ran into the house. She told Rosy what was going on, then ran to her room and changed into a split skirt and grabbed her rifle and some ammunition. She didn't want to upset Rosy, so she quietly opened the front door and placed her rifle and ammunition there, then went into the kitchen. "Rosy, I'm going to go out and wait for Wyatt."

Rosy looked at her suspiciously. "With your riding skirt on?"

"I have to feel like I'm doing something. Wyatt said he didn't care if I went riding, just not too far from the barn. I can at least do that and see if I see any horses approaching. I feel so helpless just standing here."

"Just be careful, please. I'm worried enough about where he is. I certainly don't want both of you missing."

"I'll be careful, I promise." She hurried out to the barn and quickly saddled Lilly. Checking to be sure Rosy wasn't at the window watching, she went back to retrieve her rifle and ammunition, then set out on Lilly in the direction she'd seen Dallas and Austin headed.

She watched as she rode, and soon found two sets of hoof prints that looked fresh. She followed them, hoping it was Dallas and Austin. Sure enough, they led straight to a pasture. Following the prints, it looked as though the two men rode down the side of the pasture a small distance, and went back where they had first gotten to the pasture. They went from there in another direction, and it looked as though the distance between them grew, meaning the horses were picking up speed.

Apparently they decided Wyatt had moved on, and so did they. She could see some cattle at the other end of the pasture, but nothing looked out of place. She wasn't sure how large this pasture was, but she went down along the side of it to see if there was more to it than she could see, and make sure it all looked okay.

She went up a little rise, and saw something on the ground at the far end of the pasture. There was a woods at that end of it, and she knew in Missouri she had to be alert when she was near a woods, for any animals that might be around. With that in mind, she approached carefully, looking in all directions as she went. The closer she got, the more concerned she became. Whatever was on the ground at the end of the pasture wasn't moving. She spurred Lilly on a bit faster, while still watching all around. As she got closer, she released the breath she'd been holding. The object was a dead animal.

She had to check it out closer, so she found a gate and went into the pasture, making sure to close the gate behind her. She went to the dead animal, stopped next to it, but didn't dismount. From atop Lilly she could see one set of hoof prints, and she wondered if it was from Wyatt. What worried her was she also saw prints from some kind of large cat. She wasn't sure what all animals were in this area, but it looked to her like a mountain lion. Whatever it was, it was not a small animal. She stood studying the tracks, and the dead animal.

It looked to her as though the animal had killed the steer. Her guess was that Wyatt came upon it and the cat ran off. Looking at the tracks, it looked to her as though the animal fled and Wyatt followed on Thunder. She knew from growing up on the farm in Missouri that if a wild animal killed a farm animal he saw it as an easy meal and would do it again if he wasn't stopped. No doubt Wyatt knew that and went after the cat before it could kill another of his animals.

Without hesitation, Martha set off in the same direction. Something happened or Wyatt would have been home for dinner. She went as quickly as she could, keeping an eye on the tracks she was following, but also watching for this wild cat or any other predators that could be out there. The tracks led into another wooded area, and as she approached the edge of the trees she saw movement up ahead.

She stopped momentarily and unfastened her rifle from behind her and checked again to be sure it was loaded. She turned again to the area she'd seen movement, but didn't see anything. Her eyes roamed the area carefully as she started ahead slowly, constantly scanning the area. As she entered the woods her horse became skittish, which put her on high alert. She kept her rifle handy, while trying to control Lilly and watch her surroundings.

She heard a low growl, and Lilly started prancing, bringing her front feet a little ways off the ground. Martha tried to quiet her horse, but got down from her. Since she wasn't familiar with this horse, she wasn't sure how she would act, and rather than get thrown off, she felt it would be safer on foot. Keeping her eyes moving, watching for any movement, she tied Lilly to a tree branch and slowly made her way forward, rifle at the ready.

She heard the low growl again and swiveled her head quickly

in that direction. She gasped as she saw the very thing she'd been fearing most; a mountain lion. It was crouched down and looked to her like it was getting ready to pounce. It was focused on something straight ahead, staring right at it as it crept slowly forward, and she could tell now it was obviously ready to pounce. She slowly and carefully moved to her right far enough to see what it had its eyes trained on. Her breath caught when she saw Wyatt, motionless, laying on the ground.

CHAPTER 14

*M*artha jumped into action, willing herself to worry about the cat first, then she could go to Wyatt and check him. He wasn't moving, which was a very bad sign, but she refused to even let her mind consider that he could be hurt badly, or even be dead. Instead, she pulled her rifle into place and trained it on the mountain lion. She shot just as the cat pounced. She screamed, and quickly went forward. Since she shot just as the cat moved, she might have missed it. As she watched, the cat fell, but she wasn't sure if it was dead, or possibly just hurt. She hurried over to Wyatt, reaching into her pocket for another bullet and reloading as she went. She had her rifle up and aimed at the cat as she neared.

Luckily, her shot had been on the mark and what she saw was nearly her undoing. The cat lay motionless, less than two feet from Wyatt, who was beginning to stir. Her knees gave out and she fell to the ground, as she gasped for air. She forced herself to stay calm enough to do what she knew she needed to do, and crawled forward, with her rifle still aimed at the cat. She nudged the large cat and heaved a huge sigh of relief when it didn't move a bit. The cat was indeed dead.

Her attention immediately went to Wyatt, and she turned back to look at him. He was groaning and just beginning to move a little. As she crawled over closer to him, now that she was sure they were safe from the cat, he began flailing. She quickly took his arms and tried to still them. "Wyatt? Wyatt, it's okay. You're safe. Try to calm down so I can see if you're hurt. Can you talk?"

He was still groaning, but seemed to react to her voice, so she kept talking to him. "Wyatt, it's me, Martha. You're safe, so try to stay calm. I have to see if you're hurt. Then we'll get you back to the house. Can you talk yet? If you can, tell me where you hurt."

As he seemed to be waking up, he became more restless. He was moving his arms and legs, and she realized he was trying to get up, or move away. She tried rubbing his arms, and kept talking calmly to him. "Wyatt, can you wake up now? You're okay, but you need to stop trying to move. I don't want you hurting yourself more."

As she kept talking to him and rubbing his arms and legs, he slowly opened his eyes. She watched carefully, and could tell he wasn't able to focus quiet yet. "Wyatt? Try to stay calm so I can check and see if you're hurt. Can you talk yet?"

After several long moments he blinked his eyes and squinted. "Martha?"

"Yes, and I'm glad to hear you say that. Are you okay, do you hurt anyplace?"

"My head hurts," he said, slurring his words a bit.

"Lie still and let me check you," she said as she felt the back of his head. "I can understand why your head hurts, Wyatt. You have quite a knot back there. You must have –"

Wyatt seemed to remember what happened, and instantly was struggling again. He brushed her hands away when she tried to keep him down. "Martha, we have to get out of here. There's a mountain lion real close, and Thunder reared up and threw me off. The only time he does that is if there's a rattlesnake close."

"Whoa," she said, again trying to stop his flailing. "Wyatt, it's okay, the mountain lion is dead. If there's a rattler around he more than likely left the area by now, but I'll watch for it. I need to see if you're hurt before you try getting up."

"What do you mean the mountain lion's dead?"

She moved to the side far enough so he could see the dead cat. He jumped, obviously startled, but she held him down. "Like I said, it's okay. It's dead."

"Who killed it?"

"I did."

His eyes went from the dead cat to meet hers. "You shot it?"

"I told you I could use a rifle," she said with a grin. "You didn't believe me, did you?"

"Is this where you shot it?" he asked in a rather soft whisper.

She knew what he was thinking, and picked up his hand. "Yes," she admitted. "When I got here it was crouched down, ready to pounce. When I saw what its eyes were trained on I aimed and shot right away. It pounced just as I shot, so I wasn't sure if I'd gotten it or not. If I didn't, I knew it would land on you, and I was so scared for you. I kept my gun trained on it while I hurried over, and I was so relieved when I saw it laying right next to you motionless."

"Martha, you saved my life."

"I'm just glad I got here in time."

"Me, too," he said with a smile. He tried again to sit up and winced. She helped him sit up slowly after he assured her he felt okay other than a headache. Once he was sitting up he took a moment to catch his breath and let his head stop spinning. "Thank you for helping me up. I feel better." He looked around. "Who did you come with?"

"I came myself," she said a bit cautiously.

"What time is it? Does Dallas know I had a problem?"

"Yes. In fact, I need to fire three shots so they know I found you and they can come help."

"Wait, don't fire them off yet, I think I'll be okay. I won't need help getting back."

"Wyatt, I could tell when you sat up your head was spinning. You can't ride back. I'm not even sure I can help you get on Lilly."

"Lilly? Where's Thunder?"

"I don't know. I haven't seen him."

"He probably went back to the barn."

"Probably. I could take you back on Lilly, but I'm not sure we can get you up on her."

"I'll be okay, just give me a minute or two. Dallas sent you out on your own?"

Martha sighed. Even injured, Wyatt didn't miss much, and he had this way of looking at her that set her nerves on edge. "Well, he didn't exactly send me out here alone."

"I didn't think so. When we're looking for someone or something we always send men in pairs. So who are you with, and where are they?"

"There isn't anyone else."

Wyatt stared at her for what seemed like an hour before saying anything. "I didn't think Dallas would let you go out with anyone yet since we didn't know you could shoot. Did you ask and he said no?"

"Yes," she admitted, "but I couldn't just sit there, not knowing where you were."

"Martha, I told you not to go far from the barn alone yet."

"I know, but it was because you didn't know I could handle a gun. I knew I could, and I also knew you could be out here somewhere hurt and would need help." She could tell by the frown on his face that he wasn't happy, so she continued before he had a chance to scold her again. "Wyatt, before you get too upset, stop and think. It's a good thing I did come out here. I barely got here in time as it was."

"We'll talk about it when we get back. Where are the rest of them?"

"I don't know. They went out in pairs, but I don't know where any of them went."

"How did you find me?"

"Dallas said you were going to check young steers in an east pasture, then were headed to check two line shacks. He was going there first. I watched which direction he went, then went in the house and changed, grabbed my rifle, and went to the barn. I saddled Lilly and went in the same direction he went until I found their tracks. I followed them to the pasture with young steers. They went on from there, but I looked further into the pasture and found the dead steer. There were some kind of large cat prints, and hoof prints from a horse leading away from the steer, so I figured you chased the cat off and followed it."

WYATT'S EYES were huge as he listened to her story. "You tracked me here?"

"Yes."

He shook his head, which caused him to wince. "Like I said, we'll talk more when we get back home. Right now, let's see if my head is okay."

"I know you were dizzy when you first sat up. I'll help you stand, but tell me how you feel, and be honest."

Again he studied her a moment, and shook his head. "Miss Martha Welch, every time I think I'm starting to know you, you surprise me again. Apparently there are numerous things we need to talk about when we get back. For now, let me remind you honesty is very important to me."

"It is to me, too. You didn't tell me you were dizzy when you sat up."

"No, I didn't, but to quote something you told me, you didn't ask me, either." He smiled, which brought a smile to her face, as well. "To address your concern, however, I will indeed tell you how I feel. Now, help me up, please."

"Of course." She looked around and pointed to a large rock not too far away. "Why don't you scoot back to that rock. Then I'll get on one side and help you to your feet. You can use that rock as leverage on your other side, and if you feel dizzy, you can sit on the rock for a few minutes before you try standing."

He looked over at the rock and nodded. "That's probably a good idea, just in case I am a little dizzy at first."

He slid himself back, and she noticed him wince when he moved. "Did something hurt or were you dizzy?" she asked, concerned.

"I'm a little sore, probably from the fall, but I will admit moving brought on a little dizziness. It's probably good to be able to sit on the rock before I stand."

"Do you want me to fire off three shots so one of the men can come help? Maybe we should get the wagon for you. I hate to think of you getting dizzy on Lilly with me."

"Help me up onto the rock and let me sit there a spell. If I'm still dizzy, we'll call for help."

She thought a few moments, but nodded her agreement. "Okay, as long as you agree we can call for help if you're still dizzy after sitting on the rock a few minutes." She looked around again, as she had been doing, checking for unwanted critters or the rattlesnake. "One of the pairs of men may come across us, as well."

"Maybe. Okay, I'm ready, let's get me up on the rock."

She nodded and leaned down next to him. "Put your arm around my shoulders. Then when I stand, you can hold onto the rock on the other side to help you stand. Sit on the rock for a few minutes, then when you're ready I'll help you stand."

He smiled over at her. "Yes, ma'am. I'll bet most people listen to you when you give orders, don't they?"

Her face turned a bit red as she nodded. "If that's your way of saying I'm being a bit bossy, I'm sorry. But yes, most people do what I say."

He laughed, but patted her hand. "They should listen to you because you've had some very good ideas, and I thank you for helping me. Now, if you're ready, I'm ready to be sitting on that rock instead of the ground."

She nodded and knelt next to him. Once he had one arm around her shoulders and the other on the rock, she slowly stood, pulling him with her. He helped with his other hand on the rock, and slid onto the rock with a sigh. "That feels better," he said. "I'll be honest and say I am a bit dizzy, but it's not as bad as I was afraid it might be. I'm pretty sure it will pass in a few minutes."

"If it does, we'll try letting you stand. We need to take this slow, though. I don't want to think you're okay, then fall off the horse on the way back."

"Agreed. Sit down here beside me a minute, and tell me more about your tracking abilities. That lion laying next to you is a testament to your shooting skills, but where did you acquire your tracking skills?"

"I'm not an expert tracker. Papa taught me how to follow tracks like hoof or paw prints. That's a pretty simple thing to do sometimes, like if there's snow or mud they're going through. If they go into a creek he showed me how to follow the creek and watch for tracks coming out along the bank. If they go through tall grass I can look for signs of grass being smashed down, even if it doesn't look like anything's passed through it." She grinned as she added, "If you want, I'll teach you how to do that sometime."

He smiled at her cheekiness. "I'll look forward to it. For now, I think I'm ready to stand up."

"Okay. You look like you're doing pretty good, so let's try it. If you're dizzy –"

"I'll sit back down, I promise."

Ten minutes later he was walking around, assuring her he was okay. "Apparently Thunder went back to the barn, or at least I hope he did, and I also hope my rifle was still fastened on behind the saddle. I don't see it around anywhere, so why don't you fire a shot from your rifle so everyone knows I'm okay. They'll all go back to the barn, and we'll meet them there."

"Are you sure you'll be able to get up onto Lilly? Maybe I should wait until you're on her to shoot."

"I guess maybe that might be better. We'll have to both ride her back because it's too far for us to walk. Are you okay with that?"

"Of course I am, as long as you can direct us back. I followed your tracks here, but I'm not sure I could get us back."

He tried unsuccessfully to hide his laugh. "You do seem to have a bit of a problem with getting turned around and going the wrong way."

"I did that one time," she objected.

"So are you saying you're normally good with directions?"

"Okay, I'll be honest, too. No, I'm not good with directions. I tend to remember things more by remembering landmarks, and I haven't been out here before, so I'm not sure which direction the barn is from here." She stopped and looked around before pointing. "I think it's that direction, but I'd rather follow your directions."

He laughed again, glad to see she was able to laugh at herself and not get hurt that he laughed. "Let's make a deal. I'll get on Lilly, and I'll hold her while you go over a ways away and shoot a shot to tell them we're on our way back. Then I'll lend you a hand and help you up in front of me. I'm okay to lead her back to the barn."

"Are you sure you're okay?"

"Yes, Miss Worry Wart, I'm sure." He stopped and looked up at her sheepishly. "That is, as long as I can make it up on her without getting dizzy. Maybe you better stay close by while I get up on her."

Now it was her turn to laugh. "Miss Worry Wart planned on doing that all along," she admitted. "If you're ready, let's go back to where I tied Lilly. What about the mountain lion?"

"I'll send a couple men out to take care of it." They started over toward Lilly, when they heard her, and she wasn't happy about something. She was prancing and pawing at the ground. "Be careful, there may be another lion in the area. Where's your rifle?"

"Right here," she said, as she checked to be sure it was loaded and ready to shoot. She stepped in front of him and carefully made her way toward the horse. He watched as she very quickly snapped the gun up, aimed and shot. Lilly pulled back at the sound of the shot, but settled down. They both moved closer, and Wyatt was surprised to see a rather large, but dead, rattlesnake laying in the grass.

"You've definitely proven you can use that rifle," he said with obvious pride. "Martha, I'm sorry I didn't check that out sooner. I can understand why you've been wanting to go riding, and after what you've done today, I don't have any concern about your ability to ride a horse or shoot your rifle. We'll talk about your sense of direction a little later, but if we can figure out something there, I won't keep you from going out now. I will ask you still let one of us know when you're leaving and where you're headed."

"I understand that, especially after today," Martha said. "After you came up missing, I don't have any problem with telling someone where I'm headed and when I leave. I just want to be able to get out some and see your ranch."

"We'll talk more on our way back, but let me make sure I can get up on Lilly." She helped, and they were both glad to see he didn't have much trouble, and within a couple of minutes he was fine, no dizziness. She walked a ways away and warned Wyatt so he could hold Lilly and comfort her as she fired one shot in the air, but paused. "Are you sure I should do this? I just shot the snake. They won't know that shot was to kill a snake."

"You're right. That shot was probably all we need. Another one might bring them running. Let me help you up so we can get headed back."

Once Lilly was settled again, he helped Martha up in front of him, and they set off toward the barn, which was not in exactly the direction she thought, but not too far from it, either.

"You're planning on walking Lilly, aren't you?"

"Yes, I am," he assured her. "I realize going faster is apt to bring my dizziness back, and trust me, I don't want that any more than you do."

"Good. Thank you, and I'm sorry if I'm worrying too much."

"Don't apologize for that. I like that you're concerned about me. Now, let's talk a little more about your growing up years. Something is telling me you're not originally from New York, or at least not from the city. Am I right about that?"

"You are." She explained about growing up on a farm and moving to New York with her uncle less than three years ago, when her father died. She explained that since her mother died when she was young, her father took her with him wherever he went, and her aunt and uncle were often there to help, as well, since they never had any children. He learned that she was used to working with all the animals on their farm. He was surprised to hear she worked alongside her father and uncle doing whatever they did on the farm, including breaking horses.

"When you say you've helped break horses," he started hesitantly, "what exactly did you do?"

She chuckled before answering. "Knowing you as I do now, I know you won't want to hear this. You asked, though, so I'm going to answer honestly. I did it all. There were horses that I was there when they were born, I helped feed and care for them, and when they were old enough to break, I did it all, from getting them used to a halter, and used to a blanket on them, then a saddle, to being the first one to sit on their back."

A quick intake of breath behind her let her know Wyatt wasn't real happy with hearing that, so she tried to reassure him. "Now, you have to be aware of a few things that go along with that. Every single time I did any of those things for the first time with a horse, Papa or Uncle Franklin or both were there with me. If I had a problem with the horse they were there to help, and if I did get thrown off a horse, which I did occasionally, they were there to protect me from the horse, and help me up."

"I'm glad to hear that."

"I thought you would be. It's also important that you know that we were a farm, not a ranch. The difference there is that we didn't have as many animals as you do here, and the animals we had were more used to us. It was often my job to feed the animals. Plus, I love being around animals. When I had extra time you could often find me out at the barn or the pasture, talking to or petting the animals, or sneaking them a carrot or corn from our garden."

"I have no trouble believing that," Wyatt said with a little chuckle. "It also explains why so many of the men have told me you have such a way with animals, and they take to you right off."

"They said that?" she asked, trying to turn around to see him.

"They have."

They continued talking, and he learned more about her growing up years as they continued their slow walk back to the barn.

DALLAS AND AUSTIN were the second set of men to get back to the barn after hearing the single shot. They were all relieved to know he was okay, and found themselves discussing what could have happened, who found them, and where. They watched the next pair of riders approach, also eager for answers. As they got close enough to see who it was, Dallas greeted them.

"Is he back yet?" Clay asked. "What happened?"

"Don't know yet," Dallas said. "The only ones not back yet are Cord and Garrett, so they must have been the ones to find them. I'm interested to know what happened, too, so I hope they get back soon."

"They must have found him at the far edge of the property," Austin said. "The rest of us are all back, and I don't know about you guys, but we were out quite a ways."

"That's true," Clay said. "We were way over at the west edge of the property, and here we are. I wonder where they are."

"Maybe he's hurt, but they didn't think they needed help to get him here," Dallas suggested. "They might be moving slowly so he doesn't get hurt worse."

They talked about different possibilities that thought conjured up, until one of them pointed. "Is that them now?"

They all turned to watch, holding their hands up to shield the sun from their eyes as they squinted to see better. "It looks like it might be, but I only see two horses," Clay said. "I wonder if something happened to Thunder and one of them is bringing Wyatt back."

"I hope not," Dallas said. "Wyatt's awfully fond of that horse, and he's only four or five years old. He'll be heartbroken if something happened to him."

Austin slipped around to the back of the barn and returned leading Thunder. "Guess who I found at the back door to the barn."

"That doesn't make me feel any better," Dallas said. "I hope they found Wyatt and have him on one of their horses."

"Me, too," Austin agreed, "because otherwise he's out there without a horse."

Austin took Thunder into the barn and put him in his stall so he could get some oats and water. He quickly removed his saddle and went back out to see if Wyatt was back yet.

As the two horses got closer, Dallas shook his head. "I see two men on two horses."

"That's all I see, as well," Clay agreed.

They watched and waited while the two men, Cord and Garrett, made it back to the barn. "Is Wyatt okay?" Garrett asked.

Dallas's mouth dropped open. "Are you saying you two aren't the ones that fired the shot?"

"No, we didn't," Cord answered. "We heard it and came in, glad he was found and is okay. What's going on?"

"I don't know," Dallas admitted. "You two were the last ones to return. If you didn't fire the shot and none of us did, who did?"

There was silence while the men all looked around, thinking. Cord looked to Dallas. "You don't suppose it could have been a drifter passing through, getting a rabbit or something for a meal, do you?"

"I was just wondering the same thing," Dallas admitted.

"In fact," Cord continued, "I thought I heard a shot fifteen, maybe twenty minutes earlier, but I wasn't sure. When I heard the last one, I thought maybe it was simply repeating that he was okay. Did anyone else hear a single shot earlier?"

A couple of the men nodded, while others shook their heads in denial. "I don't know what any of this means, but I have to wonder who did fire it off."

"If none of us did, that means Wyatt's still out there, and we need to go find him," Dallas said. "Everybody get your horses again, we need to keep looking. I guess we'll keep the same teams and go in the same directions. Again, fire one shot if you find him and he's okay, three shots if you need help, and repeat the three shots every five to ten minutes until someone gets there to help. Any questions?"

Everyone agreed and went to saddle their horses back up. Cord and Garrett rested their horses a few minutes while the rest were getting ready. They were all saddled and ready to go out when Garrett stopped them. "Wait a minute. What's that coming over the hill down there?"

All eyes turned in the direction he was pointing, and everyone was quiet, trying to make out what they were all watching. "It's a single horse," Garrett said. "Maybe Wyatt rescued himself, and fired a shot off in case we were all out looking for him."

"That's not Thunder," Cord said.

"No, it's not," Dallas agreed, "but it looks like two people. Who the heck is that?"

"It can't be a coincidence," Garrett said. "It's got to have something to do with Wyatt being missing and the single shot we all heard."

"Let's go meet them," Dallas suggested. "If it's not Wyatt or news about him, we'll spread out from there and keep looking." All agreed, the large group headed toward the single horse headed their way.

CHAPTER 15

"It looks like we're going to have company," Martha said.

"I think you're right," Wyatt agreed with a little laugh. "Think about this. They probably all heard the single shot and went back to the barn. They probably all beat us back since we're just walking, and now they're wondering who we are."

"And more importantly, where you are and who fired the shot." Martha giggled a little. "Think they'll be surprised?"

Wyatt laughed out loud at that. "I'd definitely say you're not the hero they'll be expecting."

"Maybe everyone needs to get to know me better."

"I think that would be a good idea," Wyatt said, after a good laugh. He surprised her when she felt him reach down and place a kiss in her hair. "I certainly know I hope to get to know you a lot better."

"That sounds like a good plan to me," she said rather quietly.

"I might have hit my head, Martha, but I didn't lose my mind or memory. I still love you, and hope you soon feel the same way about me. I'm still not going to rush you any, but I just wanted to let you know my fall didn't change my feelings for you one bit. I now owe my life to the little lady I've fallen in love with, and I'm glad to learn she's so good with a gun and tracking. I loved you before I learned that, and I still love you now. Maybe a little more. I have to admit I liked how it felt when you were worrying about me out there."

"Worrying about you is why I went out looking for you, Wyatt, even though I knew you said you didn't want me going far from the barn."

"We'll talk more about that when we have privacy."

She nodded as Wyatt's men approached, and they put their conversation on hold. All of the men, especially Dallas, were surprised to see Martha bringing Wyatt back. He eyed her, but didn't say anything to her, choosing instead to speak to Wyatt. "What happened? You okay?"

"I'm fine."

"No, he's not. He was knocked out and has been getting dizzy."

"That's true," Wyatt admitted, but I'm much better now, thanks to Martha. As it turns out, she saved my life."

Martha's face turned red and she shook her head. "I was just in the right place at the right time. We were both lucky."

"Lucky, yes, but your skills saved me. That reminds me, I need two of you men to go out and pick up a dead mountain lion. The smell of a dead animal will draw other animals to it looking for a meal, and it's too close to some of our pastures. I don't want predators that close to our cattle."

"We'll get that taken care of," Dallas assured him. "Did you shoot it out of safety for you or the stock?"

"I didn't shoot it. It killed one of our steers and I followed it with the intent to kill it. A rattlesnake spooked Thunder and threw me."

"That's how you hit your head?" Austin asked.

"It is. I was knocked out."

Austin shook his head. "So what happened with the mountain lion?"

"Martha tracked me, and the mountain lion. I was knocked out cold, but when I woke up Martha was there, along with a dead mountain lion that was literally a foot away from me."

The men all turned to look at Martha, who again felt her face warm. What bothered her the most was the look Dallas gave her. She couldn't decipher it exactly. It certainly wasn't one of surprise mixed with pride or relief, like she saw on the faces of the other men. He looked more upset, aggravated. She had to concentrate and turn her attention back to the men, who were asking her questions, asking what exactly happened while their boss was unconscious.

She quickly explained that when she came upon them the cat was ready to pounce, and she shot just as it pounced. "I was lucky that I got it. I hate to think what could have happened if I would have shot half a second later."

"Well, I for one am impressed," Garrett said. "Thank you, Miss Martha. I have a question, if I can ask?"

"Certainly," Wyatt assured him.

"Where did you find him, and how?" He turned then to his boss. "Wyatt, did you say she tracked you there?"

"She did," Wyatt answered. "She heard I was going to the small east pasture to check the young steers first, so she went there. She saw the same thing I saw there; a dead steer."

Austin tilted his head and looked at Wyatt. "In the east pasture with the small steers? We went there first, but we didn't see it. How could we have missed it?"

Wyatt looked at Martha, but when it was obvious she didn't want to answer, he did. "It was at the far end of the pasture, over the small rise. A mountain lion ran off from it as it saw me approach. Once they kill an animal in a fence, they know where to come back for another easy meal, so I set off after it. She saw the tracks and followed them."

Austin was shaking his head as he smiled at her. "So you're a tracker, huh? I wouldn't have guessed that, but I wouldn't have guessed you're a sharp shooter, either. I'm glad you are both, though," he added with a chuckle.

"I've got a question, too," Cord said with a grin. "I take it the rattler that spooked Thunder left, not causing any problems after you fell?"

"I'm lucky he didn't strike. I was knocked out so I can't say where it went, but it showed up again when we were ready to leave. Lilly was pawing the ground, so we went to see what was wrong. The snake was back and getting too close to the horse."

"So you shot it?" Dallas asked.

"Nope, but Martha did."

The men laughed, all except Dallas, who again was eying Martha in a way that made her uncomfortable. He looked right at her. "You were lucky, both of you."

"I was lucky," Wyatt said. "Martha was very impressive."

"Well, now I know why we heard two separate shots," Garrett said. "We heard one single shot, so we assumed someone found Wyatt. We both heaved a sigh of relief and headed back to the barn. A little while later we heard another single shot."

"We were the same way," Austin said. "They were both single shots, not too close together, so we assumed they were all telling us Wyatt's okay and coming back to the barn."

Martha's eyes were wide as she looked at the men. "I never even thought of that first shot. When I shot the mountain lion, that was actually the first shot." She turned to Wyatt, who was also thinking the situation through, she could tell.

"I never thought of it, either." He turned to Austin. "She going to fire a single shot before we left, but then she realized when she shot that rattlesnake, that in effect was a single shot." He laughed a little. "If she wouldn't have thought about that, you would have heard three single shots. That could have confused everyone." He chuckled, then turned back to Martha. "You wanted to fire off three shots to call for help, but thinking about it now, that would have confused everyone, too. A single shot, then three together not real long after that."

Cord looked from Wyatt to her. "Why did you want to call for help, Martha?"

"Because he was unconscious when I shot the cat. He came to shortly thereafter, maybe from the sound of the shot, but he was really dizzy. He tried to hide it, but I could tell. I was afraid he wouldn't be able to ride back, assuming we could even get him up onto Lilly."

"He told you not to call us, that he'd be fine?" Cord asked. "That sounds like our boss." Most of the men laughed as they agreed.

"Have your laughs, boys," Wyatt warned, "but I was okay. I just needed to sit up a few minutes, and the dizziness left."

"I'm just glad everything turned out okay," Austin said, then turned to Martha. "Can I ask, how did a little lady from New York learn to shoot like that?"

"I grew up on a farm in Missouri, and moved to New York to live with my uncle almost three years ago when my father died."

"Ah, that makes sense seeing how good you are with animals," Austin said.

The men talked a few minutes about her way with animals, and their shock that she can shoot and even track. Martha didn't like the attention, but she especially didn't like the looks she'd been catching from Dallas. He wasn't saying much, and several times she'd caught him looking at her with an unreadable expression, but he hadn't looked happy. She knew it had something to do with the fact that he told her she couldn't go with them, but she would have thought he would have been okay with it once he saw she's the one that found Wyatt.

She needed to get the attention off of her, and she was also concerned about the man she'd fallen in love with. Seeing him laying there unconscious, then extremely dizzy was still weighing on her mind. "Wyatt, I'm glad you're feeling better and were able to get back here, but I can tell you're exhausted. I can see it in your eyes. After what you've been through, I think we should have the doctor check you out."

"Don't worry so much about me, Martha. I'm fine, thanks to you."

"No, you're not fine," she insisted. "You're exhausted, and rightfully so. But I still think we should have the doctor look at you. If he says you're fine, then I'll believe you, and I'll feel a lot better."

Austin agreed right away. "I think she's right, Wyatt. My brother got thrown from a horse and hit his head when he fell. The doctor told him he had to take it easy for a couple of weeks. The stubborn guy insisted he was fine, and went back to doing his normal work the next day. Two days later he went to fix a fence, and didn't come back for supper. We went in search and found him laying in the pasture, out cold. This time the doc told him if he didn't give his head time to recover, he was likely to pass out again, but he could lose his sight. I agree with Martha. I think we need to get Doc Campbell out here to check you over. We'd all feel better if we heard him say you're okay."

The men all nodded in agreement. "She's right, Wyatt, you do look exhausted," Garrett said. "At least go in the house and rest a little. I'll run in and see if the doc's free to come look at you."

"If I need to see a doctor I can go in to him. There's no need to drag him out here."

"No, Wyatt, I have to agree with Garrett," Dallas said, finally speaking up. "You look so tired right now I'm not sure you have it in you to get in there and back. And what happens if you get dizzy while you're riding? No, you go in and rest and let Garrett go fetch the doctor. If he can't come out, a couple of us will go with you after you have a chance to rest. That way if you get dizzy, we'll be there to help."

Wyatt was about to argue, but Martha stopped him. "I like

that idea, Wyatt. I really would feel better. Since I'm the one that found you and was scared half out of my mind, I feel like I have a little bit of a stake in this, too. Please do as Dallas suggested."

He studied her eyes a couple of moments, and nodded. "Okay. I guess if it was the other way around and I was the one who found someone knocked out I'd feel better hearing a clean bill of health from the doctor. And you guys have all told me I'm tired so much that you have me convinced of it now, too. I'll go in and rest a spell, and by the time Doc gets here I'll be fine."

"Good. I hope he agrees," Martha said with a big smile.

"Wyatt, we found Thunder at the door to the barn, so we put him in his stall," Cord said. "I'll brush him out good, and I'll take care of Lilly, Miss Martha. You take this stubborn man inside and make sure he lays down to rest."

"Thank you, Cord," Martha said. "Thank you, all of you, for going out looking for him. It's nice to see how this ranch looks out for everyone."

They all nodded and gave her a friendly look, except for Dallas. He looked at her, but it wasn't the friendly expression the rest had. She turned and walked in the house with Wyatt, more concerned about him right at the moment. She'd worry about Dallas and his change in attitude later.

Not too surprisingly, although Rosy had dinner ready for them, which she'd held for almost three hours, Wyatt thanked her, but said he would rather lie down and rest. When he saw the look of concern in Martha's eyes, he pulled her to him outside his door. "Martha, please don't worry. Thanks to you, I'll be fine. You were right when you said I look tired, and I will admit that, but I really think I just need to rest a little while. If Cord gets back with Dr. Campbell, send him in and wake me up. You go eat some dinner with Rosy, and don't worry. After I get the all clear from the doctor we're going to have a talk."

"I thought you learned everything you wanted to talk about on our trip back. Since we went slow we had lots of time, and I thought we talked out everything you wanted to talk about."

"Most things, but not all. We still need to deal with the fact that you ignored what I told you about staying close to the house. That was meant to keep you safe, and you flat out ignored it."

Her eyes shot wide open. "Wyatt, we did talk about that. I told you I understood why you said that when you didn't know I could shoot a rifle, but I knew I could protect myself. I wouldn't have gone out alone until I could prove that to you, but you were missing. I was more worried about you than making sure you knew I could shoot well before going out. As it turns out, it's a good thing I did go."

"Honey, we'll talk when I wake up. I understand all that, but you have to see it from my perspective. I have to know I can count on you to listen to what I tell you to keep you safe. But right now, I really am tired. Can we talk about this after I wake up?"

"Yes, of course. You sleep well, Wyatt." She turned to leave, but stopped and turned back around. "I'm really glad you're okay."

He reached out and pulled her back to him and kissed her. This wasn't a quick kiss on her cheek, or even in her hair, as he'd done during their trip back to the barn. He kissed her on the lips, with a kiss full of meaning. There was nothing accidental or flippant about it. That kiss meant something. She knew it, and returned his kiss with the concern and emotion she'd been holding inside her all afternoon, from the moment she saw him lying motionless, with a mountain lion ready to pounce. He pulled her in closer to him, gently cupping the back of her head with one hand.

Against his own wishes, but knowing he had to, he pulled apart, and their eyes met. It was as if the kiss was continuing, they were each saying so much to each other with their eyes. Rosy came around the corner, giving them warning ahead of time by coughing. "There you are, Martha. I asked if you wanted some dinner, and you'd disappeared."

"She'll be down in a second, Rosy," Wyatt said, which had Rosy, who was way more to him than his cook and housekeeper, nodding as she went back down the steps.

"Again, thank you for what you did out there for me. We'll talk later, but remember, I love you." He gave her one more quick kiss, and opened the door to his room.

"Okay. Sleep well." She hurried down the steps, catching up with Rosy as she was going into the kitchen.

"Sit down and eat something," Rosy said. "I want to know what happened out there. Wyatt said you found him just in the knick of time. I need more details than that."

Martha chuckled and sat down, suddenly realizing she was famished. While the two ladies ate their meal Martha explained their adventures. Martha was totally honest, confessing she'd talked to Dallas, who had told her to stay home. She told Rosy about the looks he'd been giving her after they returned. "What should I do, Rosy? I know he's upset that I went to look for Wyatt after he told me not to, but shouldn't he be happy that I found him?"

Rosy nodded her head a bit as she considered the situation. "Dallas is a good man, but he wants – no, he expects people to listen to him. He sees it as being respectful. If someone doesn't listen to him, to him they're being disrespectful. This might just take time; time for him to see you still respect him. I think once he sees that, he'll be okay again."

"You don't think there's anything I can do in the meantime? Could I talk to him?"

She shook her head. "I don't think so. I think it's just going to take time." She grinned a bit before adding, "I think once he sees how much you care about Wyatt he'll understand that played a big part in your going against his command." She winked at her and patted her hand. "He'll see that soon enough and put the pieces together. Once he works it out in his mind he'll be okay again."

"I hope it's soon. I don't like the looks he's been giving me. They make me feel uneasy."

"My guess is that's intentional on his part. But I wouldn't worry too much. As far as I've been able to tell, his bark is worse than his bite. Though I wouldn't want to be married to him. He has definite opinions as to what's right and what's wrong, and I have a feeling his wife would have to toe the line."

"Then I wouldn't want to be married to him, either. I always thought he seemed like a nice man, but I'm seeing a totally different side of him today, after we got back."

"Don't get me wrong, Dallas is a good man. He's a very nice man and I'm sure he would treat his wife well. In fact, I can see him treating her like she is very special, even fawning over her – as long as she listened to everything he told her about her safety and his sense of right and wrong, without questioning him. And when I say everything he told her, I mean every single word."

"Without questioning him? I'd love to have a man treat me like something special, but I'm not sure I could give in to everything he might expect without questioning some of it. I mean, if I agree with it, that's fine. But if I don't agree with something he says, I'm not sure I could accept it without at least telling him what I think and why. I mean, we'd have to discuss it and come to an agreement."

Rosy laughed. "I'm not sure you and Dallas would ever make it as a pair. Now, you and Wyatt on the other hand, I could see that. He is a lot like his father, and a little like Dallas. They want people to listen to them if they tell them something for their own good or to keep them safe. He's more willing to listen if they have differing views, though. I'm not sure he'd change his mind, but he would listen and see it from the other person's perspective."

Martha had realized that Rosy was a very attentive and very smart lady, and she knew she was trying to tell her something. She appreciated it and was eager to hear any advice the lady who had known Wyatt way longer than she had was willing to offer. She met Rosy's eyes and smiled. "So you think Wyatt will be willing to listen to why I took Lilly and rode further than he'd told me to. He might see it through my eyes and understand, but it might not change his mind any?"

Rosy laughed out loud. "I knew there was a reason I liked you from the moment I met you. You and Wyatt would be good for each other. To answer your question, yes, that's exactly what I'm saying. I think he will see it from your point of view and understand. In fact, I think he might even appreciate it. But I'm not sure it will change his mind any on the fact that you didn't heed his words. If I were you, I would be ready for a good scolding from him."

"Even if my skirting his wishes a bit ended up saving his life?"

"Even if," she said with no hesitation. "He has never had a lady he cared about as much as he cares for you, so I can't say for certain or from past experiences. However, he's cut from the same cloth as his father, and I've seen similar situations with him, and he never once wavered. He saw himself as the head of his household and responsible for everyone's safety. As such, he set down rules that everyone was to follow. Those rules were meant to keep everyone safe and were well thought through. They were also very fair. Now, if something happened to prove one of his rules was too stringent, he would admit that and take responsibility for it. That rule would be altered. But that didn't mean it was okay for someone to ignore the rule. If someone 'skirted his wishes' they would be held accountable. In his mind, if they ignored one rule, what was to say they would follow the rest?"

Martha grinned as Rosy threw her words back at her. "Hearing it that way, I have to admit it makes sense, even if I would rather it didn't."

Now it was Rosy's turn to grin. "As one woman to another, I understand." She got serious again before adding, "But I would still prepare for a scolding. The one good thing I will tell you about that, though, is –"

She paused, and Martha couldn't help stepping in. "He wouldn't do it if he didn't care about me?"

Rosy's smile was full of understanding. "I'm guessing you might have already received a scolding from Wyatt. I'm not sure if it's something you're used to or not, or how you feel about it, and that's not really any of my business, unless you want to share it. Let me assure you, though, he is sincere when he told you that. He would never scold a lady if he didn't care a great deal for her."

"Unless I want to share it," Martha mumbled, more to herself.

"Martha, I like you. I think we're more alike in some ways than you would think. I also know what it's like out here, and that it's different than it is in New York. It's more dangerous here, and men take responsibility for keeping their wives safe. I haven't been to New York, but I was born and raised in Boston, and that doesn't happen there. I doubt it's much different than New York in that sense. You also said your mother died at a young age, so you didn't have a mother to talk to growing up. If you ever want to talk about this subject, or anything else that's on your mind, I want you to know you can come to me. We can talk openly and I will be honest with you."

"Thank you, Rosy. That means more to me than you know."

"This might sound silly, but you've meant a lot to me, as well. My husband and I never were able to have children, and you've been like the daughter I never had. I hope you decide to stay here. I hope you and Wyatt see how good you would be for each other and find your way to marriage some day, but if that happens or not, I would like to see you stay here. I know that's selfish of me to feel that way, and if you ever leave, I'll give you my blessings. I'll miss you terribly, but I'll not hold you back."

"Oh, Rosy," Martha said as she got up and went to the other side of the table with her arms open. Rosy stood and the two embraced in a hug they'd both needed.

CHAPTER 16

*D*r. Campbell arrived at the ranch almost three hours later. He apologized for not getting there sooner, but explained he was delivering a baby outside of town when Cole got to the office. His wife gave him the message as soon as he got back, and he headed straight to check on Wyatt. Martha led him to Wyatt's room, and Dr. Campbell woke him up.

When he emerged later, Martha and Rosy had some food warmed up for him, as they guessed he'd missed his dinner. They set the food out for him as he explained his findings. "Miss Welch, it sounds as though you found Wyatt just in time. He's certainly singing your praises."

"I'm glad I got there when I did," she said, "but how is he? He was awfully dizzy when he first came to. Is he going to be okay?"

"Yes, I think he will be. He needs to rest first, though. He hit his head when he fell, which means he has a head injury. They need rest in order to heal, just like any other injury."

"How long should we try to keep him down before he goes back to work?" Martha asked, leery that he would listen, but determined to try.

"I'd like to see him stay down and rest for a couple of weeks.

I've known Wyatt since he was little, so I'm doubting you'll be able to talk him into staying inside that long. If you can keep him in for a week, and then slowly go back to his work, I would be okay with that. I'll wish you luck now, and ask you do your best." He had a smile on his face, which told Martha he knew she had her work cut out for her.

"Is he sleeping again now?" Rosy asked.

"He's resting. He might well go to sleep again, but I won't guarantee it. He was sleeping pretty sound when I got here, which tells me he was pretty worn out. The first few days he'll more than likely want to sleep more, which is good. After that is when you'll have more trouble keeping him down."

"I understand, Doctor, and thank you for coming," Rosy said. "How much do we owe you?"

"Wyatt already took care of it. I'll stop by and check on him in a few days. If you need me before that, send someone in for me."

ROSY AND MARTHA checked on him occasionally during the afternoon, while he slept. They fixed supper, assuming he would be hungry when he woke up. As expected, he walked into the kitchen as they were finishing the meal. "Something certainly smells good," he said.

"You sit down at the table and we'll have this out in no time," Rosy instructed.

"How are you feeling?" Martha asked.

"I'm feeling good, but a bit foolish. I can't remember the last time I slept during the day, but I slept the whole afternoon away. I probably won't be able to sleep tonight now."

"You might be surprised," Rosy said. "Your body knows when you need rest. According to the doctor, that's exactly what you need right now."

"We'll see," he said, as he sat down. "I know for sure my body's telling me it needs food, and this looks and smells delicious. Thank you, ladies."

As they ate their supper, Wyatt insisted he felt good, but admitted he had been awfully sleepy. He also told them he understood Dr. Campbell wanted him to rest. "I'll try, but as my strength and stamina return I know it's going to be hard to stay here and watch my men do work I should be helping with."

"That's not quite true, Wyatt," Martha admonished. "You shouldn't be helping them until the doctor says it's okay for you to."

"Like I said, I will try." Rosy and Martha looked at each other, knowing this was going to be difficult.

As they finished the pie Martha had made so she could stay busy, Wyatt took her hand in his, but turned to face the lady who had been like a second mother to him. "Rosy, I know this is asking a lot, but Martha and I need to have a talk about what happened today. I'm asking not only if I can steal her away when I know she would normally help you clean up the kitchen, but for you to allow us some privacy, as well. I give you my word her virtue and reputation are not in jeopardy."

"I believe you, Wyatt, and I trust both of you. Martha is our guest here and while I appreciate her help, I don't expect it. Of course she can go with you now, but let me just remind you, like I said, she is our guest, and an out-of-state guest, not familiar with the way things are done around here."

"I hear and understand what you're saying, and I'll keep it in mind. Thank you. We're going to be in my office." Rosy nodded and took some dishes to the kitchen. His office was on the other side of the house, which would ensure their privacy. She hoped things went well for both of them and they would be able to talk through this.

Wyatt stood and led Martha to his office. He motioned for her to have a seat on the sofa, and sat down next to her. He took her hand in his and rubbed the back of it with his thumb, taking a few moments to pull his thoughts together. After he'd slept earlier he'd spent a lot of time thinking about this moment. He knew they had to have a talk, but after the first time he'd had this kind of talk with her, he wanted to be sure he handled this one correctly. He'd gone over it in his mind several times to be sure he hadn't missed something, from either her perspective or his.

She had gone against his instructions and had done what he'd told her not to do, and he couldn't simply let it go. Granted, he was extremely glad in this case she had. She had saved his life, and there was no doubt about that. But he didn't feel it was okay to ignore a wrong simply because it turned out fine this time. What about the next time? And what would that say to her going forward? As long as nothing bad happens, it's okay for you to ignore my rules?

But when he looked at the situation through her eyes, he had to admit it looked differently. She was obviously very capable of not only riding a horse, but also handling a gun, which he would admit was the main reason he didn't want her riding far from the barn. The fact that she saw the lion tracks and hoof tracks and assumed he was after the mountain lion told him she knew her way around this kind of country. Taking all those things into account, he could easily understand why she went out looking for him. If things were reversed and she was missing he certainly wouldn't have thought twice before going. He didn't like the idea of her going alone, but to her credit, she'd asked Dallas to go with the men and had been turned down. The fact she went on her own was actually rather heart warming, that she cared enough about him to do that.

So, after considering all those things, he'd decided they would talk about what happened. He had to let her know he understood why she did it this time, since she was indeed capable. However, in the future she had to listen to his rules in order for him to keep her safe. He would give her a few examples of things that could get her hurt, and as long as she understood his rules had to be followed, he would tell her in this case he would let her go with a warning, since he'd given her that rule not knowing her abilities with a gun. He would also point out that this is why they need to talk, and why he now saw how important it was for him to hear her side of things before he took her over his knee. Hopefully this talk would get them on more stable ground in that regard. Now he just had to be sure he said what he meant and didn't mess up again.

MARTHA HAD GIVEN Rosy's words a lot of thought. In fact, that's about all she thought about all afternoon. She tried to do as Rosy suggested and get herself prepared for a good scolding. She could tell by Rosy's words that a good scolding more than likely meant a spanking to go along with that scolding. Wyatt's words from her first spanking came back to her, and she kept reminding herself of them. As much as she'd hated that spanking, his explanation, once she got past his awkward way of blurting the words out initially, had melted her heart. He did it because he loved her and felt a need to protect her.

Even now she couldn't say that didn't make her feel good. Just thinking about them made her feel like she was wrapped in a safety net of some kind. She also remembered with some detail how good it felt afterwards when he held her in his arms. If there had been any doubt as to the truth in his words when he declared his love for her, that time when he held her in his arms would have dispelled that doubt. She felt his love then, and it felt wonderful.

As much as she tried to convince herself another spanking would be worth it to feel that again, there was one thing she couldn't seem to get over. She didn't deserve one, not this time. She could admit she had indeed gone against his wishes in going after him, but this was a special circumstance. He was in danger. She knew he wanted her to stay close to the barn until he had a chance to see for himself that she could handle a gun. She understood that, as well. It was his way of keeping her safe, and she could not only accept it, but it made her feel cherished.

But even though he might not know yet that she was quite capable, she did. She and her father went out hunting regularly. Her father had allowed her to go out alone as long as she had her rifle with her. Often during these times when she was out alone she would bring back a rabbit for supper, or occasionally something larger like a deer. If they were getting low on meat she would watch for something like that while she was riding. They both did, to make sure they always had meat for their table.

So in this case, knowing she could handle a gun to protect herself, and knowing the man she'd fallen in love with was in danger, in her mind there was nothing wrong with her going after him. She tried to go with the men, but when Dallas refused, she had no other choice. She paused at that thought. She could admit that the fact that Dallas had dismissed her, wouldn't allow her to go out, and was now acting less than friendly toward her upset her. Again, in her mind she'd done nothing wrong. She was safe, and going to look for the man she loved. To be treated like she was being treated by Dallas was upsetting, and it was wrong in her mind. Now she was facing a possible spanking by Wyatt. That would be two things, both of them wrong, when she had in fact done nothing wrong herself.

She now realized that that was the reason she couldn't get it through her head to simply accept a spanking from Wyatt. She understood his reasons for it, but this would be the second thing she would have to endure for doing something she not only didn't see as being wrong, but given the same circumstances, she would do again.

Still, she knew that in his mind he was trying to look out for her, which was endearing. What a dilemma.

Now here she was, being led into his office, a room she hadn't been in before. It was a large room with definitely a masculine feel, yet very comfortable looking. It had a large wooden desk with a chair, and shelves full of books behind it, with a few tasteful knickknacks placed here and there. There were two nice leather chairs facing the desk, and a leather couch along one wall. That was where he led her. When he motioned for her to sit down, she did, nervous about what was about to happen. Luckily, he was quiet for several moments, which gave her some time to try to collect herself.

Finally, he cleared his throat and began. "Martha, we need to talk about what happened today. As thankful as I am that you were there, and in fact you saved my life, you ignored my rule about not going far from the barn until I could see for myself that you could use a gun to protect yourself."

"But I could."

"I realize that now, but I didn't know it then. Martha, I will do what I feel I need to do to protect you. That's why I make rules. In order for those rules to protect you they have to be followed."

"I understand that, but you don't understand –"

"Martha, I made the rules according to what I knew at that time, and I expected them to be followed."

"And I expected a little respect from you, but apparently I'm not going to get it." His face went pale, which bothered her, but if he thought he was going to explain why she deserved this and expected her to sit idly by and accept it all, he needed to think again. She was upset now and couldn't always control herself when that happened. Especially once she'd worked herself into a tizzy, like now. "Look, I admit I did go further than you wanted me to, and under normal circumstances I would have waited until I could show you I can handle a gun. But damn it, this was not normal."

He reached out for her, but she stood and turned from him.

"The man I've come to care a great deal about was missing. Knowing I could keep myself as safe out there as any man, safer than many men, if you expected me to sit back like a ninny and do nothing, you're an idiot or you don't know me very well. You're not the only one that has opinions. Just because I'm a woman, that doesn't mean I can't take care of myself and I don't have an opinion about things, and if you don't have enough respect for me to even listen to what I have to say – "

"Martha, please let me finish. I expected those rules to be followed. But in this case, it seems I didn't have all the information I needed to set sufficient but fair rules to be followed. If I had known how good you are with a rifle I wouldn't have made that rule. Therefore, in this case, which I agree was a special situation, I understand why you didn't follow it."

She turned back around and looked at him. "You do?"

"Yes, I do. In fact, it warms my heart to know you cared enough about me to go out looking for me."

She sat back down next to him again. "Of course I do."

He sighed and studied her for several moments before going on. "My dear Martha, you've made this very difficult for me. What I had planned on saying next was to tell you that as long as you understand why I make rules and how important it is for me to know you'll follow them, I'm willing to say this was a very unusual incident and therefore, I'm willing to treat it differently."

"I do understand, and Wyatt, I assure you that if I hadn't been so worried about you I wouldn't have gone out alone."

"I believe you."

"Good," she said, leaning against his chest and wrapping her arms around him.

"But Martha, you've made this difficult for me because now I feel we've settled that, but we have something else we need to discuss."

"We do?"

"Yes. While I was trying to explain my feelings to you just now, you were very rude and disrespectful to me, and I can't allow that."

She pulled back, her eyes wide as she looked up at him. "But that was when I thought you were going to spank me for something I didn't feel I deserved to be spanked for."

"But you didn't respect me enough to hear me out and give me a chance to tell you how I actually was feeling."

Her shoulders slumped and she looked down at her lap. He gave her some time, wanting to see what her response would be. Just as he was about to assume she wasn't going to say anything further, she looked back up. "You're right, and I'm sorry. I couldn't bear the thought of paying twice for doing something I didn't feel was wrong."

He took her by her shoulders so she was looking at him. "What do you mean paying twice?"

"If you would have spanked me for it, that would have been the second punishment. Dallas is already upset with me, so much that he's giving me looks I'm very uncomfortable with."

"Dallas is?"

"Yes. I know he's upset that he told me I couldn't go with them, then went out on my own. But I had to. He's giving me these looks of pure evil, and I don't feel I deserve that."

"Wait a minute. Has he said anything to you?"

"No, and that's part of the problem. He was always friendly with me before, but since we got back, the only thing he's said is when Austin said the two of them missed the dead steer, and he was glad I saw it and followed the tracks, Dallas said I was lucky. Lucky! Austin appreciated what I'd done, and that I found you in time to keep that mountain lion from attacking, but all Dallas said was that I was lucky. Not only that, but he had a hateful expression on his face when he said it."

"Martha, are you sure you aren't imagining some of this?"

"No! Wyatt, are you saying you don't believe me?"

"Calm down, honey. No, I'm not saying that at all. That doesn't sound like Dallas, but I believe you. I'll talk to him about it."

"Rosy said he expects everyone to listen to him, and that's probably why he's upset."

"You talked to Rosy about this?"

"Yes, I did, because it hurts. I planned on apologizing to him for going out on my own after he wouldn't allow me to go with the men, but after the looks he's given me, I'm afraid of what he'll say or do. I don't think I deserve that."

"No, I don't, either, and I will talk to him. But I don't think I deserved the disrespect you showed me a few minutes ago, either. If you would have given me the benefit of hearing me out you would have learned that I did think about it from your point of view this time, and I agree with you." He picked her hands up and held them in his. After the mistake I made the last time when I spanked you, I wasn't about to do the same thing again, so I took quite a bit of time this afternoon while I was laying in bed to look at this through your eyes, as well."

"Thank you for that," she said sincerely. "And I do apologize for the way I acted. Like I said, I thought you were going to spank me, and I couldn't stand the thought of paying twice for something I did that I didn't then, and still don't think was wrong."

He took a deep breath and exhaled slowly, while squaring his shoulders. Still holding her hands, he looked into her eyes. "Unfortunately, Martha, I am going to spank you, but not for going out looking for me."

Her eyes filled with moisture as she listened to him continue. "We've covered that and I don't feel you deserve to be spanked for that. I can't ignore the disrespect you showed me when I was trying to talk to you about it, however."

A few tears slipped from her eyes as she continued to look at him, but she never turned away. "This is very difficult for me," he continued, "because in a way this is exactly what I did with you the first time I spanked you, and it was wrong. You pointed out to me that you deserved to be heard before I spanked you, and I hadn't allowed that. I agreed, it was wrong of me to do that, and I apologized for it. But now you went beyond that and spoke to me very disrespectfully, after you were the one pointing out to me the importance of listening to each other."

She was quiet for several moments, with tears continuing to slide down her face. Finally, she nodded. "I understand, and you're right. I don't like it, but I can't say I don't deserve it. I let my temper get away from me, and by doing that I did the exact thing I complained about you doing. I can't have it both ways. I truly am sorry."

"I know you are, Martha, and that's what makes this hard for me. It's not like you to be disrespectful, or to use that kind of language or raise your voice, and I'm glad. But you did this time. Now that I've heard why, what upset you so much, I understand that, as well. It doesn't give you the right to speak like you did, though."

"I know."

With no further words, he pulled her over his lap. It was hard enough for both of them, so he saw no reason to extend it. He was happy that she'd changed out of her riding skirt while he was sleeping and back into a dress. He laid the skirt up over her back, along with her petticoats or whatever ladies called all those other layers of material beneath their skirt. He laid his hand on her pretty little drawers with the little lace around the edging. "I don't think we need to talk any more about why you're here, unless you have any questions."

"No, I understand, and I'm sorry."

"I know," he assured her as he lifted his hand. He started the spanking, and was both a little surprised and impressed that she didn't fight it. She let him know it hurt, but she never tried to wriggle away or tell him to stop. He continued until he felt sure she would remember it and think twice before speaking to him that way again, which wasn't as long as it would normally have been since she had already admitted she deserved it and apologized. He wanted to be sure she knew from the start that he wouldn't allow her to speak to him that way, nor would he speak that way to her. If they were to be man and wife, honesty and respect were both very, very important in his mind.

That thought, of them as man and wife, brought a smile to his face and he stopped the spanking. He immediately helped her up and onto his lap, where he wrapped her in his arms. He needed to feel her close to him, but he also needed to know she knew he loved her. He kept his arms tight around her, but rocked her back and forth slowly, giving her time to catch her breath. He leaned down and kissed her temple. "Are you okay, my sweet lady?"

"That really hurt," she said between hiccups. "I'm sore, but okay."

"Good," he said, giving her a little squeeze. "If I loosen my hold on you are you going to try to run from me?"

"No," she said, "but do you have to loosen it?"

"I certainly don't. I prefer not to, but I didn't want to hurt you."

"You're not hurting me. It makes me feel safe, like you're here for me."

"I am here for you, sweetheart. I'm here for whatever you need." He held her, thinking back over what all they'd said to each other. "The last time we did this you wanted to run away from me. You aren't going to this time?"

"No."

"Why not?"

"Because, well, you see – I guess I love you."

He paused from rocking her back and forth, and stayed still for a few moments, until he heard a little giggle. "You what?"

"I guess I love you, too."

He moved his hands to her shoulders so he could move her back far enough to look into her eyes. "You guess?"

"Yes," she said with a mischievous grin. "I love you and I guess that's why I'm willing to accept it, since I understand now why you did it." She let a small giggle escape before adding, "Oh, that might not have come out quite the way I meant it."

He laughed out loud, knowing now that she was throwing his own words back at him when he'd bungled so badly the first time he told her he loved her. "Or it might have come out exactly the way my feisty little lady meant it. I love you, Martha, and there's no guessing about it."

He leaned down to kiss her, but she stopped him. "I love you, too, Wyatt, and there's no guessing about that, either. I was so worried when you were missing."

He leaned down to kiss her again, but instead of stopping him, she welcomed him, leaning up toward him. This kiss was full of passion, and full of love. He forced himself to pull back, while he still could. "Martha, it seems we have one more thing we need to talk about."

"We do?" she asked with wide open eyes.

"Yes. If you return the love I have for you, I think it's going to be difficult knowing that and living in the same house without getting married."

She looked up at him with a little grin. "Wyatt, in your awkward way of being about as unromantic as possible, are you asking me to marry you?"

His face turned red and he shook his head. "I just did it again, didn't I? I don't think that quite came out the way I meant it."

She giggled, and had a mischievous look on her face. "Or maybe it came out just the way you meant it."

He laughed, but nodded. "I certainly meant what I said, but let me try to explain it a little better. When we were taking about the decision you had to make as to what you want to do with your life, you said something that made a big impact on me."

"I did?"

"Yes. You said you thought once you had a purpose for your life you would be happier. I thought about that. The last two years my purpose in life has been the ranch."

"That's not a bad purpose, and it gives you something to feel proud of."

"You're right. I knew all the men were counting on me for their living, so that made it a good purpose. But I also wanted to prove to my father I could do this. Again, that made me proud to be able to do that."

"You should be proud because you have done that."

"Thank you. But Rosy told me several times there's more to life than the ranch. I knew she wanted me to find a lady to share my life with. I wasn't opposed to that, but never found anyone that felt right to me. Until now. You've managed to steal my heart, but I see now that it's more than that. We have the same thoughts and feelings about many things, including this ranch. You care about the hands, but you also care about the animals. I realized that with you by my side, we will share a purpose in life, to make the ranch the best it can be. We will also be living our lives, not just floating through, and hopefully we'll raise a wonderful family. Another wonderful purpose in life. Realizing that has made me that much more eager for you to agree to become my wife and make that happen."

He sat her down on the couch beside him and got down on one knee in front of her. He took one of her hands and held it in his. "Martha Welch, I love you with all my heart. Would you please do me the honor of becoming my wife and sharing my purpose in life?" To her complete surprise, he reached into his shirt pocket and pulled out a ring.

Her eyes went from his to the ring and back again. "Wyatt, I love you with all my heart, as well, and yes, I will marry you. I love having a purpose in life again, and especially being able to share it with you. That was the most romantic thing I've ever heard."

He was smiling ear to ear as he slipped the ring on her finger, then pulled her in tight against him again. This time when he kissed her he didn't feel the need to hold back. It was again filled with passion and love, but when he finished, he simply leaned his forehead against hers a few moments, seeing the love in her eyes, and kissed her again.

CHAPTER 17

*W*hen Wyatt finally managed to pull back from their kiss this time, he looked at Martha's finger. "If we need to get that ring made smaller or larger, I'm sure we can do that."

"No, it fits fine, and it's beautiful. But where did you get it and when? You had it in your pocket," she said as a few tears ran down her face yet again.

He used his thumb to dry the tears, then picked her up, sat down and settled her on his lap once again. "I'm glad you like the ring. It was my mother's, and had been my father's mother's before that. You'll be the third generation Mrs. Peterson to wear it."

"Mrs. Peterson. I like the sound of that," she said, "and I'll wear it with pride. It's beautiful, but now it has a special meaning, knowing it's been handed down."

"I wish my parents could have met you. I'm sure they would have loved you."

"I was having similar thoughts," she admitted. "I never knew my mother, but I'm sure Papa and Uncle Franklin and Aunt Helen would have loved you."

"Now we'll be our own family, and hopefully start a bigger family soon." He held her against his chest, and they clung to each other. A few minutes later they heard a noise out in the hall.

"What was that?" Martha asked, looking toward the door. "It sounded like something fell."

Wyatt grinned. "It was probably a book or something. I'd say it was Rosy letting us know she's still keeping an eye on us and the clock."

Martha looked at him, confused, but then smiled. "Her way of saying we shouldn't be in here too long without a chaperon?"

"Yep."

Martha giggled. "I've heard she is rather particular about that."

"Oh, that she is. She certainly is. Are you ready to go tell her our good news?"

"Absolutely."

"Okay." He helped her stand, but turned her toward him. "Martha, I'm going to talk to Dallas, but I don't want you worrying about him. I'd say he's just a little upset that he told you no, but you went anyway. I'll explain that the only reason I told you not to go far on your own is because I didn't know you could shoot. That obviously is no longer a concern, so he should be okay with it, especially once I tell him we've worked it out and I'm fine with it."

"Thank you. I don't want him upset with me."

"I don't want to see you two having any trouble, either. You're both very important to me. Now, let's go tell the world you've agreed to become my wife." He gave her one more kiss, and turned her toward the door.

When they emerged a minute or two later, they startled Rosy, who had just dropped another book. Wyatt was laughing as it clattered to the ground. "We got the hint when you dropped the first book, Rosy."

She turned to look at them, startled, and turned around quickly. "I'm not sure what you're talking about. I was doing a little dusting, and I accidentally dropped my book."

"It's okay, Rosy," Martha said, coming over to hug the older lady. "I'm glad you're here because we have something to tell you."

She turned, looking at both of them. "You do?"

"Yes, we do," Wyatt said, "and I think you'll like it."

Before he could say anything else, Martha held up her hand. "We're getting married!"

Rosy's eyes grew exponentially as she looked from Martha to the ring, to Wyatt, and back to Martha. "Oh, I'm so happy for both of you. I've been praying that you two would soon see how much you love each other and how good you'll be together. I swear God made you two for each other, to be together forever. I don't know any two young people more suited for each other." She pulled both of them in for a big hug. "Wyatt, your mama and papa would be so happy right now. They would absolutely love this little lady you've found for yourself."

"That's what I told her," Wyatt said as he laughed.

"So how soon is this going to happen? Martha, we have a lot of planning and a lot of work to do. We'll have to get some fabric and make you a dress, and plan a nice meal. And oh, my, how shall we decorate? And I assume you want to have it here, at the ranch, but where? Do you have a spot picked out yet, or should we be looking for one?"

"Whoa, slow down," Wyatt said. "We haven't talked about a date yet." He pulled Martha in next to him and said, "I'm hoping she's willing to have it soon, though, because I'm sure we'll drive you crazy living in the same house until it happens."

"Oh, I hadn't even thought of that, but you're right. I'll have to keep a close eye on you two until then, so I hope you decide on a date soon."

"I don't know about you," Martha said, looking at her husband-to-be, "but I'm ready anytime."

"Well, you'll need time to make a dress and –"

"I don't need anything fancy like that, Wyatt. You and Rosy are the closest thing I have to family now, so as long as you're both there, I don't care about a new dress or any other fancy things."

"Every bride should have a new dress to wear," Rosy said, putting her arm around Martha's shoulders. "I can help you make one and it won't take long. You two talk it over, but you at least need a new dress. Wyatt, you might not have any family left, either, but there are several people in town that would probably like to be invited to your wedding. You've grown up in this area and some might be hurt if you got married without inviting anyone."

"That's probably true," Wyatt agreed. "Weddings are something special out here, and people tend to gather together and celebrate them."

"I'm fine with that," Martha assured him. "I certainly don't want to hurt anyone's feelings before I even have a chance to get to know them. The only people around here I've actually had a chance to meet are the few you introduced me to the day my uncle died, and Mr. Hawkins, the lawyer, and the ones from church, and I've just met them. How long do you think we should wait?"

Wyatt turned to Rosy for advice. "Maybe a couple of weeks or so? Would that be sufficient time for word to get around, and for you two to be ready for a wedding?"

"It won't take long for word to get around," Rosy said, "but I'm thinking it might be a good idea to take Martha into town a few more times so people can get to know her before the wedding. The only thing most of them know about her now is that she and her uncle were on the wagon train, and because of the people hurt when the building collapsed, she came here to the ranch because the hotel was full. I know once they get to know her they'll like her and know exactly how you fell in love with her so quickly."

Martha thought about Rosy's words, and turned to her. "We did fall in love quickly. You don't think anyone will think Wyatt's marrying me because he feels sorry for me, alone and nowhere to go, do you? I hadn't thought of that before, but of course they will. I mean, it makes sense."

"But that's not why I'm marrying you," he said, squeezing her shoulders and bringing her closer to him. "I'm marrying you because I love you. You're the first lady that's ever gotten my attention, and once you got it, I couldn't get you out of my head."

She turned her head up to stare at him, and as she did, she watched his face turn red. "Okay, I might have done it again, and not said that exactly the way I meant it. I meant, once I got to know you I fell in love with you and haven't been able to think of much else since." He paused, looked away a few moments, and back at her. "Was that any better, or was it just as bad?"

Martha started laughing, and Rosy looked from one to the other. "See what I mean? You were made for each other. That's why I think you should take her into town a few more times and let people meet her and see the two of you together. Once that happens I don't think it will take long for everyone to see how much you love each other, and they'll fall in love with her, as well. That will make for a nicer wedding day for you, surrounded by people you both know and who think a lot of both of you."

"That makes sense," Wyatt said.

"It does. Thank you, Rosy. I feel like you're the mother I never had. I appreciate you looking out for me, and that's a wonderful suggestion."

"Let's go in tomorrow and talk to Reverend Mellinger," Wyatt suggested. "We'll see if he has a suggestion for a date."

"I think that's a wonderful idea," Rosy said. "Then in a couple of days maybe you can take us into town again and we'll get the fabric we need for a new dress."

"Get enough for a new dress for you, too, Rosy," Wyatt said. "I'll pay for it. I know you're going to be helping us get ready for this, and I want you to have a new dress to wear, too." They spent the next few minutes talking about other plans they would have to make, and possible future trips into Green Falls to allow people to become friends with Martha. After making a few notes to be sure they remembered some details, they all went to bed with smiles on their faces.

MARTHA WAS a little surprised when she went down to help Rosy with breakfast the next morning and learned Wyatt hadn't come down yet. "He's probably just sleeping in while he has the chance," she told Martha.

Before Martha could answer, there was a knock on their kitchen door. Martha was closer, so she opened the door. "Good morning, Dallas. Come on in."

"Martha," Dallas said rather curtly. "I'd like to speak to Rosy."

"Come on in, Dallas," Rosy said. "What can I do for you?"

"I'm here to check on Wyatt. How is he doing?"

Rosy's eyebrows furrowed together as she looked from Dallas to Martha. "He seems okay to me, but you should probably ask Martha. The two of them had a nice chat last evening."

"He insisted he was fine," Martha offered. "He was tired and went to bed a little earlier than normal, but he seemed good when he went upstairs."

"He certainly did," Rosy confirmed. "In fact, he was smiling and in a real good mood."

Martha struggled to keep from laughing, but simply nodded and agreed. "Yes, he was."

"Okay, good. The boys and I wanted to be sure he was okay.

Miss Rosy, you let me know if there's anything I can do to help you, especially if you need help with him."

"Thank you, Dallas, for your offer. We'll let you know if we need anything."

He left, and once Rosy saw he was halfway back to the barn, she turned to Martha. "I see what you mean now when you said he was giving you looks you didn't like. There was no reason he couldn't have asked you that. That's not like Dallas."

"I know," Martha said quietly. "He was always friendly to me before. I'm not sure what I can do, other than apologize. I'll do that after we get back from town."

"What do you have to apologize for?"

"He told me to stay here yesterday, but I didn't. You said he expects people to listen to him. Maybe he's upset about that."

"Maybe," Rosy said thoughtfully, "but he should be glad you did go, and found Wyatt. I can't think he'd be this upset about that. He'll probably be okay in a day or so. Now, let's get break-fast finished. I'm guessing Wyatt will be down any minute now."

"Probably. It's not like him to sleep this late. You think he's okay, don't you?" she asked.

"I think so. Dr. Campbell said he would want to sleep a lot the next few days, and that would be the best thing for him. I know my husband fell and hit his head one time and for about a week he slept a lot more than normal. He was a lot like Wyatt, busy all the time, but not for about a week after he fell. He slept late in the morning, went to bed early in the evening, and took one or two naps during the day."

"We shouldn't go to Green Falls today then," Martha said. "We can let him sleep in and rest as much as he needs to. We can go to town in a few days when he's got more strength."

"Nonsense," came a deep voice from the doorway. Both ladies turned to see Wyatt smiling. "I slept late this morning, but I feel fine. I feel like telling the world you've agreed to become my wife," he said, moving over to hold her gently in his arms. "I don't want to put that off. I'll be fine."

"What if you get tired before we get back home?" she asked, smiling when he placed a small kiss on her cheek, even in front of Rosy.

"Then I'll rest on the way back home. I might not have said that yesterday, but now I happen to know there will be a young lady in the buggy that is quite capable of driving us back home. The only thing she might need is some directions how to get back home," he added with a little laugh, "and Rosy will be able to provide them."

"Are you sure you're up to it?" she asked as she finished cooking the scrambled eggs.

"I'm positive. Besides, if I can't go out and help the men today, this will be better for me. It will keep me busy."

"And away from the barn," Rosy said with a nod. "I agree, this will be good in that sense. Just don't push yourself or wear yourself down."

"I give you two ladies my word. Now, stop worrying about me and let's eat. This looks good."

Rosy went with them to Green Falls after breakfast, which didn't surprise anyone. They might be planning a wedding, but until then, she was not about to let them be seen riding into town together, alone, this soon after they'd met. They took the buggy and she sat in the back seat, watching the interaction between Wyatt and Martha. She wasn't stopping them, but enjoying watching them.

Reverend and Mrs. Mellinger were surprised to see the three of them, but invited them into their home. "It's nice to see all of you," Thelma said. "Are you settling in okay, Miss Welch? I hope you're finding Green Falls to your liking. We'd love to have you stay."

"Actually, Thelma, that's why we're here," Rosy said with a big smile for her long-time friend.

Wyatt turned to Jed. "We're here to ask you if you would perform a marriage ceremony for us."

"Marriage?" Thelma gasped. "Wyatt, you're getting married?"

"I certainly am, ma'am," he said proudly, squeezing Martha's hand. He then turned back to Jed. "Last night this lovely little lady agreed to marry me. I'm so happy I want to go outside and announce it to the world. I thought it might be a little more civilized, though, if we announce it at church Sunday. I'm hoping you'll agree to perform the ceremony and help us set a date, so we can announce the date Sunday, as well."

"I didn't even know you two were courting," Thelma said. She looked down at his hand wrapped around hers. "I see you must be, though."

"Yes, ma'am," Wyatt said. "To be honest, this might seem rather sudden to some people, because I admit I've only known her for a matter of weeks. But with her staying with us, we've seen each other every day, and have gotten to know each other over meals and talking in the evening."

"I could tell right off there was a spark between them," Rosy said, "and the more I got to know Martha, the happier I was to see that spark grow. She's a fine young lady, but the two of them were just meant to be together. I've seen many a young couple courting, but I've never seen a couple that I felt was as suited for each other as these two."

"I think God was looking out for me when he sent Wyatt my way on that awful day when my uncle passed away," Martha said. "He's a wonderful man."

"I would agree with that," Reverend Mellinger said. "His father was a wonderful man, and Wyatt has grown up to be the same kind of man. He'd be proud of you, Wyatt."

"Thank you, sir."

The group visited for a while, when Thelma looked at the clock. "Oh, my, look what time it is. Please say you'll all stay for dinner. I'm enjoying our visit and would love for it to continue over the noon meal."

"Wonderful idea," Jed said. "Wyatt, while the ladies see what they can scrounge up in the kitchen, why don't we go to my office and look at my calendar. Let's see if we can find a date that would work."

The men went down the hall to his office while the ladies went to the kitchen. They enjoyed each other's company and were soon talking and laughing while they put together a meal. Rosy carefully worked in several stories about Wyatt and Martha, showcasing to Thelma how close they'd become already. Thelma asked Martha several questions, as well, and it wasn't long before Rosy felt sure Thelma could see for herself they were indeed in love.

While this was happening in the kitchen, Jed was asking Wyatt questions about his relationship with Martha. Wyatt saw through his actions, and gladly gave him little insights into things they'd talked about, and the reverend could easily see his happiness as he talked about her. By the time the three of them had eaten their meal and left, they had not only an agreement to perform the wedding, but also a date. Moreover, they had Jed and Thelma's blessings.

That was what Rosy was hoping for. She knew Thelma would spread the word, and when they came in to Green Falls the next few times people would be eager to get to know Martha, the one woman that was able to catch Wyatt's eye.

They were headed for their buggy, and Wyatt took Martha's hand and squeezed it a bit. "Would you mind driving us back home?"

"Of course not," she answered quickly. "I haven't gotten to do this in a long time and I miss it. Are you feeling okay?"

"I'm feeling fine, but I will admit I'm a bit tired. I don't know why, I haven't done anything all day."

"Dr. Campbell said you would want to rest a lot the next few days, and that you should. I'll be happy to drive us. Besides, if you let me drive the rig home today, you'll feel better about letting me take it in the future. If Rosy and I need some things in town, if you feel confident in my abilities, it can save you making a trip to town and back."

"That's a good point. This will ease my mind the first time you ask to do that, and I know you well enough to know that I'm sure you will," he said with a smile for her.

Wyatt was about to help Rosy into the buggy when Dr. Campbell came down the boardwalk and greeted them. "Wyatt, Rosy, Miss Welch, I'm a little surprised to see you in town today. How are you feeling, Wyatt?"

"Like I just told the ladies, I feel fine, but I will admit I'm a bit tired." Dr. Campbell looked from him to the horse and buggy, obviously concerned. "Don't worry, Doc, I'm going to let Martha drive us home."

Dr. Campbell's expression changed from concern to surprise. "Miss Welch, from New York?"

Wyatt laughed out loud. "That was my thought, as well, Doc, but it turns out Martha grew up on a farm and moved to New York a couple of years ago. She's missed living in the country, and she's quite adept at working with and riding horses."

"You don't say."

"I'm also happy to announce that as of last night she's agreed to become my wife."

Now Dr. Campbell truly was surprised. "Well, I'll be. The little lady with good horse skills has won you over, huh?"

"Her abilities with horses is just one of her many talents I've fallen in love with," he said as he pulled her close to his side. "She is quite a lady. I feel fortunate to have met her and won her over before anyone else in this area had a chance to get to know her. I stole her from them before they even had a chance to meet her."

Dr. Campbell laughed, watching Wyatt closely. After studying him several moments longer, he nodded his head. "I can tell you mean that sincerely, Wyatt, and that's great. It seems to me you've found that one special lady for you, and I'm very happy for both of you."

"You are right about that, Doctor," Rosy said. "These two were meant to be together. I'm thoroughly convinced of that."

"Rosy, you don't say something unless you mean it, so that's saying a lot." He turned to Martha next. "Congratulations, Miss Welch, you've got a good man here that will take care of you. You take good care of him the next few days."

"I intend to," she said with a smile for the doctor. She watched Wyatt help Rosy into the buggy, but brushed off his hands when she knew he meant to lift her into the buggy. "I'm capable of getting in myself, and you need to rest," she told Wyatt, whose mouth was open and his eyes were wide.

Dr. Campbell was chuckling as he tipped his hat at them and went on down the boardwalk. "They'll do well together," he mumbled.

Martha backed the horse up and headed them home effortlessly, which didn't go unnoticed by Wyatt.

Once they were on the road home she commented on how friendly Jed and Thelma were, and they carried on an easy conversation as they traveled. Wyatt didn't participate a lot, but the ladies knew he was tired and didn't push him any.

Wyatt was tired, but he watched Martha as she casually steered the horse around holes in the road, and he could tell she was comfortable driving them home. After yesterday and seeing the skills she possessed that he wasn't aware of, he expected her to be more than capable of getting them home. What he didn't expect was when she pulled up to the house. "You two go on into the house, and I'll be in shortly. I'm going to put the buggy up and brush the horse out. Wyatt, why don't you go upstairs and rest a while? I can tell you're sleepy."

The look on his face had Rosy laughing. "What?" Martha asked. "Did I say something wrong?"

"No," Rosy assured her. "Wyatt's just not used to a lady offering to do what he normally does."

"But you know I don't mind brushing out a horse," she said as she turned to him. "In fact, it's something I've always enjoyed. You go rest and let me put the buggy up and pamper the horse. I promise when you're feeling better I'll not only let you do it, but I'll appreciate it, as well."

That brought more laughter from Wyatt, but he leaned over and kissed her cheek. "Yes, ma'am," he said as he climbed down and helped Rosy down. "Make a man feel good, though, and if one of the men is out there, at least let him put the buggy up for you, please?"

Now it was Martha's turn to laugh, along with Wyatt and Rosy. "Okay, if one of them is out there and offers, I will allow it. In fact, I'll even thank him for it. But trust me, if no one is out there, I can handle it."

"Oh, I don't doubt that for a minute," he said. "Don't take too long pampering the horse, or I'll worry."

"Deal," she said as she backed the horse up and headed to the barn.

CHAPTER 18

*M*artha took the horse and buggy to the barn, and saw Dallas working in the back. He glanced up and quickly slipped out the back of the barn, which upset her. She didn't expect or necessarily want him to offer to unfasten the buggy and put it up, but the fact that he left so he could avoid talking to her was unsettling. She wasn't sure what had him so upset with her, but she didn't like it. Wyatt was close to him, and she didn't want to cause any problem between them. She wasn't sure she could simply ignore his rudeness to her, though, without saying a word.

She unhitched the buggy and pushed it back in its place, then walked the horse to his stall, thinking about Dallas the whole time. She had no idea how she should handle this, but as she brushed the horse down she decided she would see if he was still around the barn. If so she would approach him. Hopefully an apology would help, and they could move beyond this suddenly strained atmosphere that seemed to exist around them.

Determined to put an end to this, she finished brushing the horse and went in search of Dallas. She easily found him and approached, greeting him before he could turn and leave again. "Hello, Dallas. Could I have a minute of your time, please?"

He turned to glare at her, certainly not looking very inviting. "What is it?"

"I wanted to apologize to you for yesterday. I know you told me to go in the house and wait there, and I didn't listen to you."

"No, you didn't." he said, not very graciously.

"I didn't mean to upset you, and I certainly didn't do it out of disrespect for you," she went on, trying to soothe his anger. "I knew Wyatt hadn't yet said it was okay for me to go out alone, but I knew the reason for his hesitancy was he hadn't yet seen that I can handle a gun. I wasn't concerned about that, so when everyone set out in search of him, I couldn't simply sit in the house and wait, knowing I was quite capable of aiding in the search."

"When I told you to stay here, I was doing that in my position as foreman on this ranch. It's Wyatt's ranch, so ultimately it was him you disrespected."

He turned to walk away, but Martha hurried around to stand in front of him. "I have apologized to him, Dallas. He accepted my apology, and even thanked me for caring enough to go out looking for him, and was glad I found him in time."

"Then it sounds like your apologies have been taken care of. I have work to do. Some of us do as we're told." He dodged past her and walked out of the barn.

Martha was livid. She'd never had a man be so rude to her. She stomped out of the barn toward the house, trying to clear her head. She didn't want Wyatt worrying about anything right now, so she would just have to work this out herself, although at this moment she had no idea how. She stood outside the kitchen door a couple of minutes and forced herself to take some deep breaths to calm down. When she felt ready to conceal her anger, she put a smile on her face and walked in the kitchen.

"What's got you so upset?" Wyatt asked as he took her hand

and led her to a chair at the table, where he sat down and pulled her down on his lap.

"Oh," she said, surprised. "I'm not upset."

With no hesitation Wyatt reached around and gave her bottom, or hip, a good swat. "Do we need to talk about honesty, Miss Martha?"

"Ouch," she said, reaching back to rub her hip. "No." She looked around quickly as her face turned red.

"Rosy's not here, you can relax. She went outside to check on her garden."

"Thank heavens. I would have been so embarrassed."

"I wouldn't do that if anyone was around. It's not my intent to embarrass you, but I do expect the truth when I ask you a question."

"I know, but you startled me. What makes you think I'm upset?"

He reached back and swatted her again, though not as hard. "I don't think you're upset, I know you're upset. Martha, I was sitting here at the table watching out the window. I'm not sure why you were in the machine shop, but I saw you come out of it. Seeing the look on your face and the way you were stomping up here, it's not hard to see something has you upset. Are you ready to tell me what it is yet, or do you want to deny it again? You should keep in mind, though, if you choose the latter we'll be making a quick trip to my office to have a longer discussion about honesty."

"No," she quickly responded. "That's not necessary, but I don't want you getting upset. It's my problem, not yours, and I'll handle it."

He reached out and used one finger and his thumb to gently guide her face up so she was looking at him. "That's where you're wrong, my sweet lady. You've agreed to become my wife. That means I plan on doing everything I can to make sure you're safe, healthy and happy. Happy is very important to me, and if something is bothering you, you're not happy, and I want to know about it. If I can help you with the problem, whatever it is, I will. If not, I will at least be here and we will get through whatever it is together. Now, let me ask you again, what has you upset?"

She sighed. "Wyatt, it really isn't your problem and I don't want to upset you."

His eyebrows lifted as he looked at her. "You're upsetting me more than you realize by keeping whatever it is from me. Please, Martha, tell me so I can help you."

"Okay, I'll tell you, but please let me try to fix it before you jump in and he gets even more upset with me."

"He? You must be talking about Dallas. Are you still thinking he's upset with you?"

"No, I know he's upset with me," she said as she tried to stand up.

He tightened his hold on her. "Stay still. What makes you think he's upset with you?"

"Wyatt, I know Dallas is a friend of yours."

"He's more than a friend."

"He is?"

"My father hired him as one of the hands on this ranch when I was ten. At that time my father was just beginning to let me start working alongside the men. Dallas was twenty-five. Even though he was trying to impress my father, prove that he was a good worker and knew what he was doing on a ranch, he never hesitated to take extra time to teach me something. Two years later the foreman quit to take care of his father, who had been injured. Pa made Dallas his new foreman. He was the youngest foreman my father had ever had, but he said when he met Dallas he saw something special in him, and said someday he would make a good foreman. He didn't think it would be that soon, but he took a chance on him even though he was so young."

"And he's been the foreman ever since," Martha said rather than asked.

"He has. But when my father passed away and the ranch fell into my hands, Dallas was there for me. He agreed to stay on as foreman, but he did much more than that. He encouraged me, kept telling me I could do it, I just had to believe in myself, trust myself. Owning a ranch this size was overwhelming to me at that age, but Dallas kept telling me not just that I could do it, but that he knew I'd do it good."

"That's impressive."

"It certainly is to me," Wyatt agreed with a proud smile. "He kept the ranch running smoothly because in a sense he stepped in and became a second father to me and taught me how to be the owner of a large ranch."

"Now I know why you said you were going to ask him to stand up with you at our wedding. I don't blame you."

"We got off track, though. You feel as though he's upset with you, and I asked what makes you feel that way."

Martha hesitated a moment before saying, "Maybe I'm reading him wrong."

"No, I don't think you are," Rosy said as she came through the door. She paused and her eyes grew a bit and she frowned when she saw Martha sitting on Wyatt's lap, but she didn't say anything.

Wyatt ignored her expression, tightened his arms around Martha, and looked at her. "Why do you say that, Rosy?"

"Because I've seen it, Wyatt. I don't understand it because it's not like Dallas, but she's not imagining it. He came to the house this morning to see how you're doing. Martha was at the door so she answered his knock. Instead of talking to her he said he wanted to talk to me. All he did was ask how you were. I'm telling you, he ignored her."

"That doesn't sound like Dallas. Are you sure –"

"No, it doesn't," Rosy said, cutting him off, "but I saw it. And that's not all. I was standing at the window when she took the buggy out just now, and Dallas was in the barn. As soon as she went in, he sneaked out the back door and went in the machine shop."

"He must not have seen her." Rosy just looked at him, her eyebrows raised. "Okay, I admit that's probably not likely, but why would he do that? I would have expected him to help her unhitch the horse."

"Me, too. I'm telling you, Wyatt, she's not imagining it. I didn't hear anything you two have said other than she said maybe she was reading him wrong. When I saw him this morning and out there a little bit ago, no, she's not imagining anything. I don't know what's going on, but he's not acting like himself."

Wyatt turned to Martha again. "What happened out there that had you so upset?"

"After I brushed the horse out I went looking for him, since I knew he was around."

"You'd seen him leave the barn?"

"Yes. When I went in with the horse he looked up, saw me and hurried out the back door. While I brushed the horse out I thought about what to do to fix this. I decided I would apologize to him for not listening yesterday when he told me to go in the house and stay there while they all went looking for you. I thought maybe that would help."

"It didn't?"

"No. He told me I should apologize to you, not him. I told him I did, and he said he had work to do, that some people do as they're told, and brushed past me."

Wyatt sat up straighter. "Dallas did that?"

"Yes. Honest, Wyatt, I was trying to set things right between us."

"I believe you, Martha. I'm sorry I didn't believe you right away, but it just doesn't sound like Dallas. Let me talk to him and see if I can find out what upset him so much yesterday."

"Wyatt, I'm worried if you do he'll get more upset with me, that I ran to you. Can we give it a day or two and see if he gets over it?"

"He should have helped you with the horse and buggy, and I don't like hearing he's treating you that way. At the same time, I understand what you're saying, and agree it would be better if he can work this out in his head without me stepping in. I will agree to give it a day or two, but if he does or says anything disrespectful to you I want to know about it. That includes you, Rosy. If you see or hear him treat her wrong, please tell me about it."

"I will, Wyatt," Rosy promised.

"And you?" he asked, turning Martha's face toward his again.

"Okay. Hopefully he just needs a little time to accept my apology."

"Now that we've come to an agreement on that," Rosy said, the frown back on her face, "I will remind you that you are not married yet, Wyatt. What if one of the men were to come to the house to ask a question and saw you two?"

"He might be jealous, but he would get over it," Wyatt said with a smirk.

"And what if he were to go into Green Falls on Saturday night and drink a little more then he should and starts talking? I'll not have people hearing something from a drunk cowboy and spreading gossip that will hurt her."

Wyatt sobered quickly and helped Martha to her feet. "You're right, Rosy. Thank you." He turned to Martha. "The last thing I want to do is harm you in any way. I'm sorry, and I'll try harder to make myself wait until you're my wife. This is going to be a long month, though."

"It will be worth it in the end, Wyatt," Rosy said with a friendly warning on her face.

"Yes, ma'am," he said. He leaned down and gave Martha a quick kiss on her nose. "Now that you're in and I know you got the horse taken care of, I'm going upstairs to lay down a bit. I am a little tired."

"Sleep well. We'll wake you for supper."

Rosy waited until Wyatt was upstairs before addressing Martha. "I'm sorry I interrupted the conversation you were having with Wyatt, but I knew he would have a hard time believing what you were saying about Dallas. It's not because he doesn't trust your word, but because this is such unusual behavior from Dallas."

"You don't need to apologize, Rosy. I'm glad you spoke up because you were right, I don't think he quite believed me."

"I don't think you were being untruthful, but this goes against what Dallas is generally like, so I understand Wyatt thinking maybe you were mistaken about his words or deeds. I don't know what's gotten into him, but I hope he gets it worked out of his system, and soon."

"Me, as well. I feel like this is becoming a me against Dallas thing, and I don't want it to be that way at all. I really hoped my apology would set us to rights again."

"It still may. After he thinks it over today, maybe he'll work it out in his head. We'll just have to hope, and wait and see."

"I certainly can hope. It's the wait and see part that's going to be the problem."

THE NEXT MORNING Wyatt was feeling better and wanting to get back to work, but after seeing how worried Martha was about that, he agreed to simply go to the barn for a little while before lunch. He was happy to see Dallas in the tack room repairing a harness. He went in and sat down beside him. "Good to see you out again, Wyatt. How are you feeling?"

"I'm feeling good. I feel ready to get back to work, but Martha didn't think I was ready yet."

Dallas looked over at him, but although Wyatt was watching his expression, he couldn't tell what he was thinking. "Is she in charge now?"

When the corner of his mouth lifted a bit, Wyatt was more confused about his thoughts toward Martha. Watching his response, he said, "In a way, yes. Dallas, I wanted to find you and talk to you today, and it concerns Martha."

Again, though he was watching his reaction closely, he couldn't tell a thing. "Oh?"

"I think you knew we've been getting closer." Dallas nodded, but didn't say anything. "Well, she's agreed to marry me."

Dallas looked over at him, and Wyatt thought he looked a little leery. "Are you sure about this? It seems awfully soon. She's the first lady you've shown much interest in, and you're ready to marry her already?"

"Yes, I am sure," he said confidently.

"Do you feel you know her well enough?"

"I admit I don't know everything about her yet. She's definitely thrown a few surprises at me lately, but –"

"I have to say she surprised me the other day, for certain. She asked if she could go out with us looking for you. I certainly wasn't expecting that."

"She wanted to go along?"

"Yes, she did. I told her no and sent her into the house. I didn't know how well she could ride or that she could handle a gun."

"I understand why you told her no," Wyatt assured him. "I probably would have done the same thing."

"Does it bother you any that she didn't listen? There are a lot of things out here that could get a lady from New York in trouble if she doesn't listen."

"There are, and to be honest, I was upset about it at first, but once we talked, I came to terms with it. In fact, now that I know she grew up on a farm and that's where she became as capable as she is, I couldn't be upset with her. I might not be here right now if she hadn't gone. In fact, I feel sure I wouldn't be."

"That's true enough. I didn't know she grew up on a farm."

"I didn't, either, until after all this happened and we talked."

"But she still didn't listen. Do you think that will be a problem going forward?"

"I don't really think it will be, but we'll find out," he said with a little smile. "I understand why she didn't listen this time, and I have to say if the tables were turned, I no doubt would have done the same thing. We talked about it and she understands the importance of heeding my warnings, so I think she'll be okay. To be honest, she is feisty, which is why she couldn't sit still while everyone else was looking for me, but that feistiness is one of the things about her I find becoming."

Dallas looked off in the distance a few moments. "I can see that matching you. You did your fair share of getting into things when you were younger, as well. Maybe that's why she seems to be the only one to catch your attention."

"You're right that no other lady has caught my interest, until Martha. But with her, I know she's the one I'm meant to spend my life with. We have very similar thoughts about so many things, and being with her feels right to me. And you know me, I know what I want and I go after it. In this case, I was lucky because she developed similar feelings for me."

"Well, you sound pretty sure of yourself, so congratulations. I hope it works out well for both of you."

"Thank you, Dallas. We're getting married four weeks from tomorrow, on Saturday afternoon. I'd like to have you stand up with me."

Dallas turned to look at him again. He hesitated a moment longer than Wyatt would have liked before nodding. "I'd be honored to, Wyatt."

"Thank you. The ceremony will be on Saturday afternoon, with a meal following. We'll have more plans in a couple of days, but I wanted to talk to you, tell you my good news and make sure you'll be willing to stand up for me."

"I certainly will." He paused a moment before saying, "I'm glad you're feeling better. How soon do you think you'll be back to work?"

"I should know more tomorrow. I'm taking the ladies into Green Falls then so they can get some fabric to make new dresses for the wedding. I'm going to stop in and see Dr. Campbell while I'm there. He'll let me know then. I feel good enough to go back, but I will admit I still get tired quicker than normal."

"Maybe you can start back in the mornings, and take it easy in the afternoons for a few days."

"That's what I'm hoping, too." Wyatt asked about the ranch, what they've been getting done and what needed doing yet, before going back to the house. He went back over their conversation on his way back to the house. He hadn't detected anything amiss about the way Dallas was acting, and he didn't say a thing that seemed out of place. Maybe now that he knew he'd talked to Martha and was okay with what she did, Dallas would be able to come to terms with it, as well. He certainly hoped so.

LATER THAT AFTERNOON Martha went to the barn to visit the animals. There was a young calf that had gotten attacked by a coyote. Its mother was able to run the coyote off before it killed the calf, but it was injured. Wyatt and the men had brought both it and its mother to the barn so they could treat the cuts on the calf and give it a safe place to heal. Wyatt had warned her she could look at them, but these were beef cows, and they weren't used to interacting with people. Therefore, if the mother got agitated with her at the pen trying to pet the calf, she needed to stop. Some mothers would get so agitated if they felt someone was too close to their calf they would try to chase them away, sometimes stepping on the calf in the process.

She'd been out there on several occasions and the mother had watched her closely, but hadn't seemed upset with her. As she neared the barn she stopped to pick some tall grass by the side of the barn. She went to the stall and stood on the bottom rung, talking softly to the cow and her calf. She leaned over a bit to offer some of the grass to the mother cow, but it backed away at first. She kept talking to her, holding the grass there, but not moving. Eventually the cow inched close enough to sniff the grass. Martha stayed still, holding the grass out. After another minute or two the cow pulled the grass out of her hand.

Martha praised her and offered her more of the grass she'd picked. Before long the cow trusted her enough to eat the grass without hesitation. She didn't come any closer to Martha, but she did eat the grass as she offered it.

Austin came into the barn to start the evening chores, and stopped at the door when he saw Martha at the pen. He'd seen her there several times over the last couple of days, and he could tell she was slowly gaining the cow's trust, which was pretty remarkable in his eyes. While these cows were generally not aggressive toward people out in the open, they weren't used to being penned up. Unless they were around people on a regular basis as a calf, they seldom became comfortable around them. As he'd watched her the last few days, he could tell the cow was becoming more comfortable with her.

He was stunned to see the cow eating out of her hand, and stayed at the door, simply watching. There was no doubt that Martha had a way with animals, but even knowing that, he hadn't expected to see the cow eating out of her hands. As he watched, she reached down with her other hand and gently stroked the calf, who had come closer to her, as well. The mother kept an eye on her calf, but didn't seem to mind Martha petting it at all. Even after the cow ate all the grass Martha had, she didn't seem upset at all when the calf moved closer to Martha and allowed her to pet it.

Austin was standing off to the side at the back door, in the shadows, watching the proceedings with awe. Dallas came in the front door and with a quick glance around the barn saw Martha standing on the bottom rail, petting the calf. After glancing around again and seeing no one else around, he yelled, "Martha, get away from that pen!" The loud, gruff voice he used scared not only Martha, but the cow and calf, as well. The cow became more agitated the closer Dallas came, as he continued to scold Martha for being there. "Look how agitated you have this cow. Get out of here right now and maybe she'll calm down before she hurts the calf."

"But Dallas –"

"Go!" he yelled, pointing to the door.

Her eyes misted with tears, and although she wanted to argue with Dallas, right now, right here was not the place to do it. The cow was becoming agitated. She was certain it was because of him, and not her, but arguing now would only make it worse. She fled from the barn, tears escaping from her eyes. This was certainly not going to help her relationship with Dallas. She ran out the front door, and behind the machine shed so she could have a little time alone to think.

She started walking along the path close by, debating what she should do. Should she confront Dallas and ask why he did that? Did he honestly believe she was upsetting them before he came in, or was this simply more of his new way of treating her? She had to figure out what was going on and fix it. She didn't want to come between Wyatt and Dallas, especially now, after Wyatt explained why Dallas was so important to him.

CHAPTER 19

*A*ustin couldn't believe what he'd just seen. Dallas was very good with the animals, and generally a very even-tempered man, which made him a good foreman. What he'd just witnessed was anything but that. Martha had done nothing wrong. That cow and her calf were fine, as were all the animals in the barn. To him, it had often seemed as though Martha had a calming effect on animals. She talked to them all in a soothing voice, and would only get close to an animal and pet it if it was amenable to the attention.

When Dallas yelled from across the barn it riled several of the animals up. Austin had never seen or heard Dallas act that way around animals, and couldn't imagine why he had now. It was certainly unprovoked. When he ran toward her, yelling the whole way, it not only upset the cow, but he could see what it had done to Martha. She ran from the building. If it would have been him he would have stayed and asked Dallas what the hell he was doing. As soon as the thought entered his mind, though, he realized that would have made the matter worse, and Martha probably knew that. A quick glance at the barn showed most of the animals were now upset, and he was torn as to which way to go. He decided to let Dallas deal with the mess he'd made and go talk to Martha.

He hurried to the side of the barn where he would be most able to see her after she left the front door of the barn. He looked around, but didn't see her. Finally he saw her going down the trail behind the machine shed. She was moving pretty quickly, probably running. He felt bad for her, but wasn't sure he should go after her. He knew Wyatt had eyes for Martha, and how would it look if someone saw him escorting her down a trail? Although he could explain it to Wyatt and hopefully he would understand, gossip could be dangerous. What if one of the other men saw the two of them together alone, and said something to someone in town, who took it the wrong way?

He could still hear the commotion inside the barn, so he decided to go in and try to help calm the animals instead. He would give this whole thing some thought. Maybe he could come up with a better way to help Martha, and to try to find out what was wrong with Dallas. His best chance of that, he decided, was to play dumb. He wouldn't tell Dallas he saw the whole thing, and ask what happened. That might give him some insight into it.

WYATT WOKE from his afternoon nap and went downstairs. When Rosy told him Martha had gone to the barn, he went out, as well, hoping to get a chance to watch her interact with the animals. When he got to the barn, however, he heard a ruckus going on and hurried inside. Dallas was at the stall of the cow and her injured calf. Something obviously had the cow upset, as she was shaking her head back and forth, and even rammed into the stall near Dallas. He headed in that direction.

Now that Austin had a plan, he turned and went back inside the barn. He headed toward the cow and calf, which were on the opposite side of the barn, walking slowly and trying to talk calmly as he went. He was glad to see other animals around him beginning to calm down. He was surprised to see Wyatt heading toward Dallas, as well, but was glad. He was good with the animals and hopefully would be able to calm them down, as well.

He got to Dallas about the same time Wyatt did, and heard Wyatt asked what was going on. What he heard shocked him again. "Not sure," Dallas said. "Martha was over here when I came in the barn. The cow was becoming agitated, so I headed over to see what was wrong. I couldn't believe what I saw. Wyatt, Martha was inside the pen, trying to get close enough to pet the calf."

Wyatt looked stunned. "She was inside the pen?"

"Yes. I couldn't believe it, but she was inside. I hurried over and calmly told her to get out of the pen. I kept the cow on one side as much as possible while she climbed out. She wasn't happy that I made her get out of the pen, and after letting me know that, she ran out of the barn. I've been trying to get them calmed down since."

"That doesn't sound like Martha," Wyatt said. "I'm going to go talk to her. She needs to know that is not something I will allow on this ranch. Do you know where she went?"

"No idea. She ran out of the barn, but I was too busy trying to settle things down here to see where she went."

"I understand. I'm going to go see if she went in the house. We need to have a serious talk."

Austin couldn't believe what he'd just heard, but hopefully if Wyatt talked to her she would tell him what actually happened. He would try to get a chance later to talk to Wyatt, as well, in case he had any question as to which story to believe. "Wyatt, I saw her walking down the trail behind the machine shed," he offered. "I just came in from that direction. She was walking quick or maybe running, but she was on that trail."

"Thanks, Austin," Wyatt said. "If I miss her and either of you sees her, please tell her I want to talk to her." Both men nodded and Wyatt made his way quickly out of the barn.

"So what happened?" Austin asked. "I heard you say Martha was in the barn, but I didn't hear it all. She seems so good with animals, I can't imagine she'd do something to upset them."

"I couldn't believe it at first, either, but she sure did have them upset. I hope Wyatt can convince her she has to listen to us. We can't have her roaming around here doing as she pleases." He turned and walked off, leaving Austin staring after him.

WYATT HURRIED out of the barn and straight toward the trail. He considered saddling Thunder first, but if she was walking she shouldn't be far away, and Dr. Campbell had advised against riding until he saw him again. It would be unfair of him to have a talk with her about listening and following directions aimed at keeping her safe, if he ignored his doctor's orders. With that in mind, he set off at a brisk pace, looking from side to side as he went, and calling out for her.

He was moving so quickly he just about missed her calling out. "Wyatt?" She got up from the large rock she was sitting on and ran out to the trail to meet him. "Wyatt, you look upset. Is something wrong?"

"Yes, it is," he said as he took her hand. He saw the rock she'd been sitting on and led her back to it. They sat down facing each other, and he started right in. "Martha, I was outside and heard a commotion out at the barn and went to see what was going on. I understand you were in there before you came on your walk. What happened?"

She took a moment before she answered. "You sound like you're accusing me of something. Is that what you're doing?"

He sighed and made himself relax a bit before answering.

"Martha, I'm not accusing you of anything, but I would like to know what happened, in your words."

"In my words," she repeated. "That sounds accusatory to me, so let me ask, what have you been told happened?"

Wyatt saw something in her eyes he didn't like. She was hurting, but he didn't know why. He had to wonder if it had something to do with the spat that seemed to be ongoing between Martha and Dallas, though after talking to Dallas he still wasn't convinced the whole thing wasn't a misunderstanding on Martha's part. Dallas didn't seem to be upset. On the other hand, Martha had never given him a reason to doubt anything she said, so he had to be careful. "Dallas said the cow wasn't happy, got upset when you got in their pen to pet her calf."

Her mouth dropped open and he could tell she wasn't expecting to hear that. He could also see her getting upset, and tried to calm her down. "Okay, Martha, I can tell you have a different version. I want to hear your side of it, but please remember to be respectful."

"What do you mean by that?"

"In the past I've seen you get upset and lose your temper. You've had very few spankings, but the ones you have had have been for that very thing. We've talked about it before. You lose your temper and use words that aren't becoming to a young lady, or things you regret saying later. I'm reminding you, watch that you don't do that now, because I don't want to have to spank you again for the same thing. I will if I have to, though, so consider this a warning."

He was sure she was about to argue, but he raised his eyebrows and met her eyes, not budging until she sighed and slumped her shoulders. "You're right. This isn't your fault and it's not fair to take it out on you."

"Thank you. Martha, I want to get to the bottom of this. I can tell your version of what happened is different from what Dallas said, so please tell me what happened as you saw it."

"I don't know why Dallas is doing this," she said, looking far off. "He must hate me for some reason."

"What happened, Martha?"

"I was out with the cow and her calf, but they were fine. I pulled some grass and took it in for the cow, and when she felt comfortable enough with me she came forward to take it from me. She was eating the grass, and her calf came over to the side so I could reach in and pet it. Neither of them were at all agitated."

"How about when you got in the pen; did she get riled up then?"

"That's the thing, Wyatt; I never got in the pen."

Dallas tilted his head and stared at her. "Well, she certainly was agitated when I got there."

"Yes. Dallas came in the barn and screamed at me to get away from there. He came over to the pen, yelling and screaming at me the whole time. That's what upset the cow. Her calf was scared, too. He had several animals in there prancing in their stalls."

Wyatt put his hands on his hips and looked right at her, not believing what he was hearing. "You're saying you never got in the pen?"

"Of course not! You explained that your cattle aren't used to interacting with people like our few cows were, so they're not as friendly."

"Then why would Dallas say the cow got upset when you got in the pen?"

"How am I supposed to know?" she demanded. "He hates me or something. I'm not sure why, but he's treating me horribly. That's what I've been trying to tell you." She stood and started to pace.

"I've never known Dallas to lie."

She whirled around and glared at him. "So if he isn't, I must be? That's what you're saying, isn't it?"

"Martha, all I'm saying is –"

"Is that precious Dallas couldn't possibly lie, so that means I did! Well, I didn't, and if you think I did, you can both go to Hell. I don't lie!"

She turned and started stomping away, but he caught her arm and swirled her back around to face him. "No, that's not what I'm saying, but you don't seem to be able to listen long enough to hear what I am saying, so let's try it like this." He sat down and pulled her over his knees.

"Wyatt, no, you can't do this. Someone might see or hear us, and I didn't do what Dallas is saying I did. He should be the one in trouble, not me."

He easily held her in position while he lifted her skirts over her back. "Martha, settle down. The men are all on the other side of the ranch working, so no one's going to see us. Now, listen to what I have to say and maybe we can avoid having to do this again. I don't like hearing you say Dallas should be in trouble instead of you. This isn't about one or the other because I refuse to pit you against him. You two are the most important people in my life, and we have to work this out somehow. To do that, though, I have to be able to talk to you, without you telling me to go to Hell."

"Well, tell him that! He's the one that lied, not me!"

He lifted his arm and brought it down with a sharp smack on her bottom, and followed it with several more. "You're not listening. I'm not saying one of you has to be lying. Isn't it possible there was a misunderstanding?"

"How could that be? I never got in that pen. He says I did, so the only thing I could be misunderstanding is why he's lying. Is he trying to get me in trouble with you, trying to break us up? If you think I'm misunderstanding something else, please tell me what it could be."

He brought his hand down several more times. "Watch your

attitude. You're acting like I'm taking his side over yours. I'm not. I'm simply trying to get to the bottom of this."

He continued spanking, and talking about her attitude, until he could tell she'd finally heard what he was trying to tell her. She slumped over his knees and whispered, "I'm sorry, Wyatt. I know it's not your fault."

"No, it's not," he said with three more swats. He lifted her then, helping her to settle on his lap, and she immediately snuggled in against him. "Sweetie, you have to learn to keep your temper. When we have a problem we'll talk about it. You have to talk respectfully, though, so we can get to the bottom of it. Are you ready to do that now?"

"Yes."

He rubbed her back and gave her a few minutes to recover. "Are you okay now?"

"Sore, but yes, I'm okay. Wyatt, why do you suppose he hates me?"

He tightened his arms around her and tried to reassure her. "I don't think he hates you. I can't imagine what's going on, but I simply can't believe he could hate you. I don't know how anyone could hate you, Dallas included."

She giggled and when she looked up at him he kissed her forehead. "I'm going to talk to Dallas again and get to the bottom of this."

"Maybe I should talk to him about it. What if it just makes it worse if you do?"

"I don't know how it could make it any worse. I want to know why he said you were in the pen if you weren't. If he thought it looked like it from where he was, that's one thing. He shouldn't have yelled at you for it if that's the case."

"Wyatt, he shouldn't have yelled at me regardless. I wanted to stay and have it out with him right then and there, but he had the animals so upset, they needed to settle down. Us yelling at each other or arguing would have simply made it worse. I couldn't believe he did that."

"That's been bothering me, too. It doesn't sound like something he would do." He looked down at the frown on her face and quickly added, "I'm not saying he didn't do it. All I'm saying is he knows better than to do that and it's not normally how he acts around animals. If he did, I have to wonder why. Maybe something's on his mind."

"Do you think he would talk to me if I tried?"

"I don't know. I appreciate that you want to settle it between you without getting me in the middle, but I'm not sure if that's possible. Let me think about it a little. We'll go into Green Falls tomorrow morning so you and Rosy can get your fabric and whatever you need to make your new dresses. When we get home I'll let you know what I think."

"Okay, that's fair enough."

"Let's get back to the house before Rosy finds out we're out here alone and comes looking for us," he said with a chuckle. He stood, taking her with him, and took her hand as they turned and started back. She was quiet on the way back, and he was pretty sure it was more from worrying about the problem with Dallas than from the spanking.

THE REST of the afternoon and evening Martha was quiet. She was attentive and answered questions Rosy and Wyatt asked, but didn't engage in other conversation, which drew a concerned look from Rosy on a couple occasions. Wyatt could admit he wasn't himself yet, as he got tired much quicker than normal and had been going to bed early every evening.

Before he went to bed that evening, though, he pulled Martha out onto the porch for a conversation. "You've been awfully quiet ever since we came back from our walk." She looked up at him, but instead of saying anything, she waited for him to go on. "You aren't upset or pouting about receiving a spanking, are you?"

Her expression remained aloof, telling Wyatt nothing. "No."

Again, a single word answer didn't tell him much, so he tried again. "Pouting after a spanking is something I won't allow. If you're pouting because you don't feel you deserved the spanking, I didn't do my job properly. My job is to not only correct what needs to be corrected, but to make sure you know why I feel it needs to change. If you understand why you're getting spanked and are still pouting, we need to talk about why. If it's simply because you didn't like being spanked, we might not be meant to be together, because I believe spanking is a very effective way of keeping the lady I love safe."

Finally, she responded. "No, it's not that, Wyatt. I'm not pouting, I'm just thinking."

"So you're not pouting at all?" he asked hesitantly.

"Well, okay, maybe a bit, but not why you think."

His eyebrows raised. "What do I think?"

She shrugged her shoulders and smiled a bit. "I guess I really don't know what I'm thinking right now," she admitted. "The only reason the spanking bothers me is that I feel like Dallas is out to get me for some unknown reason, and in this case, he won."

"Martha, you don't think I spanked you because of what Dallas said, do you?"

"No, it's not that. But he got me so upset that I lost my temper again. I know that's why I got spanked, and I admit my temper is a problem, so I'm not upset about getting spanked for losing it. What bothers me about it is that Dallas is the reason I lost my temper, so I feel like he won this battle."

"Ah," Wyatt said as understanding settled over him. "Then you need to make sure he doesn't win again. Talk to me if anything else happens, but do it in a calm, respectful way. Then we'll get to the bottom of it without your bottom being involved."

"Not funny," she said with a little chuckle, "but I understand what you're saying, and I intend to do just that. But I've been thinking about this problem with Dallas. I don't just want to win this next battle, I want to settle the whole war. Before I can do that, though, I have to figure out why we're at war in the first place."

"I'll talk to him tomorrow after we get back from Green Falls, and maybe I can help get to the bottom of it."

"I just hope you talking to him doesn't make it worse."

"Why would it make it worse?"

"If he's upset with me, he might take offense to me going to you to fight my battles for me. I mean, you might be friends, but you are still his boss."

"I don't think he'll be upset, but we'll see. If it comes down to it, I won't allow him to lie to me, especially about something he says you did. If he has a problem with you, I want to know about it, and we'll deal with it."

"Thank you, but I don't want to come between you and him."

"Martha, you've done nothing that should do that. At least not that I know of. If something did upset him that much, he can tell me about it. Otherwise, he needs to come to terms with it, or this ranch won't run smoothly. You are going to be my wife, and he needs to be okay with that."

Martha nodded, but Wyatt could tell it was still bothering her. Hopefully he would get some answers tomorrow. He fell asleep that night wondering how to approach it with his long time friend and foreman.

Down the hall, Martha had a difficult time falling asleep, as well. In her mind, she had to figure out what had Dallas so upset, and then fix it. The last thing she wanted to do was be the cause of a long time friendship and working relationship coming to an end.

What neither of them knew was that downstairs in her little two-room suite off the kitchen, Rosy was having trouble falling asleep, as well. She'd known Dallas for a long time, and although she hadn't said a whole lot about the situation to Wyatt, she'd seen enough to know something was amiss. Dallas was being downright rude to Martha, and it wasn't like Dallas at all. She couldn't imagine anything Martha could have done to spark such animosity, and especially from him, who was generally a very calm, very fair man.

The more she witnessed and heard about the way Dallas was treating Martha and things he said to her, the more she was convinced something was terribly wrong, and that was a problem. Dallas a good foreman for the ranch, and that was important for Wyatt. The ranch was big enough that one person would have a very difficult time trying to run it and manage all the cowboys working on it himself. Wyatt and Dallas made a good team, with Dallas managing the men, and he and Wyatt talking over and agreeing on major decisions, while Wyatt handled the books and other managerial type duties.

Beyond that, though, Dallas had been like a big brother, or even a father figure to Wyatt when his father died. It would be difficult for Wyatt to lose that, especially as he was about to enter into a new phase of his life. It would be nearly impossible for him to do well with his new marriage and the ranch if those two aspects of his life were at odds with each other. She lay awake trying to figure out what was going on and how to fix it.

The next morning all three of them were up, though none had slept well. They had breakfast and Wyatt went out to the barn to harness a horse and buggy, hoping to catch Dallas out there. Maybe he could have a quick chat and get this whole thing settled. Dallas wasn't around, though, which was just as well. This was a conversation that could take longer than a few minutes.

Martha was quiet on the way to town, and Wyatt assumed it was the same reason he wasn't as talkative as usual. When he noticed Rosy was quiet, as well, he became concerned. "Okay, everyone, let's get this out in the open and talk about it before we get to Green Falls. Rosy, you said we need to go to town a few times before the wedding so everyone can get to know my future wife."

"I know once they get to know her a little bit and see the two of you together, they'll know you've indeed fallen in love with her this quickly, and they'll know why. Everyone will love her, I'm sure."

"Not if she's this sullen," he said, surprising the two ladies.

"I'm sorry, Wyatt," Martha said after thinking about his

words for a few minutes. "You're right, though. If the idea of this trip is to let people get to know me, they won't do it this way."

"Exactly," Wyatt agreed. "Now, we're all going to put this problem with Dallas behind us. As you said last evening, my dear Martha, we're not going to let him win this round. We'll figure this out when we get home and I have a chance to talk to him. For now, though, we need to put it out of our minds."

"He's right," Rosy told Martha. "Tell me, dear, have you given much thought to what kind of dress you want for your wedding? And we've talked a bit about where to have this wedding, but we haven't decided for sure. You two need to decide on that quickly so we have time to come up with some decorations for it. Do you want it inside the house or outside?"

Wyatt looked at his bride-to-be with a big smile. "I'll let that up to you, because I'm fine with anywhere, just as long as you become my wife."

"I'd love to have it outside, but I think if we plan that we will also need to have a backup plan in case it rains."

"We will," Rosy agreed, "but I think we can do that. The grand staircase opens into the front room, and we could always have it in there. You could come down the stairs and straight into the front sitting room. We could put chairs on each side, leaving an aisle for you to walk straight down the stairs, across the front entrance and right straight through the room and up to the mantle."

"That would be a straight walk, wouldn't it?" Martha said, obviously picturing it in her mind. "The entryway could hold extra people if we need more room."

"My thought, too," Rosy said. "I know you both said you don't have family, so a small wedding would be fine for you, but I think folks in town will be hurt if they're not invited. You've been part of this town and surrounding area long enough that they consider you family, Wyatt, and I'm sure they'll think of Martha the same way soon. When the reverend announces it at

church Sunday, you'll want him to make sure to let everyone there know they're invited."

"Yes, of course, and you're right, I don't want anyone to feel left out or hurt," Wyatt said.

"I agree totally," Martha said. "I'll trust you two to invite anyone you think we should. If it rains, I love the idea of getting married in front of the fireplace in the front room. I've always loved that room."

"Okay, that's our backup plan then," Rosy said. "Now you have to pick a place to have it outside if the weather is nice. Once we know that we can get started on the decorations."

"Wyatt, you know the ranch much better than me," Martha said, squeezing his arm a bit. "Where would you suggest?" After a conversation that lasted until they reached the edge of town, they had decided on a spot in the backyard that showcased a waterfalls. Martha often sat on the bank of the creek there, watching the water as it fell over the edge and onto the rocks below. Even though it was smaller than their bigger magical green falls, it was still a beautiful sight, and the quiet but very distinguishable sound of the water was very calming.

"We can make some benches to put out there for the guests," Wyatt offered.

"Good idea," Martha said enthusiastically, "and with the falls as a backdrop, we won't need a lot of decorations. Some nice potted flowers around the edges will make it beautiful."

By the time Wyatt pulled up in front of the mercantile, all three of them were talking excitedly about the upcoming wedding and how pretty it would be. That was what people in town saw as he helped the ladies down and they went inside to pick out their fabric.

Eloise looked up as the three of them were still talking and planning as they entered. "Well, hello. You all look excited. I'm guessing it might have something to do with the wonderful news we've heard, that you two are getting married. Am I right?"

"You are indeed," Wyatt said, pulling Martha closer against him. "Little did I know that fateful day I came across her in a wagon that in less than two months she would steal my heart."

"Oh, how romantic," Eloise said as she clasped her hands under her chin.

"Yes, it was," Martha said as she and Wyatt's eyes met and they both chuckled at irony.

"It was also very unusual," he whispered into her ear, which caused them both to chuckle again. Facing Eloise and raising his voice back to a normal level, he pointed to the ladies. "In fact, the wedding is what brings us here today. We need to get whatever they need to make some new dresses."

"Well, of course you do," Eloise said, catching their excitement. "Let's go look at what we have in stock. We just got some new fabric in yesterday that you might like."

"While you ladies are looking at that, I'm going to go see if Hank is in the sheriff's office," Wyatt said. "I need to thank him for convincing me to take you to the ranch when the hotel was full."

Joseph came out from the back room, chuckling. "Congratulations, you two," he said. "We heard the good news. And now that you mentioned Hank, he was in here yesterday, puffing his chest out, asking if we'd heard the good news, trying to take credit for it."

"Oh, he was, huh?" Wyatt asked with a little laugh.

"Yes, in a joking way. In reality, he's really glad it worked out. He said he had to convince you to take Miss Welch to your ranch for a while. At the time he was looking for someone that had an extra room for her, and he thought your ranch had the room, but Rosy would be a good person for her to talk to. Together he thought it would give Miss Welch a safe place to stay and a friendly lady to talk to while she decided what she wanted to do."

"Well, he was certainly right about that," Martha said. "The ranch was the perfect spot, and Rosy is so easy to talk with. Then there's Wyatt," she said, looking at him dreamily.

Rosy laughed out loud. "It was fun watching these two. I could tell right away there was a spark between them, but it took them a little more time to figure it out. I had to keep an eye on them, and it kept me busy. I'm so glad they figured out how right they are for each other."

"Well, I know Reverend Jed and Thelma feel good about it, and they're a good judge of character," Joseph said.

"Good to hear," Wyatt said. He leaned down and gave Martha a quick kiss on her cheek. "You and Rosy pick out whatever you like for dresses for the wedding. Get the prettiest fabric and lace they have, and I'll be back after I talk to Hank."

"Can we go see if Dr. Campbell is in his office then?" Martha asked. "I'd like to hear what he says about you starting to work again. I know you want to, but I'd like to hear him say it's okay first."

Joseph had to laugh. "It sounds like she's going to be keeping you on the straight and narrow, Wyatt, or at least try to."

"She's been taking very good care of me. She won't let me do much yet, but I have to admit she's just following the doctor's suggestions. Hopefully he'll give me a clean bill of health today so I can get back to working on my own ranch," he added with a chuckle.

True to his word, once he'd talked to Hank and the ladies were done shopping, they went to see the doctor. After checking him out, he told him, and Martha, that he was doing well and could start back on a limited basis. "Wyatt, I think you'll find you still tire easily, and listen to your body. When it's tired, rest. Maybe work half a day and rest the other half."

"I'll try to do that," Wyatt assured him. "I will admit I tire quicker than I used to, but it sure will feel good to get back to something closer to normal." They both thanked the doctor and left.

Like the last time they were in town, after they finished their business, Wyatt took the ladies to the restaurant for some dinner before heading home. Word of their marriage had indeed gotten out, and several people went to their table to congratulate them and meet or talk to Martha again. By the time they were driving the buggy home they were all in a good mood, with a full belly. Martha could tell Wyatt was beginning to wear down, and once they were out of town she took over the driving of the horses, without much objection.

When they got home he agreed to lay down and rest a little while, but insisted he at least let her help this time with unharnessing the horse. She was brushing the horse out when he finished putting the buggy up and came looking for her. They hadn't seen any of the men, so they finished brushing the horse and put her in her stall before going into the house.

As they were going to the house, they heard a horse galloping toward the barn, and someone yelling. They turned to see Austin heading toward them. When he got close enough he slid down from his horse. "Good afternoon, Miss Martha. Wyatt, I'm sorry to bother you, but could I have a word with you, please?"

"Of course you can. Tie your horse up at the house and come on inside. We can talk in my office."

"Thank you."

The three of them walked into the house and the men made their way into his office.

"I wonder what that's all about," Rosy said.

"I was wondering the same thing," Martha said with a chuckle. "I hope nothing's wrong."

"That's for sure. Dallas is enough of a problem for right now." Martha helped Rosy wash clothes, even though she insisted she didn't need help.

"I know you don't," Martha said, "but I need something to keep myself busy, at least until I know there's no problem with Austin."

The men came out fifteen or twenty minutes later and Wyatt thanked Austin for filling him in. Austin nodded to the ladies, grabbed his hat off the peg by the door and left.

Both ladies turned to face Wyatt. "Everything okay?" Martha asked.

"I don't know. Austin was worried about you."

"About me?" Martha looked shocked. "What did I do?"

"Nothing, and that's why he's concerned. It seems he was at the back of the barn when the fiasco with the cow and her calf took place. He told me he watched you a few minutes, amazed at how you had that cow eating out of your hand and not at all upset when you pet her calf. He was shocked when Dallas came in screaming, upsetting all the animals there."

"So he confirmed what I said?"

"Every word of it. He couldn't believe Dallas lied to me, and those are his words. He was going to follow you down the path, but was afraid I would get upset if I saw him walking my girl back to the house, the two of you alone. So instead he went to try to calm the animals down."

"So you believe me now," she said more than asked.

"Martha, I believed you then. Like I told you when we talked about it, I had no reason to doubt what you said. I was confused because I never had a reason to doubt Dallas's word before. That didn't mean I didn't believe you. I'm glad he told me this, though, so when I talk to Dallas, there will be no doubt in my mind as to exactly what happened. He gave me a few more details that you didn't mention, like the fact that the cow was eating grass out of your hand. I'm glad I heard both of your stories before I talk to him. I better go see if I can find him and get this over with."

"You look exhausted," Martha said, and Rosy agreed. "Why don't you go rest before you talk to Dallas."

Wyatt agreed without arguing, which told both ladies just how tired he was. He went to lay down to rest, while Martha went to the kitchen. She wanted something to keep her hands busy while still giving her a chance to think. Cooking or baking normally did that for her, so with Rosy's blessing, she set out to make several pies. They would have one with their supper, and she was sure Will would be happy to have pies for the men at supper.

She was so busy baking and thinking that Wyatt startled her when he came up behind her and put his arms around her waist. She jumped, until he kissed her hair and she inhaled the wonderful smell of her future husband. She turned in his arms, with flour on her hands, and touched his nose, grinning. "You scared me."

"I'm sorry. I didn't mean to scare you," he said, wiping the flour off his nose. "I wanted to tell you I'm awake and I'm going out to the barn. Dallas should be in now, or shortly."

"Thanks for telling me. I'll make sure I'm nowhere near, but please don't upset him even more."

He frowned. "Of course I won't try to, but what I say will all depend on what he says."

She nodded in understanding. "Good luck."

"Thanks. I love you, Martha. Don't forget that."

"I love you, too, Wyatt."

He gave her cheek a quick kiss as Rosy walked in and cleared her throat. "I'm leaving, Rosy," he said as he grabbed his hat off the peg by the door and walked out, chuckling.

"I heard him say he was going to talk to Dallas," Rosy said. "Let's hope it goes well and this whole thing can be over with."

"I hope that happens. I've thought and thought, and I just don't know what has him so upset with me. I apologized for going out to look for Wyatt after he told me not to, but since Wyatt understands why I did and isn't upset, I wouldn't think that's what Dallas is so upset about."

"If that is what's eating at him, he needs to get past it. That's certainly not worth causing all this fuss about." Rosy handed

Martha the pies to put in the oven, and the ladies cleaned up the kitchen and started supper.

Half an hour later Martha glanced out toward the barn, and every ten minutes or so thereafter. "They must be having quite a talk," she said after looking again and not seeing Wyatt yet.

"That or Dallas wasn't back in yet and Wyatt had to wait for him," Rosy suggested.

It was well over half an hour later before Wyatt returned to the house, and both ladies were alarmed as soon as they saw him. He hung his hat on the peg by the door and practically fell into a chair at the kitchen table. His face was pale and he turned to Martha, who had hurried over to him when she saw him come in. "Wyatt, what's wrong?" she asked.

"Dallas quit."

Both ladies sat down at the table to talk with him. Martha was upset. "He quit? But why? What did I do to cause this?"

"That's the part that has me the most upset," he said. "I don't know. He said you flat out ignored him when he told you to stay home, and that's not safe."

"Hogwash," Rosy said. "Surely you told him why she did, and that you would have allowed her to go about the ranch alone if you had known her abilities?"

"Of course I did."

"He didn't care?" Martha asked.

"No. Apparently not knowing your abilities with a gun had nothing to do with it. He said one of his main jobs as foreman is to keep everyone on this ranch safe, and that includes you. He told you that based on the knowledge he had at the time, but regardless, it was to keep you safe. If he can't count on you to listen to what he says, he can't guarantee your safety."

"But I will," Martha insisted. "The only reason I didn't this time is because you were missing, and I knew I could protect myself with a gun. Wyatt, I couldn't stay in here knowing you might be out there hurt or in trouble."

"Sh, sweetheart, I know. I think he knows that, too."

"Then why is he still acting this way?" Rosy asked. "This just doesn't sound like Dallas."

"I know it doesn't, and that's what bothers me. He didn't deny anything, says he hasn't been treating you well, but he can't get over you not listening to him. According to him, if he doesn't have a belief that someone will listen to him, he can't be responsible for keeping them safe."

"But I don't hold him responsible for keeping me safe. If something would have happened, I wouldn't have blamed him," Martha said.

"I know," Wyatt said in an attempt to soothe her, "and I think he knows that. I just don't know what to make of him, but something's not right."

"Did he really quit?"

"Yes, he sure did," Wyatt said. "I just don't understand it."

"Is he going to stand up with you at our wedding?"

"No, and this is part of what I don't understand about this whole thing. He said it wouldn't be fair for him to stand by me at our wedding after the way he's treated you."

Rosy shook her head. "Not only does that not sound like Dallas, it doesn't make any sense. So he's admitting he's been treating Martha wrong?"

"Yes. He said he hasn't been a bit friendly to her, and it wouldn't be fair to her for him to stand with me at our wedding. When he said he's been treating her bad, I had to agree with him. It wouldn't be fair to you, my dear Martha, to have him next to me."

"But if he admitted he's been treating her badly, and he knows you're going to marry her, why can't he simply apologize?" Rosy asked. "Martha would have accepted it and we could have all moved on."

"I've had similar thoughts," Wyatt said.

They all sat there for several minutes, stunned.

"We're missing something," Martha finally said. "From everything you two have said, he's not acting like himself. I don't know him as well, but I do know when we first met he seemed nice, we got along fine. So it seems to me as though something has happened that we're missing. How do we find out what it is?"

"I don't know," Wyatt said, "but if we can't find it before he leaves tomorrow morning, I'll be out a good friend, and a foreman."

Martha forgot about her pies she'd made for the men, as they were busy discussing something much more important. They talked about this dilemma as they ate supper, and afterward until they had exhausted themselves and went to bed, hoping an idea would come to them in their sleep.

At breakfast they decided their best shot was simply for Wyatt to talk to him again, and try and get him to change his mind. He went out to the barn, with the ladies watching the window, waiting for his return. It wasn't long before he headed back to the house, and they could tell he hadn't been successful.

"He looks so lost," Martha said. "I worry about him. The doctor said he could start back today, working half a day. He hasn't even mentioned that."

"I noticed that, too," Rosy said. "This is really bothering him. Maybe I should go talk to Dallas before he leaves."

"If he's decided he's leaving, I don't see what your talking to him could hurt. You never know when someone will say just the words he needs to hear."

"I'll do that right after I hear what Wyatt has to say."

They turned to Wyatt, waiting to hear what happened. "He's not budging and says there's no need for us to talk any more, that we've said all there is to be said."

"I'm going to go talk to him," Rosy said. "It certainly can't hurt."

"No, it can't, but give him a little time first," Wyatt suggested. "He's just starting to pull his things together."

Rosy nodded. "I can give him a little room. It'll give me time to decide what I want to say to him."

"While you do that, I'm going to take these pies out to Will. I forgot them last night, but the men will still enjoy them tonight."

"They'll love them," Wyatt said. "It's nice of you to make them special things for desert now and then."

"I enjoy making them," Martha said as she put the pies in a basket and headed to the door.

She reached the bunkhouse and started to open the door, but paused. Will was talking to someone. She debated whether she should interrupt them, or wait a few minutes. While she was debating she heard another voice. It was Dallas, which gave her pause. Maybe she should try talking to him again. She hadn't actually considered that before. Once she apologized and he didn't accept it, she didn't think there was anything else she could say that would make a difference. Rosy's words came to her mind, and she was right. At this point, what could it hurt?

Her mind made up, she decided when Will and Dallas were done talking, she would give Will the pies, then hurry in and catch Dallas. If she couldn't change his mind, she could at least tell him what was on her mind. Did he realize that after Wyatt and his father had given him a good job for so many years, and Wyatt had thought so much of him, it was hurting him badly for Dallas to just walk away from all of it without a good explanation? Maybe that was what he needed to hear. If he would just tell Wyatt what was really wrong before he left, Wyatt would at least know why he was leaving. That would at least answer the question he's been struggling with.

As she reached that decision, Dallas's words caught her attention. She wasn't one to eavesdrop, generally didn't think much of people who did, but in this case, she couldn't seem to pull herself away. Instead, she found herself stepping a bit closer to the door so she could hear better.

"Thank you for coming to say good-bye to me before you left," Will said, "but could you do me one better and answer a question or two for me?"

"I'll try," Dallas said reluctantly. "I probably know what you're going to ask, and it's hard for me to talk about. You encouraged me a lot when I first came to work here, though, and I've always appreciated that. You told me to stick with it and I'd be foreman some day, and you were right. Sticking with it paid off for me, and I have you to thank for that, so I guess maybe I do owe you one."

"You certainly do," Will said, "and I'm calling in that one favor right now. Why in tarnation are you leaving, and why have you been treating that little lady like shit?"

"You never did mince words, Will."

"No need to, and no need to avoid the question, neither. That little lady Wyatt found is good as gold, and you know it. Any man would be lucky to find a woman like that, and I would think you'd be happy for Wyatt."

"I am."

"Then why are you making his life so dang miserable?"

"I'm not making his life miserable. I'm leaving so it's not."

"There you go again, making not a damn bit of sense. Why aren't you happy that he found a woman like that, and why can't you be civil to her, like you were before Wyatt come up missing and she found him? Is that what's eating at you, that she found him instead of you?"

"No, that isn't it at all."

"Then what is it? Are you jealous that he found such a good lady and not you?"

"No. I found a lady like that once, and that's why I've got to leave."

"Dat burn it, Dallas, say something that makes sense. What the hell does that mean?"

Dallas sighed and was quiet several moments. Martha was beginning to think he wasn't going to answer Will, either, but she was wrong. "I guess if I'm leaving, I might as well tell you what my problem with Martha is. I suppose you deserve that much."

"Damn right I do. It might make you feel better, too."

"I don't know about that, but you've been good to me, so I'll tell you. Everyone that knows me and what happened wants to talk about it all the time, says I'm looking at it wrong, and I don't want to hear that. I don't even want to think about it, so that's why I left town and haven't spoken of it since. But I'm leaving today, so you won't be able to harp to me about it, so I'll tell you."

CHAPTER 21

*A*s Martha stood outside the door to the bunkhouse, she knew she was eavesdropping and should leave, but she also knew there was nothing that could tear her away. This sounded personal, so it wasn't really any of her business, but it was also the reason he was leaving the ranch because of her, so there was no way she was leaving. Instead, she stood still so no one would hear her as she listened to Dallas as he began talking to Will.

"At one time before I came to this ranch I found me a good lady. In fact, Martha reminds me a lot of her. She was pretty, kind, smart, funny, and would do whatever she could to help people. You don't find many like that. She agreed to marry me, and I was the happiest man alive. But then she died."

He stopped. After a rather long silent pause, Will said, "I'm sorry to hear she died. But I don't quite understand why that means you have to be so awful around Martha. How are the two things related?"

"Well, like I said, Lydia was a lot like Martha. She was a free spirit, wanted to try everything, and wasn't afraid of much. She was also from the city and didn't know there were hidden dangers out here. I had my hands full with her, trying to keep her safe. I walloped her little behind on several occasions for not listening to my rules to keep her safe. Oh, she hated them, but by the time I was done with each one, she finally understood how dangerous she'd been acting. Well, one time she ignored one of my rules for her safety, and she died before I could save her."

"I'm sorry, Dallas, but I doubt it was your fault. What exactly happened?"

"She was the owner's niece. Her parents had died and she'd come to stay with them. She wanted to take a horse out alone, but her uncle and I both told her not to, that she didn't know how to use a gun, and she wasn't experienced enough riding a horse yet to go out alone. Well, she went anyway, and she went way further than she should have."

"You weren't the only one that told her not to go, Dallas."

"No, but I was the man marrying her. I should have made her listen to me."

"I'm not sure you could have, but go on."

"One of the ranch hands saw her pushing her horse, and knew she wasn't experienced enough to be doing that, so he went to slow her down or see if there was a reason she was doing that. As he neared her, he saw a pack of wolves following her. He took his gun out and was just about to shoot at the wolves to scare them off, when a wolf came running out of the woods right toward her horse, who reared up on his hind legs, throwing her off."

"Oh, no."

"He shot one of the wolves, which sent the rest of them running the other direction, but when he got to her, she was motionless. It turned out when she fell she broke her neck and died right then."

Martha didn't move an inch. Poor Dallas. No wonder he was so upset about her going off after he told her not to. She couldn't imagine how that had to have made him feel. Her thoughts were pulled back to their conversation, as Will was speaking again.

"So you were okay with Martha until she did the same thing Lydia had done."

"Exactly. It brought all those memories of Lydia back to the front of my mind, after I'd tried my best to bury them. For so long I wouldn't even allow myself to think about her and how I'd failed her. I instantly blamed Martha for what happened to Lydia, but I hadn't even realized it until Wyatt talked to me last night. Now that I see what I did, though, I have to leave. I treated Martha horribly, and she didn't deserve it. Neither does Wyatt, who loves the lady I've been treating so badly."

"Dallas, I understand what you're saying, but I think you're wrong. Martha and Wyatt are good people, and I think you're underestimating them. I think if you explain to them what happened and apologize –"

"No," Dallas said, interrupting. "The way I treated them I don't deserve to be forgiven, just like I don't deserve to be forgiven for Lydia's death. I need to move on before I hurt someone else."

Martha couldn't stand still any longer, and pulled the door open and marched right over to face Dallas. "No, you don't, Dallas. If you move on you'll be hurting people that care about you, and we don't deserve that."

Both men looked at her, their mouths dropping open. Dallas was the first to respond. "Martha, how much of that did you hear?"

"Enough to know you're making a big mistake if you leave. Do you know how upset Wyatt is right now? He's not just losing his foreman, at a time he's not able to even work a whole day yet, but he's losing his best friend. That's hurting him terribly."

"But after the way I treated you, it wouldn't be fair to you to allow me to stay."

"Dallas, why don't you let me decide what's fair to me? I don't think it's fair to me for you to leave after making the man I'm going to marry this upset. What's he done to deserve that? Is that fair to him?"

"I thought it would be better for him, yes. I treated you badly, and he's upset about that. I know that because he told me so, and I don't blame him. He should be upset."

"Yes, you treated me badly. I won't argue that point. But that can be fixed. A simple apology will take care of that, especially now that I know why. Running off and leaving Wyatt hurting is treating me way worse. I love him, Dallas, and I don't want to see him hurting like that. He has no idea why you're actually leaving and he's worried about you. He wanted you to stand up with him at our wedding because he's considered you more than just a good friend. He looks up to you."

"You could forgive me, just like that, even though I don't deserve it?"

"It's not just like that. I heard your story, and while I'm very sorry you had to go through that, I now understand why you got so upset. In fact, I'm sorry I brought all those memories back. But knowing that, yes, of course I can forgive you. And so can Wyatt. Please stop underestimating us and give us a chance. I have to say one more thing, though, Dallas."

"What's that?"

"Will's right. It wasn't your fault Lydia didn't listen to you. But saying you don't deserve to be forgiven for it is a bunch of hogwash. We all make mistakes. Heaven knows I have. One mistake I made could have possibly prevented all this."

"How?"

"Papa told me men prefer ladies who can cook and sew and things like that. I prefer being out with the horses and working on a farm. Papa said that's why I never caught the eye of a man, so when I meet someone new I don't say anything about knowing how to ride a horse or shoot a gun. I never lied if someone asked, but if they didn't ask I didn't volunteer the information. Looking back on it, when Wyatt so kindly brought me to the ranch to stay while I decided what to do with my life, I should have told him I was comfortable riding and shooting. That would have changed things. You wouldn't have told me I couldn't go out, so this never would have happened."

"Nonsense," Dallas said. "You can't be held responsible for that; you had no way of knowing something like this would happen."

"Likewise, you can't be held responsible for what happened to Lydia since you didn't know she wouldn't listen to you or her uncle, or that a pack of wolves would start trailing her. You had no way of knowing something like that would happen."

"It's not the same."

"Yes, it is. If you don't believe me, ask Will."

Dallas looked over at Will, who was nodding his head. "Martha's a smart lady, Dallas. She's right, it is the same. It's pretty much exactly the same. That wasn't your fault, and it's about time you get your damn fool head wrapped around that fact and stop tormenting yourself."

After a long silent spell where Martha could tell Dallas was thinking over what she'd said, he spoke. "I really am sorry for the way I treated you," he said rather quietly.

"I know," she said just as quietly. "I can tell, which is also why I know you're sincere. If you want to make it up to me, you can do that by going in the house with me and telling Wyatt what happened all those years ago so he knows. Then you can tell him you'll stand up with him at our wedding."

"Do you really think he would –"

"Dallas, I know he would be thrilled to have things back to normal with you. You know him well enough to know that, too, if you could get past that crazy idea you have about you not deserving to be forgiven, and I think I know how to do that."

"How would that be?"

"It sounds to me as though it upset you, which I completely

understand. But you blamed it on yourself, which is wrong, and then tried to put it out of your mind. You tried not to think about it. That means you never took the time or allowed yourself to grieve." She put her basket of pies down on Will's table and moved closer and laid a gentle hand on Dallas's arm. "Dallas, grieving for someone you love is important. I've lost my mama, my aunt, my papa, and finally my uncle. I learned it's not easy or fun, but grieving is important. If you don't go through that grieving process, you can't move on. Things will keep reminding you of it. If you allow yourself to grieve for that person you loved, eventually when things remind you of them, it will be good memories that come to you. You still miss them, but you remember the good instead of the bad and it doesn't hurt as much."

Dallas sighed again. "I don't know. I don't know if I can."

"It's hard, I know, but you can get through it if you let your friends, like me and Wyatt and Will and Rosy help."

"Rosy?"

"Yes, of course Rosy. She's been worried about you, as well, saying something's not right."

"I didn't know."

"People here care about you and are willing to help you. Give it some thought. Tonight when you go to sleep, in the foreman's cabin here on the ranch where you belong, give it some thought."

He smiled a little, but nodded.

"Good. But for right now, please tell me you'll go in and talk to Wyatt."

Dallas looked unsure, but Will spoke up. "Dallas, I think you owe her that much. You owe it to Wyatt, too."

He looked from Will to Martha. "Okay, you're right. He's apt to send me away, but I guess I have nothing to lose at this point."

"Thank you," Martha said as she grabbed his arm and started pulling him toward the house. "Come on."

"Right now?"

"No time like the present. Wyatt's in there hurting, and we should be planning a wedding instead of worrying about him losing a dear friend. You can fix that."

"You are a persistent little thing, aren't you?" Dallas asked.

"That she is," Will said, "but in this case that's a good thing. And she brought us pies. Now go on."

Will chuckled as Martha tried to pull Dallas out the door, but he moved enough to let her go first, even putting his hand on her elbow, leading her. Will was smiling until he heard them both gasp. He moved to the window and saw Rosy heading toward them, and she didn't look happy. He stepped over to the door in case he was needed. "Rosy," Dallas and Martha said together.

"Dallas, you take your hand off that poor girl. She's done nothing –"

"Whoa, Rosy," Dallas tried.

"It's okay, Rosy," Martha said.

"No, it's not. He has no right to –" She paused when she saw Will step from the bunkhouse, looking at her and shaking his head, trying to quiet her. "Will?"

"Let them go, Rosy. Our girl done good. You'll be proud."

"Okay," Rosy said reluctantly, as the big smile on Will's face helped ease her anxiety over the situation.

She followed them to the house, where Wyatt met them at the door. "What's going on? Martha, are you okay?" he asked.

"I'm better than I've been in several days, and I think you will be, too. Dallas has something he'd like to say to you."

Wyatt cocked his head to the side as he studied Martha, then Dallas, who was looking awfully fidgety. Rosy looked just as confused as he felt. "Is that true, Dallas?"

"It is."

"Well, come on in then. Maybe we better go to my office. Do you want to speak alone?"

"We can if you want, but I'd feel better if Martha was there, as well. I think she'll be a big support for me."

Wyatt's eyes popped wide open, but he recovered quickly. "Then let's go talk."

Half an hour later the three of them had finished their talk, and Wyatt turned to face Dallas. "Now that we've got all that figured out, I have to ask you a question, again. Will you please stand up with me at our wedding?"

Dallas turned to Martha with questioning eyes. "I certainly hope you say yes pretty soon," she said with a big smile.

"Then I'd be honored to," he said. "The two of you are the best friends a man could have. I don't know how I'll ever be able to repay you."

"Actually, Dallas, I believe you might have already," Martha said.

"How?"

"I'm sorry I eavesdropped earlier, but something you said has already helped me, and I want to thank you for that."

"What did I say that could possibly help you?"

"Hearing how special Lydia was to you and how you took it personally, too personally when she died, made me realize why Wyatt worries so much about me. He told me he tells me not to do things in an attempt to keep me safe because he loves me. I believed him, though sometimes I thought he was worrying too much about me. But now I realize that when he tells me things like that, I need to see it as him showing me how much he loves me. More importantly, that goes both ways, and I need to show him I love him, as well. To do that I need to listen carefully and do exactly what he says, not just most of what he says."

Wyatt met her eyes and moved to gather her into his arms. Without a bit of hesitation, he leaned down and kissed her with so much feeling, when he pulled away she had tears in her eyes. He turned to Dallas and reached one hand out to shake his, while holding her with the other. "Thank you, my friend. I know she meant every word of that, and it means more to me than you can know. You don't owe us a thing."

Dallas nodded, understanding what Wyatt was saying. "Glad I could help," he said sincerely.

A few minutes later Wyatt emerged from his office with one arm around Martha while the other shook Dallas' hand, and he had a big smile on his face. Rosy still wasn't sure what went on, but the smiles on all their faces told her all she needed to know. "I have cookies and coffee or milk on the table," she said.

"Thank you, Rosy," Dallas said, "but I need to get back out there. I have a ranch to run."

"You do?" she asked, looking from him to Wyatt, who nodded.

"I certainly do," Dallas confirmed.

"Oh, that's good to hear," she said, coming forward and giving him a hug. "Take some cookies with you. You can eat them while you work."

He took several cookies and laughed. "Thank you, Rosy." He paused just a moment before leaning down and giving her a quick kiss on her cheek, surprising them all. He grabbed his hat from the pegs next to the door and left, leaving Rosy shocked and looking at the other two for answers.

They just smiled at each other, so Rosy looked to Wyatt. "Will said she did good. Can I assume he was right?"

"He certainly was," Wyatt said, leaning down to kiss the top of her head. Sit down and let's have some of those cookies while we explain it to you."

LATER THAT EVENING after supper Wyatt and Martha were both feeing more relaxed. They went out to sit on the porch and enjoy the evening breeze and go over some plans for the wedding. She was fine with anyone he wanted to invite or felt they should invite, but she wanted to know who they were, so when she saw them, or in some cases met them for the first time, she would know how they knew Wyatt. He was naming the various people and telling her a little about them.

He started to pause a little longer between explanations. She assumed he was trying to think of who all he'd put on his list of names, but she didn't mind. She loved being out there with him, enjoying the breeze. When he paused for several minutes without naming anyone else, she asked, "Can't think of anyone else?"

"What? Oh, I'm sorry, I guess I got sidetracked."

She giggled. "You looked like you were deep in thought. If you weren't trying to remember who is on your list, where were you thinking about?"

"You, and what we're doing right now."

"What do you mean? I just want to know who these people are so when I meet them I know why they're special to you."

"I know, and that's what I'm talking about. This is one of the many things that makes me feel so lucky to know you're going to be my wife," he said.

"What is?"

"The fact that you care about the people who will be there. You're new here and no one will expect you to know everyone or their connection to me or my family. You want to know because you care, which doesn't surprise me. You care about everyone. Sometimes I'm just plain overwhelmed. I'm a lucky man indeed."

"I don't understand. Why do you feel overwhelmed?"

"Because you care so much about – you make pies and do things for everyone no matter – you try to help everyone you – you impress everyone with your – they all love you because of –"

Martha looked at him, totally confused. "What?"

Wyatt looked at her and threw his arms in the air, as if surrendering. "I can't find the right words. I guess I love you."

She stared at him, laughing. "Again?"

He shook his head as his face turned red. "Okay, maybe I should try that again. "I have a hard time finding the right words to explain why I feel so lucky to be planning a wedding with you because of how much I love you. Does that sound any better?"

"Much," she said with a giggle.

He stood and pulled her up to stand in front of him, pulling her close with his hands around her waist. "I might not always be good with words, but I want you to know I love you very much, and I'm very sure of that."

"I know you do," she said, "and that means a great deal to me because, well, you see, it seems – I guess I love you, too."

"You can be a feisty little brat sometimes," he said as he reached around and landed a swat on her bottom, "but that's actually another thing I love about you." He leaned down and his lips gently met hers, just as Rosy opened the door to join them outside. She watched a few moments, and witnessed what she knew was a very passionate kiss full of emotion. She smiled and turned around and went back inside.

MISTY MALONE

Writing has been a dream of Misty's for several years. She's finally following that dream, and began writing in 2013. She enjoys writing romance stories, with a handsome man who falls in love with a lovely lady in need of a strong man who can take her in hand. Having grown up on a farm, she especially enjoys writing about strong cowboys. She lives in the Midwest with her husband and son, not far from where she grew up. Misty hopes you enjoy reading her books as much as she enjoys writing them. Reviews to her books are very much appreciated, and she would like to thank you for each one of them. She invites you to leave a message for her at authormistymalone@gmail.com.

Don't miss these exciting titles by Misty Malone and Blushing Books!

Pine Falls Series
The Town's Inheritance
Say Something
Nothing Average

Western Camping series
The Camping Cowgirl, Book 1
The Camping Cowboy, Book 2

Holiday House Series
Finding Holly
Warning Merry
Convincing Sarah

A Beautiful Ranch
Being Schooled
Nice to Meet You
Stealing Her Breath
Mail Order Mystery
The Best Accident Ever
She Did What?
Never Again
Not Lonely Now
Top Cop
Darn Noisy Neighbors
Listen Here, Cowboy
Can't Argue with That
Hidden Talents
It'll Work Out
Work and Play

Anthologies
Tamed By The Cowboy
12 Naughty Days of Christmas 2018
Love of a Cowboy, Two
Sweet Town Love

Audio Books
The Real Prize
It's My Ranch?
Mail Order Surprise

Connect with Misty Malone
authormistymalone@gmail.com

BLUSHING BOOKS

Blushing Books is the oldest eBook publisher on the web. We've been running websites that publish steamy romance and erotica since 1999, and we have been selling eBooks since 2003. We have free and promotional offerings that change weekly, so please do visit us at http://www.blushingbooks.com/free.

BLUSHING BOOKS NEWSLETTER

Please join the Blushing Books newsletter
to receive updates & special promotional offers.
You can also join by using your mobile phone:
Just text BLUSHING to 22828.

Every month, one new sign up via text messaging will receive a
$25.00 Amazon gift card, so sign up today!